Praise for Joan Druett's novels

"Excellent characters in full sail amid tangy salt air and creaky timbers offer prime entertainment" — *Publisher's Weekly*, reviewing *Abigail* (*A Love of Adventure*)

"A spellbinding adventure ... an exhilarating voyage not soon to be forgotten" — Cindy Vallar, *Pirates and Privateers*, reviewing *A Promise of Gold*

"... dazzles with Druett's truly splendid prose" — George Jepson, *Quarterdeck*, reviewing *The Money Ship*

"[A] highly entertaining — and absorbing — nautical tale" — Helen Hollick, *Discovering Diamonds*, reviewing *The Money Ship*

"This impressive debut will appeal to both fans of historical mysteries and to Patrick O'Brian readers" — *Booklist*, starred review of *A Watery Grave*

"Noted maritime historian Druett blends strong plotting and scads of authentic maritime detail in an impressive debut" — *Library Journal*, reviewing *A Watery Grave*

"Brilliantly plotted, well-written thriller packed with lore about the sea" — *Booksense*, reviewing *A Watery Grave*

"[Druett] makes the vanished world she depicts come alive" — *Publishers Weekly*, reviewing *Run Afoul*

"Sharp psychological portraits and stirring, sea-swept descriptive passages remind you of - dare I say it? - Patrick O'Brian" — *Chicago Tribune*, reviewing *Shark Island*

"Not only an intricate murder puzzle but an unfolding family history, a splash of romance, plenty of crackling good dialogue, and a lively, enjoyable seafaring yarn as well" — Joan Curry, *Christchurch Press*, reviewing *Run Afoul*

"Druett continues to pepper her suspenseful plots with the same type of authentic seafaring facts and lore that so distinguished the novels of the late Patrick O'Brian" — *Booklist*, reviewing *Deadly Shoals*

"Combining historical and nautical accuracy with a fast paced mystery thriller has produced a marvelous book which is highly recommended" — David Hayes, *Historic Naval Fiction*, reviewing *The Beckoning Ice*

"[Druett] writes some of the most sparkling sailing prose I have ever read" — *Manawatu Standard*, reviewing the Wiki Coffin series.

"... compelling reading ... These stories are on a par with C.S. Forester and Patrick O'Brian" — *Launceston Examiner*, reviewing the Wiki Coffin series.

"The homicides in Joan Druett's novels are fun to follow, but fans ... will gain most enjoyment from Wiki Coffin's charm and the authentic pictures of 19th century shipboard life. Druett's books are enriched by her descriptions of the ships, social relationships on board and ashore, and the enticing bits of Maori culture and language" — *Professional Skipper*, reviewing the Wiki Coffin series.

Daughters of the Storm

JOAN DRUETT

Also by Joan Druett

Abigail (A Love of Adventure)
A Promise of Gold
Finale
The Money Ship

WIKI COFFIN MYSTERIES
A Watery Grave
Shark Island
Run Afoul
Deadly Shoals
The Beckoning Ice

NON FICTION
The Discovery of Tahiti
The Notorious Captain Hayes
Eleanor's Odyssey
Lady Castaways
The Elephant Voyage
Tupaia, Captain Cook's Polynesian Navigator
Island of the Lost
In the Wake of Madness
She Captains
Rough Medicine
Hen Frigates
Captain's Daughter, Coasterman's Wife
The Sailing Circle
She Was a Sister Sailor
Petticoat Whalers
Fulbright in New Zealand
Exotic Intruders

Daughters of the Storm

JOAN DRUETT

Published by
Old Salt Press
Jersey City, NJ, USA

Chapter one

Helen Pederson stood outside the arrivals door of Los Angeles airport terminal, and watched the trolley with her bags roll in from the concourse. She tipped the porter, and then he was gone. She shivered. The hot air outside fought with the inside air conditioning every time the glass doors slid open, which was a good reason for shivering. But she thought it was more than that. She had no idea what was ahead of her, and that made her very uneasy.

The message that her husband's new personal assistant had sent to New York had been brief to the point of curtness, but as always she had dropped everything. Back in her New York apartment the reception rooms were being prepared for a function where the hostess would not be present. It didn't really matter. Helen had faith in her own personal assistant, Lady Pamela Phillips, who would preside in her place. But a very special young author had at last been able to accept a pressing invitation to attend, and so it was natural to feel upset.

It had been happening this way for ten years. Harold would summon her and Helen would travel obediently to wherever it might be – Amsterdam, London, Paris, Dubai, Nairobi once — usually to an exclusive suite booked in a world-class hotel, but sometimes to a Pederson-owned property. The Pasadena mansion here in California was one of her favorites, but her destination made no difference. She would arrive and some important employee would be there to meet her, and then she would carry out her role as Harold's hostess. She was always superb. She knew her job down to the tiniest detail, so that he arrangement worked as smoothly as the rest of Harold's empire. But always in the past she had known what lay ahead.

The doors slid open as a family came out, and Helen shivered again. She had given up hope long ago that Harold himself would meet her, but until today there had always been the dignity of having someone waiting. Limousines swept the curb side, picking up preoccupied businessmen, but none came for her. Between cars the forecourt was empty.

Ten minutes passed. The misgiving shifted uneasily inside her. There was a long mirrored wall to her right. Helen checked her appearance unobtrusively, knowing what Harold would expect. Perfection. He was a man who demanded perfection.

Pale hair, more silver than gold, cropped into a neat cap. Pale complexion, also perfectly groomed. Helen was wearing a suit in heavy fawn silk, with a pencil skirt skimming long slender legs, unrumpled despite the long flight. Her reflection gave her no thrill of vanity — her only value to Harold, now, was her flawless manner and appearance. On this depended a lifestyle for which she had struggled, and which she valued more than almost anything else. Elegance was the keystone of her existence.

Helen Pederson, in an ironic kind of way, was a casualty of war. Her mother had been a war bride, married to one of the American servicemen who had come to the South Pacific during the war with Vietnam. Helen was born in New Zealand, but her earliest memories were of Boston, and the rarefied existence that is reserved for the most exquisitely pedigreed of Bostonian families. It was a life of perfect manners and superb taste, of lovely old mansions with plain brownstone exteriors, of the right schools and expensive vacations.

And it had all abruptly come to an end in Helen's sixteenth year, when her father had committed suicide after a well-publicized embezzlement. Helen's mother had fled back to New Zealand, taking Helen with her, and Helen's life since then had been devoted to regaining that expensive lifestyle, and then keeping it.

Was that lifestyle in danger now? Harold had grown colder and even more remote, but there had been no hint that he might feel ready to dispense with her. Maybe this was the hint now — that he had not bothered to send someone to collect her. Helen was shocked by the surge of relief she felt when she heard a man say her name.

"Mrs. Pederson." She turned. Unexpectedly, the man had come from inside the airport terminal. He had a briefcase in one hand and a soft leather bag slung over one shoulder, so he had just arrived himself. He was tall and lean, quite handsome, and he looked about forty. His hair was gray-flecked black, coarse and strong, worn unfashionably long, and his eyes were very distinctive, as pale as a wolf's. He looked tanned and fit, but also as if he spent a lot of time at a desk, or at a computer.

When he put down the briefcase and shook hands his grip was firm. "Hamilton," he said. The name meant nothing to her – which was odd, because she felt a sudden sense of recognition. Normally she had a well-trained memory for faces and names, but now she just felt bewildered.

"Skye Hamilton," he elaborated. Helen murmured a polite reply, her mind racing, trying to track down the familiarity and the unpleasant sense of danger that came with it. She was not even sure if Skye was his name, or the name of the company he represented. She had never heard it before, but somewhere ... sometime ...

Hamilton looked about, and then put his bag on the trolley. He said in casual tones, "I'm sorry you've been kept waiting, but I've come a long way. Your husband asked me to meet you. He said it was to save sending two cars."

Helen was staring at him, the sense of recognition forgotten. She was accustomed to Harold's strange small economies, and had indeed found over the years that petty thrift was characteristic of the extremely wealthy. However, it was the first time that this stinginess had been directed at her. A silver-gray Cadillac had at last drawn up – now that this stranger had arrived. Helen's stiletto heels clicked angrily as she walked across the path.

The driver loaded the bags. Hamilton got into the back and then sat with his body turned toward her, one long arm along the back of the seat. He did not speak, but studied her face as the driver threaded the big vehicle through the madhouse traffic, his brows pulled down in a frown. Helen, feeling increasingly annoyed, was about to break the deliberate silence with chilly social chat when —

The car stopped.

They were at an intersection, and the signals were against them. Helen sat very still, staring at Hamilton. A flyover arched overhead, casting a shadow that darkened the man's chin, and that nagging sense of déjà vu returned. Yet Helen felt almost certain that she had never met Hamilton – Skye Hamilton? — before. With his lower face cast in deep shadow, though, there was something disturbing about his frown and the way his tanned skin creased out over his cheekbones.

She almost blurted, "Have we met before?" — but stopped herself just in time. Instead, she said, "You have business with my husband, Mr. Hamilton?"

He looked away, the car moved forward as the lights changed, and the shadow slid away from his face. The sense of recognition was gone.

He said, "I hope so. I've been trying to negotiate a meeting for a long time, but this appointment came out of the blue."

So he, too, seemed to have no idea what Harold had in mind. Helen lapsed into silence, struggling to make sense of the situation. It was a relief when the limousine finally turned off a tree-lined street and grated over cobbles.

After Helen left the car she stood still for a long moment, gazing at the house, the Pasadena mansion that never failed to soothe her. It was far older than the billionaire bungalows all about, being a beautifully maintained relic of the pre-goldrush days of Spanish California. Curved terracotta roof tiles in warm burnt sienna colors swooped gracefully down to arched and pilastered white walls, which shone with ageless serenity in the late California sun. Everywhere there were tubs of gorgeous plants.

Ramirez was waiting for her in front of the tall carved doors, his plump hands folded in front of his black suit. His round head was balder, but otherwise he was little changed from the first time she had come here, more than twenty years ago. And that was soothing, too.

Inside, the shadowy entry hall smelled as it always had, of bowls of fresh roses and beeswax. Ahead of the entrance a long series of glass doors opened onto a pillared courtyard, where ferns and creepers rioted in boxes, urns and hanging baskets. The windows and galleries of the second level framed this lovely loggia on three sides, while the fourth side opened out to the flower-strewn gardens, with conservatories and tennis courts in the distance. Helen saw appreciation in Hamilton's expression as he looked around. Then a servant led him away to a guest room upstairs.

After he had gone the hall and loggia were empty, except for herself and Ramirez. He said softly, "Mr. Pederson's compliments, Mrs. Pederson, and he would be obliged if you could meet him in the Tudor Room at five."

Helen looked at her watch, anger and misgiving inside her again. It was four forty-five. Harold had kept her waiting at the airport, and now she had far too little time to get ready — for what?

The only sounds in the house were a distant clatter from the kitchens. She could smell food cooking, but had no way of knowing what kind of meal was being prepared. A banquet for fifty? A buffet for an informal gathering of six? But of course she could not ask Ramirez. Helen turned to the stairway that curled up to the second floor.

The staircase was the loveliest feature of this very lovely house, a broad curving flight that led past landings holding priceless antique furniture pieces, to the bedrooms on the upper floor. Helen mounted it slowly, running her fingers along the polished rosewood rail. She was very conscious that Ramirez stood still in the hall below, watching her. Perhaps he, too, wondered about Harold's intentions.

She arrived in a broad corridor where portraits of long-dead Californian dons frowned at her, her heels silent on the heavy carpet. Her room was furnished in keeping with the original oak rafters and paneling, but the ensuite bathroom had modern fittings. Her luggage had already arrived, and was being unpacked by a maid, a dark-eyed Hispanic girl Helen had never seen before. At least, she thought bleakly, Harold was not going to dismiss her as soon as whatever lay ahead was over, so she would not have to face another flight this evening.

Helen arrived at the Tudor Room precisely at five. The heavy wooden door was shut, and she paused to collect her thoughts, listening to the faint sounds of talk on the other side, trying to guess how many people were in there. Not many, she thought. She pushed open the door and stepped into the gracious old room with its artesonado paneled ceiling, and the first person she saw was Skye

Hamilton. Then she saw the two girls with him, and her heart stopped. And in that scant instant she knew where she'd seen Skye Hamilton before. It had been twenty— no, twenty-one — years ago, and he had been bearded then. And very much younger, just a teenager. He had been standing at the counter of a half-wrecked hospital, asking urgent questions, and —

Oh my God, she thought, and fought down a shudder. *The storm.* The storm that had so nearly killed both Harold and herself, and the storm when her baby was born.

But Skye Hamilton certainly didn't recognize her now. The atmosphere was silent and heavy. It was hard even to breathe, and Helen would not have been able to speak if she tried. Twenty-one years, she thought. The seeds of this meeting had been sown nearly a quarter-century ago.

Both of the girls with Skye Hamilton had very dark hair, streaked with a warm caramel color; it was obvious they used the same hairdresser. While one was a half-head taller than the other, they looked closely related — sisters, or even twins. They had the same large, dark, catlike eyes, naturally outlined with thick black lashes, and both had smooth olive skins. They were also amazingly successful, considering their youth. The journalists called them the Cinderella girls, because both had emerged from obscurity to soar to public attention, just as if some magic godmother had touched them with her wand.

Kate Giacomo, the taller girl, stood at Skye Hamilton's right. Her expression was wary, Helen thought – and well it should be, since Kate Giacomo was supposed to be the star turn at Helen's party in New York. Kate was even wearing what she had probably intended for the promotion — dark tailored slacks, and a white silk blouse with voluminous sleeves that caught at the wrists. Her hair was swept up into a chignon, and there were no dangling pendants or long sparkly earrings, because they would have distracted the audience. Despite her youth, Kate knew exactly what she was doing — so what was she doing here? One of the most prestigious social events of the season, and both hostess and star guest were here in California.

At the age of twenty, less than one year ago, Kate had published a book called *The Man Who Played With Fire*, about the unique breed of fire-fighters who specialized in oil well fires. The day it was launched there was a short and nasty war in the Middle East, and oil well fires exploded onto the front pages. Within a week *The Man Who Played With Fire* headed every bestseller list in the United States and Great Britain. The advance Kate was offered for a second book was certainly astronomical, but the paparazzi were left to guess the precise sum. Kate announced that it was far too much and demonstrated what a profit publishers made out of selling bestsellers.

Then she'd declared that she would sink all the money she made from *The Man Who Played With Fire* into her own publishing venture, and was actively seeking backing. And that was the reason Helen was staging the party in New York, to help Kate find that finance. So what, in God's name, was going on?

The other girl, often fancily called *la Cenerentola*, stood at Skye Hamilton's other side. Maggie Bacchante was wearing the 'graffiti' dress that had been her first hit: a sleeveless, high-necked shift that skimmed down to her knees, with just a loose chain belt to hold it in. What made it a stand-out was the pale, heavy silk fabric, which had been hand-painted with slogans in the pastel colors favored by taggers. Teenagers had fallen for the style in droves, and now every department store stocked cheap versions of it, machine printed, and made of silky polyester.

Like Kate, Maggie had just turned twenty-one, and she, also like Kate, had arrived in New York one year ago. On the surface, Maggie was simply joining her sister, but as all the fashion commentators now knew, underneath there was a burning ambition to be a dress designer. Her bold mantra was that every woman had the right to feel fantastic, and that if a woman was wearing the right clothes, she was able to move mountains.

That Maggie Bacchante was female in a business that, ironically, was dominated by men, and that she did not even have an influential lover, should have been against her. But she did have an amazing portfolio, including the graffiti dress, which she had been prepared to carry anywhere for meetings with buyers. That hard work had not been necessary. The New York branch of the Italian house Bellissimo had been easily persuaded to invite her to join their studio, and now, at the age of twenty-one, her career in fashion promised to be spectacular.

Then Helen's attention flicked away from the Cinderella girls. The door opened with a snap that was loud in the taut silence.

And Jewel Pederson came in, followed by Dr. Florida Sullivan.

Helen exclaimed, "Florida, why did you bring my daughter here? You should have consulted with me first!"

She was studying Jewel anxiously, searching for the signs that were often the only warning that Jewel was going to erupt into a screaming frenzy. However, Jewel merely appeared as bored as a plastic mannequin, her face quite blank. She looked better than she had in months, so perhaps the new treatment was working as well as Dr. Green had hoped it would. Helen found it impossible to keep back the familiar raging sense of injustice, though. Surely a girl with a face so beautiful, a skin so perfect, with such long pale silky hair, who moved with such grace, should have a personality to match? But God and fate had blundered.

Helen returned her gaze to her friend, saying more quietly,

"Florida, why did you bring her?" Still the pediatrician said nothing. It wasn't necessary, as Harold Pederson had come into the room.

There were two men with him. One was an elderly character with a gray ponytail whose laughter lines creased his weather-beaten face. Despite his refined surroundings, he was defiantly clad in worn jeans and a plaid shirt. Helen didn't know his name, but had seen him before, a long time ago, at the same time that she had seen Skye Hamilton. He had been standing at that hospital counter, too. They had both been asking about women and newly born babies, and the nurse had yelled back, and then —

The storm. Helen's arms were tightly folded.

The man with the ponytail marched up to Kate and engulfed her in a huge hug. Then he shook Skye Hamilton's hand, and kissed Maggie Bacchante on both cheeks before hugging her, too. It was a flamboyant display of affection. When he came to a still on the other side of Kate Giacomo, he was still grinning with pleasure.

It was a grin that slipped when he looked at Harold Pederson. Then, for a long, frowning moment, he studied Jewel, who gazed back without a hint of expression. For once, being in the same room with strangers didn't send her off into a tantrum. Instead, she had been off in some world of her own, and not listening to a single word.

There was another man with Harold, a youngish man in a dark suit. He had a blandly businesslike expression and an unnaturally pale face. He looked as if he spent his entire life at a desk, under artificial lights. Helen had definitely never seen him before. A lawyer, she thought. Bracing herself, she lifted her chin, and waited.

For a long moment Harold Pederson said nothing, staring broodingly at Skye Hamilton and the two girls. His jaw was set solid, his lower lip protruding, bristling blond eyebrows lowered. Twenty years ago he had been like a magnificent Viking; now, at almost seventy, he was like an old bull. His wide body was braced, his feet set apart, the muscles of his thick horseman's legs bulging despite the elegant cut of his suit. Despite it all, Helen still found him enormously attractive.

Then at last the small blue eyes shifted. Harold's brooding stare moved to Jewel's blank face, and then he studied the Cinderella girls again.

Finally, he looked at Helen. "I think you know these girls," he said.

"I do indeed." Helen took refuge in her hostess mode, saying brightly, "Have you met them? Kate Giacomo, Maggie Bacchante. Kate and Maggie, this is my husband, Harold Pederson."

He didn't bother to greet them. Instead, he said to Helen, "It's time you told the truth, my dear."

"The truth? I don't understand."

"You do remember the hurricane? Back when *Odyssey* was brand new and beautiful?"

The storm. Helen's mouth went dry. "Of course I remember."

"The chaos in that little fishing port in New Zealand? How the clinic where you gave birth was torn apart by the storm? How three little girls who had just been born were not identified by name or number, because the nurse was killed before she could write up the records?"

Numbly, she nodded. *The storm. The nightmare.*

"Three anonymous newborns, in three unmarked cribs. Yet, when I fought my way into the clinic, you had already claimed one as your own. Remember all that?"

Again, Helen nodded. She was fighting not to clench her eyes shut. The image of her first husband was hovering in the back of her mind. The nightmare touched her yet again.

"So, my dear," Harold went on coldly, "it is time for the truth. Which one of these girls is really our daughter?"

Chapter two

Helen had always been clear-sighted, and she acknowledged in the depths of her heart that it had probably been inevitable that she should fall for a man like her first husband, Pierce Brooke. He was well connected, apparently rich – and – most enticing of all – he was American.

Nine years after her father's arrest for embezzlement and his subsequent suicide, memories of the screaming headlines in the papers still had the power to make Helen wince. She remembered people pointing as she and her mother were driven to the wharf, and the whispering that started up each time she and her mother left any of the saloons of the ship that had carried them to New Zealand. Helen's mother had been half mad with grief, and Helen had mourned too, not just for her father, but for the life in Boston she had left behind as well.

Nothing about New Zealand seemed familiar. She had to get used to everything, the smallness, the casual lifestyle, the constant sense of isolation from what she thought of as the civilized world. She didn't complain to her grieving, prematurely aged mother, but she did rebel. Helen refused to go to school, and not just because she would have had to wear an ugly uniform that belonged to the Victorian era. Helen, at the age of sixteen, had a very clear ambition – to return to the States and make herself independently rich. The only assets she possessed were her body and her beauty, and so she set out to become a model.

She didn't expect it to be easy, which was fortunate, for the going was tough. She was shrewd enough not to waste her time with beauty pageants, but she did make the mistake of falling for the trap of photographic modeling. First she found herself modeling brief underwear, and then a highly-rated photographer in the business raped her. Instead of panicking, Helen blackmailed the man into creating a superb portfolio for her, and signed up with a reputable agency as a runway model. Then she had her first lucky break. Mini-skirts took the country by storm, and Helen had long, beautiful legs.

By the time she turned nineteen Helen was earning big money. Her modeling portfolio was breathtaking, and her portfolio of carefully acquired shares was gilt-edged. When her mother died Helen cashed in the lot, then flew to New York with no intention of flying back.

Helen had chosen New York deliberately, because her sense of self-preservation warned her not to spread her wings in Boston. As it happened, it did not matter, for she fell in love with the rough charm, the pizzazz and sheer energy of the Big Apple, that amazing city of many sirens and few children. She took an apartment on Riverside Drive, and advertised for another girl to share it with her. And so she came to meet Florida Sullivan.

Florida was thirty years old, a redhead with a pair of large cushiony breasts that she called Bust One and Bust Two. She was the daughter of a tycoon in Wyoming who had made several millions out of wheat and racehorses, but despite all that she had studied for a medical degree, and had spent the previous year living in a shack in Trinidad, working with deprived children. Now she was an assistant to a professor of psychiatry at a university in Flushing, a man who had revolutionary theories about the way children learned to speak.

She wore denim, drank beer, and talked all the time about *her* children and *her* professor, Doctor Trevor Green. Helen liked her immensely, and wished Florida wasn't so obviously and hopelessly in love with her mentor.

And it was because of Florida that Helen fell into bed with Pierce Brooke.

It was an unseasonably hot night in September. Florida phoned Helen and begged a favor. "I'm supposed to be at Claudia Vermeeren's party tonight, and I promised my mother that I would, but I can't go, truly. There's this kid — Yeah, the little Mexican girl. We'd given up hope entirely, Helen, but she's finally — My God, Helen, she cussed at us; instead of trying to kill us, she's communicating!"

The moment her cab drew up outside the apartment block on Fifth Avenue, Helen suspected that Florida had really sent her along because she was too scared to go herself. Under the delusion that Claudia Vermeeren was a school friend of Florida's, she had dressed in a soft golden knit that matched her neatly bobbed hair. The bias-cut front was demurely high-necked, but the back plunged to the curve at the base of her spine, and the hem didn't start until a full ten inches above her knees. At that awful moment, looking at the people who were processing through the high reception lobby toward the Vermeeren's private elevator, Helen knew that her choice of dress was disastrous.

Many of the faces were easily recognizable from the society pages, the men in black tie, the women in long black dresses. Most were past middle-age, and they were all turning like automatons to look at her. But, instead of taking flight, Helen lifted her chin and set off across the great mirrored lobby. No one spoke to her in the elevator, and they all stood back when it arrived at the Vermeeren apartment, to let her go in first. Still, she refused to be intimidated. Pretending to herself that she was on the runway of some great fashion house, she stepped across the lush carpet in her famous swaying walk, one foot placed neatly in front of the other.

Just as on the runway, she moved to music in her head, smiling very slightly, her gaze focused in the middle distance so that she did not quite catch anyone's eye. Instead, she studied the great room itself — and was impressed. Fifty feet long, it was arched and multi-pillared, with an ornate rococo ceiling and with world famous artworks hung along the walls. It was as if she had been transported to some palace in Italy. Then, involuntarily, she met the startled eyes of a tall dark man at the other end of the room.

He was forty-five feet away, but in that electric instant it was as if they were the only ones there. She even knew the color of his eyes — dark-brown that glinted with golden lights, like sherry. She had never seen him before, but felt as if he had been waiting all these years in the wings, to play a major, devastating role in her life. With perfect inevitability, she watched him move through the crowd toward her, his expression intent.

He shouldered his way through knots of people as if he did not see them. He arrived; he was towering over her – and long-nailed fingers grasped Helen by the upper arm.

A female voice said, "My dear, you must be Helen Howland. Florida phoned and warned me. Pierce, you bad man, you mustn't monopolize the girl." This was her hostess, Claudia Vermeeren, at least fifty years old, plump, powdered and playful, bright red mouth smiling, small eyes inquisitive. Helen could never recall afterward what she said, or the names of the people she met. The next hour passed in a blur, while she talked and listened mechanically, all the time tinglingly conscious of — Pierce? Pierce Brooke, she learned. Helen sipped champagne that tasted like water, ate delicacies that she did not want. She danced, he danced, but not together. Every time he moved her way some other man stepped into the gap.

Finally she escaped by moving into the shadow of a pair of draped curtains that veiled a balcony. The cool breeze fanned her half-naked back as she held onto the balustrade, looking at the traffic far below. She didn't know Pierce had joined her until, with total unexpectedness, his hand gripped her arm.

His fingers were blunt, hard, unmistakably masculine. Helen whirled and looked up at him. The sherry-brown eyes were brilliant with intensity, wide and fringed with thick black lashes. He said unevenly, "My dance, I think." The moment she moved into his arms he said, "Christ!" She felt him shudder. Then, in an uncontrollable rush he had yanked her close to his rigid body, and they were kissing.

It was like a delirium. Beyond the curtains Helen heard brittle social chatter and sweet music, but all of it was utterly meaningless. She clung to him as they danced, out of the balcony and onto the floor, traversing the room in slow sensuous circles, moving like a single spirit. Then Pierce had maneuvered her into the elevator, through the lobby, and out into the street. The taxi ride passed in a blur, and she scarcely saw the vestibule of his building. An elevator, a corridor, the door to his apartment, and then with frantic passion they fell onto his bed, too driven by overriding urgency to undress.

The next week they got married, and Helen went with Pierce to Washington, D.C.. She gave up her apartment, her assignments, her ambitions. For Pierce Brooke, she was willing to do anything at all.

Chapter three

Helen's first husband was a kind of diplomatic broker. Pierce Brooke advised governments on foreign aid and international loans, and organized export and import arrangements for Asian and Middle Eastern countries. It was fashionable to adapt modern capitalist economic theories to the globe at large, but even after three and a half years of marriage, Helen had never quite understood how he made his living. Pierce was reputed to be brilliant in his field, and was constantly in demand. He charged a commission for all the deals he masterminded, and should have been comfortably rich. But Helen, while she found the work itself an enigma, did discover very fast that Pierce spent money much faster than he made it.

Despite this, Helen coped well with the Washington lifestyle, as the lessons she'd absorbed in her Boston-Brahmin childhood served her well. But now, when she looked back on all this, her memories of Washington were of loneliness, as Pierce was away such a lot, on trips to far-flung capitals that did not include her. So, being practical, she had decided to do something to fill the empty space in her life, and to make the extra money they badly needed. So, the next time he was home, Helen informed Pierce she was going into business.

She described it to Pierce as a School of Modern Manners. He laughed derisively, and prophesied disaster, but to her great satisfaction, it worked. For a hefty fee she groomed the wives of new politicians, to equip them for the social minefield of Washington. She taught them how to walk, how to dress, and how to host a soiree. She did not need to advertise. The first clients did it for her, by word of mouth. The timing, also, was excellent. Within a year of a turnaround election most of the politicians and lobbyists had been replaced by men whose wives were intimidated by the unknown niceties and conventions of Washington society, and were anxious to hire an advisor.

Success piled on success, and kept Helen very busy – so preoccupied, in fact, that it wasn't until after the second anniversary of their marriage that she realized she scarcely saw her husband at all. She thought that she'd known it all along, subconsciously, but full realization came with a jolt.

It happened not long after a strange man phoned her, to make a most unusual appointment. He said he was Harold Pederson's personal assistant. Harold Pederson, the shipping baron, wished to consult with Helen Brooke on an important and very personal matter.

It was held in his office, on the penthouse floor of the Pederson building on lower Connecticut Avenue. A car was sent for her. The Pederson building was magnificent enough, but as she stepped through the great glass doors of the entrance, Helen had the feeling that if it had not been for the building laws of the city, it would have been a dozen floors higher. Oddly, she had the same first impression of Harold Pederson himself, when he rose from his seat behind his desk to greet her. He was tall, yet of such enormous presence that she felt he should have been a good six inches taller than he was.

He was very fair skinned, with a ruddy, rocky face that had considerable charm when he smiled. However, he described himself as just another rough Swede. Helen knew better, as she had read some of the many magazine articles written about this remarkable man. It was his grandfather who had been the rough Swede who had founded the family empire. Harold's father had broadened the horizons to include the United States, and Harold himself had been born on American soil.

His small blue eyes watched her all the time, studying her alertly while Helen murmured politenesses and wondered what this was all about. Harold, with an abrupt directness that she soon found was typical of him, did not leave her in the dark for long. His image as a financial giant needed improvement; he was tired of being a rough Swede. He wanted his manners polished, and he wanted Helen Brooke to work the miracle.

"I have seen you before," he said. "Though you don't remember. I was doing some business with your husband, and you were both at one of those appalling banquets. I was very impressed then, and have been even more impressed since. I know you can do this for me."

Helen almost committed the unforgivable blunder of laughing in surprise. Then, when she had control of herself, she refused, politely but firmly. She did not, she said, run courses in deportment for men. Again Harold Pederson surprised her, by not protesting. Instead, he stared at her for a long time in silence, his manner brooding. Then, abruptly, he dismissed her.

But within days Helen found that once Harold Pederson had made up his mind, his determination never wavered. He tried the same approach twice more, offering her more money each time. Then he asked her if she would advise him professionally on the redecoration of his summer home.

Helen paused before refusing, intrigued by the idea – and it was then she fully realized what a strangely small part in her life Pierce played now, because her husband was in Egypt. And, most intriguingly, Harold Pederson's summer home was on the island of Martha's Vineyard.

Again, he persisted, and finally she agreed to go. They flew there early on a Sunday morning, in Harold's executive jet. The bright summer sun highlighted quaint gingerbread houses as the Pederson limousine drove through Oak Bluffs towards the northern end of the picturesque island. The Pederson estate was surrounded by a ten foot-high ornamental wrought-iron fence, with immense gates that swung open at some electrical signal. There were deer browsing in the long grass under the live oaks, but nothing prepared Helen for the sight of the house. Immense, crouched low to the ground, built of hand-quarried stone, it spoke of uncounted millions, money that could be squandered and then forgotten, as the house was shamefully neglected.

The interior was centered on a big square hall, with a battered swooping stairway that led up to a lovely mock-Tudor gallery, where much of the railing was broken. Helen looked about at cloth-draped furniture, cobwebs and dust, and began to feel angry. She said, "Harold, you are wasting my time."

"Huh?" The grunt was abrupt, and his head had sunk down between his massive shoulders as he stared at her, but she had the strange impression that her reaction pleased him. "Why so?"

"You don't want a woman's advice. You need a professional decorator – and that decorator will want a year and a very big budget to restore this ruin."

He seemed amused. "If I don't want a woman's advice, then why did you give it to me?"

Then they flew over to Nantucket Island, simply because he wanted to eat a fish lunch at a certain restaurant on Water Street. At that time of day on a Sunday the restaurant was full and had been fully booked for months, but a table was swiftly found for Harold Pederson and his companion. Helen felt a most unaccustomed sense of being pampered, knowing that women at the other tables were glancing her way with envy.

Harold said in his abrupt way, "I need a hostess."

Helen silently agreed with him. His affairs were notorious. In his teens he had married a London debutante, who soon left him for an older man. Another marriage had ended suddenly when his blonde bombshell wife had failed to take a bend in her new Ferrari. Since then, he had taken out a series of film stars and models, mostly in a blaze of unsavory publicity. None of those would improve his image the way he wanted.

He said, "Will you do it?"

"What will it involve?"

"You will come whenever I ask, to wherever I might be entertaining people. Important people, clients, other businessmen. Politicians. Princes. Sultans. It could be anywhere in the world. It has become important to me that I entertain them in style. I know that you will do it superbly."

Stunned by the concept, Helen stared in silence, wondering why she was so attracted by this big, abrupt, ugly man. Harold Pederson's whole manner tough and experienced. He lacked all the qualities of culture and refinement that she admired, and yet he had enormous charisma, made up of total confidence in his power and virility.

She had dreamed erotically about him the night before, and now he was offering her the kind of life that had only existed in her dreams. Images filled Helen's mind, of exotic settings, gracious dinners, parties where great personalities gathered. She would be like the legendary hostesses of history – Lady Mary Wortley Montague, Madame Pompadour, Empress Josephine ...

Nevertheless, she said, "No,"

"Why not?"

"I'm married." Though of course he knew that; he had done business with her husband.

"Ah," he said, and smiled – and in that moment something told Helen, with uncanny sureness, that he meant to marry her. She had shivered, staring at him, feeling trapped in some kind of golden web, and he smiled and said, "I think your husband needs money."

Chapter four

Afterwards, Helen often thought that her life would have turned out very differently if Pierce had been at home when she got back that night. As it was, he had left Egypt, but only to go to Geneva, to organize something important there.

When Harold failed to get in touch with her the next day and then the next, she began, contrarily, to feel piqued. He was in town, she knew, but a whole week went by without hearing from him. When the envelope arrived for her, addressed in a hand that was familiar to her already, she tore it open with impatient fingers. And then froze, sick to the heart, as the photographs slipped out. Pictures of Pierce and a much talked-about French actress. Some were innocent, some were not, but what knifed Helen to the very soul was the expression in the actress's eyes as she gazed up at Pierce.

Utter, confident ownership.

The phone rang. Helen numbly picked it up. Harold's voice said, without any preliminaries, "Will you marry me?"

She said, "Yes."

"Good. I'll arrange the divorce." The phone went down, and that was that. Helen was summoned to a lawyer, signed papers and returned to her apartment, all without seeing Harold.

When there was a knock on the door at eleven at night she felt a nudge of warning, because it was so like the time when the damning photographs had been delivered. However, she ignored the premonition and rushed to the door and threw it open, saying, "Harold!" And looked straight into brilliant sherry-brown eyes.

She gasped Pierce's name and fell back. It was like the first time, at Claudia Vermeeren's party in New York. She felt as if the years were rushing back, except that this time she was terribly afraid. Pierce was dead white, his beard stubble dark against his drawn skin. She was wearing a thin gown over a diaphanous nightdress, and felt naked. When he reached out and gripped her shoulders she opened her mouth to scream, but any sound she was about to make was quenched by his furious kiss.

Her body caught fire with the old familiar lust. To her eternal shame she hollowed and clung to him, and then all humiliation was swept away in a mindless fury of desire. They made love the way they had the first time, with wordless mutual sensuality, racing together to a pinnacle of release.

When Helen came to her senses she lay still, stricken with disbelieving horror. When she turned her head, Pierce was staring at her, his expression bleak. She had the impression he'd been staring a long time. He said, "So my love, we are to divorce?"

She said nothing, but got up and fetched the photographs. She stood very still, looking down on his bent dark head as he studied them, and said bitterly, "You really did need the money, Pierce."

"What makes you think that?" He looked up, his expression puzzled, and that was when she realized the full extent of his betrayal.

Helen shut her eyes a moment, pressing down the anger and pain. Then she said very clearly, "You fool, Pierce. I thought Harold was paying you to fake grounds for our divorce. But you really were having affair with that bitch – and was she the first, Pierce, was she?" His expression told her the answer to that question, too. So she threw him out of her life. She told him to go, and Pierce dressed and went, without another word. In the morning Helen packed a bag and took a cab to Harold's apartment.

The next day, after they had made love for the first time, Harold gave her the enormous solitaire she had worn ever since. Then he told her that Pierce had flown to Mexico, where he signed the papers that completed the divorce. One week later, Helen and Harold were married, and one week after that, Pierce failed to take a corner in his brand new Porsche.

The following month, Helen realized she was pregnant.

As soon as she suspected she was to have a baby, Helen made an appointment with Dr. Jim Hansen. He was the fashionable obstetrician of the moment, but Helen would have consulted him in any case. He was Harold's first cousin, so going to anyone else would have been unthinkable.

She hadn't expected to dislike him, but Jim Hansen's demeanor was professional and chilly. While he asked her to address him by his first name, he never called her Helen, but always *My dear*. She found that subtly patronizing, and disliked the analytical expression in his blue eyes as he studied her minutely. The thorough care he took over the examination was reassuring, but nevertheless she was very aware that Harold's relatives could not have been happy about this, his third marriage. And they would certainly not be happy that he was about to have an heir.

"Harold will be over the moon," Dr. Hansen said when he finally confirmed that she was both pregnant and healthy. "He'd given up every hope of ever siring an heir. You've done very well, my dear."

Helen nodded, acutely aware that his speculative eyes were watching her as she slid off the examination table and got dressed. Then, just as she was preparing to leave, she saw him smile.

He said very softly, "I know Harold won't mind what sex the baby turns out to be – but we must hope that its eyes are blue."

Her heart jerked, but she hid it, arching one eyebrow.

"I'm not sure what you mean," she said.

"Brown eyes are dominant, my dear. If one parent is blue-eyed and the other brown-eyed, the odds are at least three to one that the baby will have brown eyes. You and Harold both have blue eyes, so the chances that your baby will have brown eyes are almost nil."

Jim Hansen paused then, leaning back in his leather chair, still smiling slightly while he twirled a gold pen in long manicured fingers. "While it is not unknown for a blue-eyed couple to have a brown-eyed baby, it is very unusual indeed. It's common knowledge, my dear. I'm amazed that you didn't know it already."

The veiled threat was unmistakable. Helen looked down and slowly brushed her skirt with the palm of her left hand, the one with the enormous diamond. She took a slow, deep breath and then proudly lifted her head, smiling coldly right into his clinical expression.

"But I did not know it – and I'm sure Harold will be fascinated, too, when I tell him," she said.

At the time, she had the satisfaction of seeing Jim Hansen's smile slip, but inside the first chill tendrils of panic were clutching at her heart.

The next day, after making an excuse to Harold, she caught the train to New York, because she desperately needed a long talk with her best friend, Dr. Florida Sullivan.

Naturally, Florida was delighted to see her. It was only the second time they had got together since Helen had married Harold. She also looked delighted when Helen revealed that she was pregnant, exclaiming that they must go to lunch to celebrate — "But no wine, sweetie!"

Helen took a deep breath. "There's more," she said, and launched onto the long, humiliating confession, while Florida's expression became increasingly serious.

When she ran to a stop, the silence seemed endless. Still without speaking, Florida stood up, and looked out the window at the building rearing up on the other side of the street. Then finally she returned to the other side of her desk.

Looking down at a pencil that she had picked up, she said, "So you slept with Pierce one night, and with Harold the next?"

"Yes." It sounded so awful that Helen added quickly, "I was still married to Pierce at the time."

"But he could be the baby's father — and you are now married to another man."

Helen winced. "It's possible that Pierce is responsible — and possible that Harold is the father, too. I fell pregnant the month I slept with them both."

"And Pierce has brown eyes." Florida knew Pierce Brooke; she had been a witness at their wedding.

"Yes." Helen vividly remembered her first husband's eyes. Brown with golden lights, rimmed with thick black lashes. Almost girlish, but his best feature.

"Both his parents had brown eyes?"

"I don't know. I never met them. By the time we got married they were dead."

The pencil rolled back and forth, back and forth. "And you are very fair, with very blue eyes. Did both your parents have blue eyes?"

"My mother's eyes were blue. I don't remember my father's eyes, but I can check from photos. His hair was dark; I do remember that. So it is likely that his eyes were dark, too."

"So, if Pierce is the father of your child, the baby's eyes are almost bound to be brown. The genes that trigger eye color are there to be linked. But what about Harold? What is his coloring?"

"He's very fair, with blue eyes."

"And his parents?"

"Both blue-eyed. Nordic stock, all the way back to his great-grandparents."

Florida grimaced. "Have you thought about an abortion?"

"No!" Helen was horrified. "Never!" She really wanted this baby. "And Harold's doctor-cousin is bound to congratulate him on the news."

"Then I am so sorry, sweetie, but you will just have to hope that Harold's sperm beat Pierce's sperm to your egg."

"Oh God," said Helen. "Oh God, oh *God.*"

They went out for lunch, and she did drink wine, She normally drank very little, but this time she needed it.

And thirty-eight weeks later she gave birth to a baby girl in a little clinic in faraway New Zealand. She was in that strange place because of Harold's fancy new motor yacht — the yacht that so nearly foundered in the storm.

Chapter five

The *Odyssey* was the kind of luxury pleasure craft that few men could dream of owning. Costing many millions of dollars to build and fit out, the motor yacht had been designed, built and outfitted in New Zealand, as that country that was considered the epitome of yacht-building – or so Harold bragged. He carried Helen along when he flew to Auckland to collect his new toy, despite her advanced pregnancy, as he claimed he wanted her to watch as the ship was launched into the water.

And that decision had very nearly cost him his precious yacht and all their lives, for, once launched, it was impossible for him to resist the urge to take the boat to sea.

When they sailed out of Waitemata Harbour, occasional squalls gusted across the sky, spitting rain and writing rainbows over the Auckland skyline, but most of the time the sun shone. The stiff south-west breeze filled flags and set banners snapping, tautened the canvas of a multitude of little sailboats, and sent the smoke of a departing freighter flying forwards. It was most breathtakingly beautiful, and Helen stood for hours on the breezy open deck, drinking it all in.

The storm warnings came over the marine radio as the *Odyssey* was negotiating the Colville Channel, at the northern tip of the Coromandel Peninsula. It didn't sound too dire, as it was April, and the south Pacific hurricane season was supposed to be over — and, anyway, the usual path for a cyclone was to the east of New Zealand, where its force normally dispersed over a set of remote atolls. The forecasters didn't expect more than a dusting.

Young Captain Castellano was less optimistic. Helen heard him say to Harold that it could get rough, and it might be a good idea to turn back. He was an Italian who hailed from Naples, a port with a long maritime history, so was bound to be a fine seaman, or so Helen thought. But Harold just laughed. He was enjoying himself immensely, and didn't want it to end. Castellano had been promoted from the first officer's job on one of Harold's freight carriers, so was easily over-ruled, but Helen could see the worry in his face.

A couple of hours later, it was definitely getting rough. The yacht, with its low profile, wasn't rolling to the same extent as the huge car-carrier that was heading for the horizon, but still the movement was uncomfortable. Then it started to rain, the water flicking across the sea with every gust. Between the gusts it was calm again, but the air outside the open side window was sultry, too warm for this time of year in the south Pacific, heavily oppressive. The shipyard foreman and the designer, who had come along on this maiden jaunt, were beginning to look as worried, too.

But then, all at once, it was too late to turn back. A dense black bank of cloud was rushing towards them from the starboard beam, coming like a wall, sweeping over the water. The car-carrier was lost to sight in the murk. The gale freshened with a roar, tearing great clouds out of the oncoming wall of the storm, and all they could do was run south.

Captain Castellano turned to Helen, and advised her that she should go back to the owner's suite, and sit somewhere secure. His brown eyes were kind, as well as worried. There was a door from the bridge that led to Harold's private office on the mezzanine level of his suite. Helen went through this, and down the steps to the lounge area of his suite, and wedged herself into one of the plush armchairs.

When she turned on the television, the newscasters were talking about the intensifying storm. Unexpectedly, there were floods in the far north of the country. Still, the expectation was that the storm would turn east, but the shaky, rain-spotted scenes of fallen trees and blocked roads were grim.

When suppertime came Helen ate from a tray of finger food that was carried to her by a Filipina steward. When Helen asked the sedate young woman about herself, she learned that the girl had been recruited at the same time as Captain Castellano. Her name, she said, was Constantia, and she hailed from Manila. Then, after telling Helen that if help was needed all she needed to do was call, she went away.

By bedtime, Helen hadn't seen Harold for some hours, and she was feeling the first symptoms of seasickness. She took a tablet when she went to bed, and slept for an hour or so, but was woken abruptly as the yacht began to surge up and down on unseen waves. When she called out, Constantia came in with another young woman, and between the two of them they helped Helen to the bathroom. When she had finished, they tucked her tightly back into bed, hauling on the covers so that she was swaddled, and would not be jerked out by the lurching of the boat.

When Helen asked for Harold, Constantia told her that the yacht was battling tremendous seas to get to a safe anchorage. It was impossible to turn north, as the cyclone was coming from that direction, so the *Odyssey* was headed south, racing to a little game-fishing port named on the charts as Homerville. The yacht designer knew it, Constantia said, as he kept his pleasure launch there, and so he was helping to navigate. And Mr. Pederson was on the bridge, keeping lookout.

Helen took another tablet, but was unable to sleep. The noise was deafening. With each cross sea the yacht pitched wildly, and the waves pounded her hull like deadly hammers. The vessel became a jar of ugly noises, of plates and ornaments crashing, loosely secured furniture sliding about, panes of glass smashing. Worst of all, however, were the sounds from above, the tons of water that washed the decks with every lurch, and the constant, awful whistling of the wind in the superstructure.

Twice, Helen had to call Constantia to help her to the bathroom again. The second time, as she was pushing a cold cloth over her hot face, a long contraction dragged at her distended belly. For a long numb moment, as she clung to the edge of the vanity, she couldn't comprehend what was happening. The contraction went on and on, rippling and peaking, easing and then worsening, so unexpectedly that her breath hissed between her teeth. Then, feeling sick, she understood.

Mercifully, it went. Trembling violently, Helen was able to stand upright, staring at her shocked reflection in the mirror as she tried to cope with the realization that she was in labor. Then, to her horror and humiliation, her waters burst in a warm scented gush down her legs. Helen whimpered with shame, and then burst into tears of fright.

The primitive protest was lost in the even more primeval thunder of the storm. She straightened, tried to calm herself, looked about, grabbed a towel and crammed it between her legs. Then she called out for Constantia. The other room steward came too, and they helped her back into the bed, and swaddled her tightly again.

Constantia's round face was kind. "Do you have children?" Helen asked.

"Fifty-seven, but none of my own," said Constantia with a smile. It didn't make sense. Then Helen forgot it, as another contraction rolled through her. Her confinement was coming fast. Soon, somehow, someone would have to help her deliver her baby. She wished fervently that Constantia had had children of her own, because then she would have known what to do.

But the next time Constantia came, it was to tell her that Captain Castellano had worked the miracle. They had rounded an important little cape, and were going to make Homerville just before it became impossible to make any landing at all. And at last Harold came into the suite. He looked dreadful, his eyes dazed and bloodshot from the long, sleepless night, but when she whispered into his ear, there was a flash of joy in his eyes. Then, he looked tense, bracing himself as he went back to the bridge to tell the captain about this new emergency.

It took yet another supreme feat of seamanship on the part of the captain and crew to hold the *Odyssey* to the wharf long enough for Harold to carry Helen down the gangway and onto the street. The designer had told him how to get to the little hospital. Mercifully, it wasn't far.

But the rain poured, and the wind howled, and once Helen had to beg Harold to hold still for a moment, as she was wracked with yet another contraction, this time accompanied by a primitive urge to bear down. Even though her clenched eyes she could see that the wild black sky was lit eerily every now and then with the blue flicker of falling power lines. Then the contraction eased, and Harold made the last sprint for the clinic door, which he pounded until they were let inside.

The district nurse examined Helen briefly, then sent a messenger for the doctor. The baby would not be born for quite a few hours yet, or so she said. Harold kissed Helen after she was settled in one of the little wards, and then went back to his precious yacht, to take part in the battle to secure her safely.

But forty minutes later Helen was moved to the surgery, her confinement unexpectedly rapid.

*****

When the eye of the hurricane arrived, bringing a strange, temporary release from the turmoil of the storm, Helen's baby girl was one hour old. Helen herself was struggling to emerge from a drug-induced sleep, beset by an overwhelming sense of unreality, knowing she'd been disturbed by some kind of commotion. For several terrible moments she could not remember where she was. Then she remembered the storm – the *storm!*

Helen lurched up in bed, trembling and chilled, close to vomiting, utterly disoriented and quite alone, even though she felt convinced that someone had come into the room and disturbed her. She was by herself – where? Helen stared wildly about at furniture, a chair upholstered in a flowered chintz that matched the curtains, a dressing table holding photographs of people she had never met in her life, a Peter Scott print of a flight of ducks. The room looked like a suburban bedroom, but had the unmistakable anesthetic-disinfectant smell of a clinic. She was alone, but could hear urgent voices echoing in the distance, and rapid footsteps, people calling out. Everything echoed – the steps, the voices, children crying, groans in the distance, the faint wail of a very young infant...

Memory returned with a rush. Helen slumped back on the pillows with a groan, aware now of the pain in the muscles of her tightly bound abdomen and the swollen numbness between her aching thighs. She remembered the barely suppressed panic in the doctor's voice as he had delivered her child, and the awful crashing sounds as the gale played havoc with the trees about the hospital. The doctor was an old man, probably retired, she thought. His trepidation had been obvious, in the way he snapped at the harried nurse, and the trembling of his liver-spotted hands. His eyes had been bloodshot, sliding about worriedly above his mask, never really looking at her, even when she cried out with the pain and fear of giving birth. Instead he had curtly instructed the nurse to give her an injection.

Then, just as her baby gave its first furious cry, a vehicle of some kind had arrived outside and Helen had heard men shouting out for help. The awful sounds of the hurricane abruptly worsened as an outer door opened, and then that door slammed back and forth like the double crash of doom. Footsteps ran along the corridor. A woman in the near distance was screaming. Helen, her heart lurching with fright, tried to sit up on the delivery table, but the doctor pushed her down again.

She had just time to glimpse her baby dangling upside down, the little legs held in the nurse's rubber-gloved hand. A girl — she was screaming, a heart-rending wail. Helen reached out her arms, but the doctor ignored her. Instead, he snapped to the flustered nurse that this was no time to fuss over a newborn baby who could easily survive a few hours unwashed, and then he ran out of the surgery.

More shouting, closer, very urgent. Helen heard the doctor cry out, "Clear the goddamn theatre, nurse!" She saw the nurse bundle the naked squalling infant into a receiving blanket and then into a crib. Helen called out in protest as the crib was rushed out of the room, but no one answered, and for a terrible moment she was left all alone in the antiseptic operating theatre. Then two nurses had hurried in with a frenzied rustling of plastic overgowns, but they ignored her too, laying out instruments and cleaning surfaces with frantic speed.

The only person who spoke to Helen was a white-coated porter, who ran in with a wheelchair. He was a scrawny middle-aged man, but he lifted her easily. As he wheeled her out of the surgery he said in a jolly voice, "It's your lucky day. Five star accommodation for you tonight." The crowded corridor went by in a blur, and then they raced through the waiting room. There was a man sitting there whose face was covered in blood, more blood running down his arms and elbows. The porter stopped, scribbled something in a big book, and then pushed Helen to a door marked Private, and through the door into this bedroom. Then he whipped back the covers, and slid her into this bed, as neatly as a sausage into its skin.

Helen, lost in shock, said nothing. Instead, she fell back against the pillows and into a deep, sick sleep where she struggled with nightmares. Then someone had come in, she was certain of it. She had been woken by the slam of the door as that person went out. And now she was awake, and the world had gone silent. Was the storm over? If so, where was Harold?

The room and bed, she deduced, must belong to the district nurse, a woman who acted as midwife and medical aide to this whole huge isolated area. When Helen had been admitted she had been put to bed in one of the two wards, each of which had three beds. Otherwise the small hospital was made up of a surgery-cum-operating theatre, a dispensary and the waiting room, seemingly adequate for normal purposes. But on a night like this one, Helen now realized, it had been necessary to bundle her in here, out of the way, to make room for the victims of the cyclone.

And now, thought Helen, struggling up on her elbows in this alien, yet strangely domestic room, her baby was born, and was in a crib somewhere in the clinic. She remembered how the baby had screamed. Was she still crying? Harold was the father of a girl. She wondered tensely if he knew it yet. Had he come back? Surely not. If he had, he would have been hovering by her bed as she awoke.

Despite his blind arrogance in making her travel to New Zealand when her pregnancy was so well advanced, Harold was besotted with delight about the prospect of being a father. Indeed, when Dr. Jim Hansen had congratulated Harold on his potential fatherhood — right after that first consultation, just as she had dreaded — Harold had been so overwhelmed with delight that he had issued a press statement to inform the world that at long last, at the age of forty-seven, and after a third marriage, he was about to be blessed with an heir. Then he had stunned both Helen and the gossip columnists with the announcement that he had made legal arrangements to endow Helen with an unconditional private income of a million dollars a year, payment to start when his baby was born, and to continue as long as the baby lived.

The news, not surprisingly, had been the sensation of the season. Making Harold Pederson a father had given Helen financial freedom. It should have felt like the fulfillment of all her dreams. Instead, Helen remembered the nightmares she had been having before she woke to the eerie silence. Nightmares about her first husband, Pierce Brooke.

She sat up, shivering despite the closeness of the air, crossing her arms over her swollen breasts. She could hear a baby whimper in a room nearby. When she turned her head she saw a door she hadn't noticed before. It was slightly ajar, and she could see that it led to a bathroom. So that was where the nurse had put her baby, she thought, and felt the old familiar dread coil in her stomach. Her head was full of unwelcome pictures, of Pierce and his dark-brown eyes.

Outside, it was weirdly silent. The eye of the hurricane, she realized then. The newscasters had discussed the science of hurricanes when she was watching television on board the yacht, and some roped-in egghead had talked brightly about the center, where the pressure was very low, and the winds whirled madly around it. Her eardrums hurt, as if she were in a plane that had descended too fast, and the silence seemed suffocating, the strangely still air hard to breathe. Helen thought she would faint if the window was not opened soon, and slowly, groggily, she began to ease her way out of bed.

Chapter six

Nurse Betty Turner spread her hands on the reception counter of the clinic, resting her weight on them and suppressing the tremble in her fingers. There were splotches of blood and mud on her white uniform, and she felt drained beyond mere exhaustion. At thirty-eight, overweight, unmarried, eternally harassed, she had often wondered why she had ever decided to be a nurse, but now she questioned it with a deep, ghastly weariness.

It was fate and her parents' fertility at fault, she brooded. She was the eldest and the only girl of a family of five, whose mother had died when she was fifteen years old. As far back as she could remember she had been a slave to her four younger brothers. It was fated that she should be either a teacher or a nurse, and nursing as a career had seemed safer. But the way it turned out, the doctors and tutors had treated her just the way her brothers had, and on top of that she was terrified of falling to pieces in emergencies. To hide all this, she treated her patients like a tyrant.

She stared at the two men who stood waiting in front of the counter, filled with anger and formless dislike, annoyed with them for hanging about when all the staff were stretched to human limits by the storm.

It was weird, what the storm had done to people. There were the expected broken legs and heads, but some of the wounds had been grotesque. Falling trees were bad but roofing iron was the worst. There was that poor fellow who had lost most of one leg when a sheet

of iron had slammed down from the roof of his barn, and the kids –
oh God, the poor little children.

Betty particularly hated to see hurt kids. All her life she had
worried about brothers who had gone off to do crazy stunts on horses
and bicycles, and who rode overpowered motorbikes and parachuted
out of airplanes. It had all been on purpose, just to torment her, she
was certain, and seeing the children who were brought in on
makeshift stretchers tonight had made her feel sick to the stomach.
Now she stared at these two men and loathed them, because they
were taking up valuable space and time, and yet were so obviously
unhurt.

She snapped at the younger one, "Yes?"

He looked startled. He was a tall, dark young man, with a scruffy
black beard. Betty had never seen him before in her life, and hated
beards, because she thought they were dirty. All her brothers had
been lazy about shaving, forcing her to nag them about their scruffy
stubble all the time. This fellow was younger than he had seemed at
first sight, too, probably only eighteen or nineteen, unusually young
to have so much facial hair. Betty decided that it probably meant he
was oversexed, and said coldly, "I assume you're here for a reason?"

He flushed. "I came here with the woman who had her baby in the
storm, and now I want to know how she is, and the baby, too."

So he was the father, Betty guessed, and no doubt the other man,
the muscular one with a droopy moustache and a ponytail, was his
dad. She fought down the remembered panic. The hospital was taxed
if ten babies were born here in the course of a normal year. It had
been incredibly bad luck that three should arrive in the middle of
disaster.

Babies meant paperwork. She'd delivered two of them and had
admitted the third, and so she was the poor bitch who had to do the
job. With abrupt movements Betty Turner pulled over a block of

forms and three baby-sized identification bracelets, and said curtly to the younger man, "Name?"

He blinked. "Hamilton. Why?"

Betty's teeth set so tight they gritted. "I have to certify the birth of your baby."

"What?" To her irritation he gave an embarrassed laugh. "The baby isn't mine, though I delivered her on the way here. I was driving the mother to the clinic when the car broke down, and the baby came while we were waiting to be rescued. The little girl is Stefano Bacchante's daughter. And I would really like to know how Stefano is, too. I reported that he was badly hurt when I got here. Was he rescued, or is he still lying hurt in his barn?"

Betty felt mortified. Stefano Bacchante was the man who had lost a major part of one leg. He had lost a lot of blood too, before some Maori farmers had heard his cry for help, and had brought him to the clinic. His wife was sitting with him now, but no one had bothered to inform Betty that one of the babies was theirs.

To save face, she turned to the other man, figuring that he must be the father of the third baby. He was a much older man, fifty if he was a day, and looked as tough as a boot as well. She thought sourly that he was really pushing it, being a new father at his age. His disgusting ponytail was gray, but he was looking at her face and breasts as if he found her sexy.

Betty Turner flushed and snapped, "Name?"

Jerry said, "Jack." The name in his passport was Giacomo, but he hated having to spell it out all the time, and, anyway, he was tired of listening to dumb jokes about barrel organs and monkeys.

"How do you spell that?"

He sighed inwardly. "Jay. Ay. Cee. Kay."

"Mother's name?"

Jerry paused. The mother was a dancer he had found in a London nightclub. After just one night he had liked her enough to invite her to come along with him on an extended jaunt to New Zealand. Back then, neither of them had known she was five months gone, but when they had been told that she was pregnant, it hadn't worried him a bit — not until now.

Her name? Her stage name was Kelly. The surname in her passport was Parkin and the given name was Debbie, but she liked to be called Kelly, as that was the name of her favorite stepfather. Over the four months of travel Jerry had gathered not only that she had been subjected to abuse for much of her life, but that there had been rather a lot of stepfathers. The one called Kelly was the one she'd liked best.

Though not enough to ask for his help when she was in trouble. Nevertheless, Jerry said, "Kelly." Then he spelled it out, watching the nurse print the name on the form.

She shouted, "I need the surname, sir. Just in case you didn't know it, the Christian name is not enough for our records."

"Kelly is the surname. It's the complete name she goes under."

When she looked up again he added, "And I'm not her baby's father."

Then he grinned, right into her eyes. Betty was trembling with fatigue and fury. He had deliberately set out to make a fool of her, she thought.

She snapped, "If neither of you are immediate relatives it would be much easier on our stretched resources if you'd go home and wait for news there. The storm might be over, but that doesn't mean that the emergency is past!"

Both men stared at her. Then the young one shook his head and said emphatically, "No, it isn't."

"I beg your pardon?"

"The hurricane isn't over. We're in the middle of it, what they call the eye. A hurricane," he explained pedantically, "is like a big whirlpool of air, formed about a centre of very low pressure. In that centre, the air is very calm, the way it is right now. But when it moves on the hurricane starts again, only the gale blows from the opposite direction. So, there is still half the storm to go."

He sounded as if he knew what he was talking about. Exhausted tears shot into Betty's eyes, and she refused to believe him. Surely God wouldn't be cruel enough to send the storm back? But the other, older, man was nodding. Half the storm to go? Betty's hands began to shake. Without knowing it, she was tearing the form she had written on into little pieces. When she realized that the door of the district nurse's bedroom was open, she whirled.

She shouted, "What the hell are you doing out of bed?"

The woman flinched. She was standing in the doorway, holding herself up with her hands braced on the frame. Her face was dead white, except for hectic splashes of color high on her cheekbones. Even in her shapeless hospital gown she was lissom and beautiful, golden haired and graceful, everything that Betty Turner wasn't. Assisting at this woman's delivery seemed a nightmare age ago. Betty's only clear memory of it was how Doc Judd had snapped and yelled, the old fool. He was well past retirement, and clumsy and irascible with age, but because of the storm they had been forced to call him in.

Betty snapped, "What are you trying to do?"

The woman was looking at the two men, staring from one to the other. Then she said in a faltering voice, "There are three babies – three. In cribs – in the bathroom. *Three* babies."

Of course there were three. All girls. By some miracle all three were alive. When she thought about the third baby, the shake in Betty's hands became uncontrollable. Doc Judd had been attending to an accident victim when the third mother – Kelly? – was rushed in, and so Betty had been in charge of the delivery. The baby had been born okay, but when Betty had been delivering the afterbirth the woman began to convulse, flopping about on the table. Luckily, Doc Judd had run in fast and taken over, as Betty had been terrified so witless that all she could do was scream.

One of the men said, "Babies? In a bathroom?"

"Where else could we put the babies?" she shouted. "There's an emergency on, you know!"

Sirens screamed outside as if in confirmation, and Betty heard the hurried grating of tires. She would put the bracelets on the babies and fill in the forms when the storm was over, she confusedly thought, as there was far too much to do right now. And, as if on cue, urgent voices called out for help.

The two men whirled and ran outside. Betty snapped at the woman, "Get back into bed." Then, without waiting to see if the woman obeyed, she ran out, leaving the door open in her hurry.

The two men who had been nagging Betty about the babies were now helping drenched policemen carry in two battered and bloodied stretchers. She could hear what they were saying, their voices ringing out in the calm. Many roads were impassable, blocked with fallen trees and mudslides. Chimneys were down, roofs whisked away. A car radio was blaring out more grim reports. The little town was unnaturally dark, lit only by a few hand-carried lanterns that were not as bright as the weird brilliance of the stars. She could see the silhouette of a man running up from the quay where the rich American's yacht had finally been secured. It was the Yank himself, she guessed, come to get his baby and his wife.

It was her last coherent thought. The stars were abruptly blotted out. It was as if a great hand had been drawn across the sky. The world went dark and the gale roared back. There was not so much as a moment's warning. One of the stretchers that the men were handling was picked up, lifted high by the wind and then dumped, along with its cargo. It knocked Betty down, slamming her head against the car, breaking her neck with an unheard snap. Jerry was blown off his feet three times while trying to get to her, and when he saw the way her head lolled he cursed and jerked away.

The hurricane's return was as murderous as it had been before, but its vicious force hit the opposite way. Trees which had leaned over in the gale earlier were now snapped back and broken, and half-peeled roofing iron was torn away completely, twisted and rolled into frenzied shapes. The tempest lunged at the hospital building, its full blast directed at the side that had been the sheltered one before.

A tremendous gust came in the window that Helen Pederson had opened, tearing the curtains off the rail with a single vicious rip. The door that Betty Turner had left half-open slammed back against the wall so hard that its knob lodged deep in the paneling, and then the doorway to the bedroom was blocked by the heavy counter, which the wind picked up like a child's wooden brick, and slammed down over its side. Rachel Bacchante, sitting by Stefano's bed in the ward at the far end of the corridor, watched in frozen disbelief as the ceiling of the corridor belled in and out with the force of the wind. Then the ceiling collapsed, falling with an endless crashing as plaster panels came down.

Walls fell, while people ran and screamed and, bit by bit, the building fell apart. Rachel's grip on Stefano's hand was convulsive, and it was through that touch that she felt him die. Oh God, her beautiful laughing Stefano. Her darling husband. They had been married only two years. How could her beloved Stefano be torn away after such a short time? In that moment's agony of bleak bereavement she thought she would never feel anything again, and then she thought, *My baby*.

Harold Pederson ran through the wreckage of the waiting room, shouting with a fury that rivaled the frenzy of the storm, tearing huge obstacles out of his way in his search for Helen. He heard her voice calling, and heaved up the counter that was lodged in her doorway, throwing it aside with an echoing thump. Then he stood in the empty bedroom, his battered hands opening and closing as he looked wildly around at wreckage that flapped in the draft. Babies cried beyond the overturned bed. Harold hauled the bed back from the bathroom door – and found Helen.

The room was undamaged. The single tiny window had been shut tight, and with no through draft for the gale, the bathroom was untouched. All three babies were safe. Two wailed loudly in their cribs, little arms waving in the air. Helen was sitting in a nest of pillows and blankets, a tiny fair child in her arms. Her face was soft with sensuous delight as the infant clung and suckled at her breast.

"Your daughter," she said, and smiled radiantly up into Harold's blue eyes.

Chapter seven

Helen blinked, returned dazedly to the present, and stared at her husband — her second husband, the husband from whom she had been estranged for the last ten years.

She exclaimed, "Harold? *What* did you say?"

"You heard me." Harold shifted his stance, just a little, but aggressively. "Which of these girls is our real daughter? Is it Jewel? Kate? Or Maggie? None of those babies were identified, because the nurse was killed before she did the paperwork. So how sure are you that you claimed the right one?"

Incredibly, he looked rational, as if he really did think he were talking sense. Kate and Maggie were staring at him with growing horror, while the two men with them were getting angry. The one with the ponytail stepped forward aggressively, but stopped when Harold put up his hand. Thank God, thought Helen, that Jewel was not listening to this craziness.

Harold had summoned her from her big promotion – and Kate, who was the star of the occasion, too – for *this*? For a terrible instant she was afraid that she would lose control and scream with frustration. How could he possibly believe that Jewel was not his? Kate and Maggie, the two girls who had been born at the same hour, in the same storm, were dark-eyed and dark-haired, while Jewel — beautiful, blue-eyed Jewel — was as fair as Harold himself.

Harold had given the baby that romantic name in his delight at being a father at last, calling her the new Jewel of his existence. That nirvana, Helen bitterly remembered, had come to an end when Jewel had been diagnosed with a congenital mental illness — at the age of ten, after years of unbelievably wild tantrums. An incurable mental illness, the specialists had said, one not treatable by any known medication. Jewel would become increasingly angry and violent, and should be institutionalized for life, they said.

Helen had fought against the diagnosis, aided by those ever-optimistic friends, Dr. Florida Sullivan and Dr. Trevor Green, but Harold had accepted it. The child had been unmanageable from the very beginning, he said, and facts were facts, and had to be faced. He had virtually disowned Jewel — why? Had he taken DNA tests without telling her?

Helen pushed the thought away, though uncomfortably reminded that it had been the end of their marriage, too. It was not with divorce, because Harold still needed a hostess, but with the total withdrawal of warmth. Over the past ten years they had learned to live successful separate lives, so why had he staged this farce now?

And why had he subjected Jewel to this unnecessary stress? Harold knew how combustible she was. Helen quickly studied her daughter, assessing her condition as she had many times before. The girl was blinking and frowning, as if she were starting to realize the strange situation. She said quickly, "Florida, please take Jewel out of the room. She doesn't need this." Florida nodded, and for once Jewel allowed herself to be led away. Thank God, a frenzied outbreak had been forestalled.

Helen turned back to Harold, and snapped, "This is private business, Harold, and should not be aired in company — particularly this company. It's embarrassing and unnecessary."

Harold merely lifted his hedgelike eyebrows. "But these people are part of the scenario, Helen. The three girls weren't given identification bracelets when they were born. There was no way of telling which was which. Any of them could have belonged to any of the three mothers. We won't know whether you took the wrong baby until we've found evidence in New Zealand. What we have to do is locate the people who were there when they were born – the two other mothers, in particular."

Helen pressed her lips tightly together to keep back the fury. So this was why he had summoned Skye Hamilton, she thought — because he had been there. But it was just so *crazy*. After all these years, did Harold expect to be able to claim Maggie Bacchante or Kate Giacomo as his rightful daughter, without either girl's permission? Just because he wanted to replace Jewel with someone better?

It fitted his personality. Harold insisted on perfection, always. Yet this abrupt confrontation after so many years was quite insane – good evidence, as Helen ironically meditated, that Harold was indeed Jewel's father. The specialists had asked many times about any family history of mental illness, as Jewel's condition was considered to be hereditary, but Helen had been at a loss for a reply. Her father had committed suicide, but not because he was mad. It was to avoid public humiliation, once his embezzlement had been uncovered.

Harold's obstinate chin lifted towards her. "And we have to find the doctor who delivered the babies."

"But the doctor was old!" Helen remembered Dr. Judd's rough, liver-spotted hands. "He must surely be dead."

At last one of the others spoke up. It was Skye Hamilton, who snapped, "I'm sorry, but this is absolute nonsense. There's no need to check up on Maggie's birth. I was the one who delivered Maggie — in the back of my car, if you want to know the grisly details. I had rescued the mother when she was trying to walk to the clinic in the storm, and the baby came before anyone could get to us. There was no doctor and no nurse, not until we arrived at the hospital. I was only nineteen, but I managed — and I know perfectly well that

Maggie was the baby I delivered."

Helen stared, thinking that delivering a baby must have been a strange experience for a boy in his late teens. Harold ignored him, however, not even bothering to turn his head. "And we have to find Kate's mother, Kelly," he said. "So we are going to New Zealand, to learn the truth. All of us, on the yacht — on the *Odyssey*."

"What?" Helen cried. The flight to New Zealand would have been bad enough, but a weeks-long voyage? She struggled for arguments, and seized the first one that rushed into her mind. "But the boat is over twenty years old!"

"Which is why she needs an overhaul in the yard where she was built, and is why it is logical to sail. The yacht might be old, but there is ample room for us all."

So he was being thrifty, Helen thought. With the peculiar eccentricity of multi-millionaires he was saving the cost of flights, because the yacht had to go back to New Zealand anyway. But then he turned his stare back to Maggie and Kate, and said in a flat voice, "Ten million dollars. Each."

Dead silence.

"And Bacchante Wines get the contract you've been lobbying so hard for, Mr. Hamilton. I've been reliably informed that you are a gifted business manager, with graduate degrees from Melbourne and Harvard, so I am sure you will see the sense of my offer."

Helen said shakily, "That's blackmail."

"It's business. The contract to stock my discovery cruise ships with Bacchante wines is worth hundreds of thousands, as Mr. Hamilton knows well. Maggie could set up her own designer studio, and Kate could found a publishing empire. Ten million dollars will set them both on the path to their dreams. Would you deny them that? I have spent a great deal more than that on Jewel, my dear."

"Would someone explain why the hell I am here?" a new voice

said. When Helen looked, it was the weather-beaten fellow with the ponytail.

"Ah, but we need you most of all, Mr. Jack."

"Oh no, no, no," the fellow said. "Not me. I took Kate's mother to the clinic, that's all — not that it wasn't a mighty struggle, what with the storm and the dog."

The dog? Helen blinked. This was getting crazier than ever.

"Exactly." There was a note of triumph in Harold's voice. "Kate's mother."

"She ran away, as she had often done before, in the course of her hard life. When I looked for her the day after Kate was born, she had gone. So I was left with a motherless infant. It could have been quite a problem for footloose me, but to our eternal good luck the baby and I were adopted into the Bacchante clan, at the same time that they collected Maggie, Rachel, and Skye. And we had no trouble raising our babies — did we, Skye?"

Maggie and Kate were holding hands, while Skye Hamilton was nodding. They were demonstrating togetherness, letting Harold know that they were family. Despite the different names they were emotionally related, Helen realized, and was struck with unexpected envy.

"But you could still identify Kate's mother when we find her, Mr. Jack," said Harold. "And never fear, I will compensate you — very generously — when the job is done."

The contempt in his tone was unhidden. The man with the ponytail flushed angrily, but Kate reached up and whispered in his ear, and after a long pause, he reluctantly nodded.

"That's set, then," Harold said, his tone becoming brisk. "We leave the day after tomorrow. My personal assistant, Steven Madden, will attend to all the details, and answer any questions." And he nodded to the silent man with him. "He already has your passport, and

Jewel's," he added, with a glance at Helen.

"Jewel?" Helen exclaimed. Surely Harold knew how dangerous Jewel could be? Back when she was just five years old, and had been taken for a short cruise on the *Odyssey*, she had destroyed furniture in the frenzy of her tantrums, and tormented the polite and hardworking crew. If anyone tried to control her, she tried to throw herself overboard. Once back on shore, Helen had sworn never to take her to sea again.

She cried, "Jewel can't sail — it's impossible!"

"Nothing is impossible," Harold said, and strode out of the room.

Chapter eight

"Oh my golly, sweetheart," said Jerry, and settled into an armchair. "I could put up with a lot of this pampering. What are your lodgings like?"

Kate stood in the centre of his stateroom. It was on the lowest deck of the luxury motor yacht *Odyssey*, so that the surface of the sea outside sparkled almost level with the three oblong portholes. There was a two-seater settee to match the chair, a television on a wall, a small table with two chairs, a desk with Jerry's laptop and an internet connection, and a refrigerator with a fully stocked minibar. A fruit basket sat on the table, and a curtained alcove led to a double bed. Beyond was a small but modern bathroom.

"I'm sorry to tell you this, Jerry, but my cabin is even grander."

"You have flowers?"

As always, she had to laugh. "Of course."

"And telephones with cords?"

"Of course — though how would they work when we are at sea?"

"Only to phone someone on the ship," he said comfortably.

"To get help, perhaps? Is that why there is one in my guest lavatory?"

"You have a guest *lavatory*?" His voice rose dramatically, and she laughed again.

"But I have to share the bed with Maggie," she reminded him. "Even if it is the VIP suite."

"As if that were a hardship," he growled.

Ever since the day the Bacchante family had arrived at Homer-ville to sweep Jerry and both babies into their warm and generous lives, the girls had slept together. When they were little, they had cried to be in the same cot, and had then slept peacefully with their fingers entwined. Then, later, it had been heart-warming to see the two dark heads on adjoining pillows, their hands still touching, even in sleep. There was the chance, he supposed, that Rachel Bacchante had taken the wrong baby, and Kate was her biological child. But even if that were the case, it would have made no difference. Rachel had mothered both children, and the Bacchantes had always treated them as twins. Indeed, when they were tiny no one had been able to tell them apart.

He looked up at Kate, who looked as fabulous as always, just as Maggie always did. It was a constant amazement that they were so alike. Kate looked a true Bacchante, olive-skinned, slim and vivacious, with dancing brown eyes. It was the same with Skye. He was not a biological Bacchante either, as the family had taken him in when he was five, but he looked and acted like a Bacchante, right down to being a connoisseur of wines, singing as lustily, and following the same arts and sports.

"But honestly, Jerry," said Kate, "don't you find this all rather strange?"

"Oh yes," he agreed amiably. "For a start, our host is as crazy as a loon."

"Well, his daughter —" Kate hesitated, then sat down and came out with it. "Do you think he really believes that Jewel is not his?"

"It would not be a surprise if he wished to disown her, considering her condition."

"You've heard about it, too?"

"Yep."

"She was so strange during that meeting — like a wax doll. Until the moment her mother asked the doctor to take her away, I don't think she heard a single word. Because if she had —"

Kate's voice drifted off again, and she grimaced.

Jerry was fingering his droopy moustache, gazing into the distance with his expression abstracted. Finally, he said, "I got the strong impression that Helen is quite certain that Jewel is her daughter."

"Of course, poor woman. After all, she was there, and she would know."

"But Pederson could have a good reason for claiming Jewel isn't his — if he's had DNA tests done."

Kate's eyes were huge. "Do you think that's possible?"

"He would be crazy not to have done it before embarking on this farce, if not sooner."

"So Helen cheated on her husband?"

Jerry shrugged. "She's a beautiful woman, a lot younger than he is. It wouldn't be surprising. But I don't think Pederson's thoughts are heading in that direction."

"He simply reckons that Helen picked the wrong baby?"

"Yep."

"But that means that either Maggie or me —" Kate shut her eyes, visibly wincing. Then she looked at him again, and said, "Jerry, what happened that day when I was born — when Kelly gave birth to me?"

Jerry settled more deeply into the armchair, and crossed his legs, his mind harking back two decades. "I mostly remember the hurricane. By God, it was a hell of a storm, you have no idea. I'd been lost in the murk for two hours or more when I hit the dog. Or, more accurately," he amended, "the dog hit me."

"Dog?"

"Yep. I should have hired a bigger car. It was a big dog, and when it ran out of the long reeds at the side of the road and smacked into the car, it made a big bump. Then it got up, shook itself and ran away again."

"It wasn't hurt?" Her tone was incredulous.

"Well, it was in much better shape than the car, which produced nothing more than a horrid grating noise when I tried to get going. So I got out into the storm, and found that the dog had crumpled the fender so that it was locked against the wheel. Hauling away with a tire iron did no good at all, so I got back inside."

"And Kelly? What was she doing?"

"Nothing. Just having a quiet time in the back."

"She wasn't in labor?"

"Didn't look like it." Though, Jerry thought now, that could have been something to do with the fact that she was smoking a joint that she had rummaged out of one of her zillion bags while he wasn't looking.

"She wasn't worried about being stranded in the storm?"

"She was a very easygoing girl."

Though it was more likely that she hadn't understood their dire situation, he mused. It hadn't taken him long to find out that classically blonde Kelly was classically dumb. It had made no difference, though, as Jerry hadn't invited her for her conversation. Even from this distance in time, he classed her as the most beautiful girl he'd ever bedded.

He had discovered Kelly in a London nightclub, where she worked as a dancer. While dinner-jacketed men and their scented companions drank exotic cocktails and nibbled at food and each other, and a jazz band blared into the smoke-laden air, Kelly and her fellow dancers pirouetted sinuously in fanciful swinging gilt cages, over their heads. Jerry, fresh into town from a grueling assignment in Saudi Arabia, where all the women were formlessly swathed in black drapery, would have found any female in briefs and sequins enticing. Kelly was the one who caught his eye, though, simply because of her sensual grace.

Like a slender birch in the wind, he thought poetically – but of course he was not going to tell her daughter any of that. It was best that she did not know that Kelly was a nightclub dancer, or that she had been available for escort duties. All Kate needed to know was that her mother was beautiful.

"But what if the car had been blown over?"

"Well, it didn't," he said, surprised at the question. "We were in the shelter of a stand of trees — macrocarpas, though I didn't know what they were called, back then. But I must admit," Jerry went on reminiscently, "that I did get a little panicked when Kelly began to rub her stomach and groan."

Jerry had always been good at handling emergencies, something he was quietly proud of now. The English-born son of an Italian itinerant farmhand, he had been born tough and grown strong. A spell in various units of the British army had hardened him further, and then he had become one of the best at one of the toughest trouble-shooting jobs in the world — that of putting out oil well fires. As he was fond of saying, he was fifty years old but could beat any man twice his size and half his age at anything, including the conquest of women – and that despite the fact that his body was criss-crossed with scars in most unexpected places.

But the prospect of delivering a baby in a storm had been very different. He loved kids; he'd fathered two children before his wife had finally given up and gone back to Manila. Her reason, she declared, was a good one — she was sick and tired of his constant absences. The big money he earned did not make up for it. Jerry, being a phlegmatic man, had accepted the situation, yet had visited her many times and had even fathered a couple more children. But, though he was a fond father, and never forgot birthdays, he had never brought a child into the world, or even been present at a birth. This was a situation he had not been prepared for at all.

"Just when I was getting desperate, I saw this light," he reminisced. "It was bobbing down the road through the dark and the storm, and I was never so glad to see anything in my life. So I hopped out of the car to scream and yell — and the light was ten feet above the ground. And there was this plod, plod, plod noise, like a heartbeat, Kate, and I tell you without a lie that my hair tried to stand on end."

"You are joking!"

"I am not. But then I saw that it was a man on a horse, holding a lantern high — so it was two faces that came up to me, a nice black horse with a white blaze on its nose, and this wonderful Maori farmer on its back. The plod, plod had been the horse's hooves. Oh boy, was I glad to see him. Never have I made a mate so fast. He trotted off to bear the news of our emergency, and twenty minutes later a truck came along, and carried Kelly and me to the clinic."

"Just in time?"

"Yep. She'd been laboring for hours, without either of us knowing it." Because of the joints, he thought, and wondered if perhaps he should have taken them away from her.

"And the baby was me."

"Of course it was you. Rachel and Skye knew right off which of the two babies was Stefano Bacchante's daughter, though sadly he died that day, and so he never got to know his Maggie. But that was set in stone, they were so sure about it, and so the other infant had to be Kelly's daughter. You, Kate, you."

"Even though there was no record, no identification."

"By the time Skye and I checked the bathroom, Helen Pederson and her husband had gone, along with their baby, so we didn't have a choice. You have to face it, Katie, we were stuck with you."

They laughed, and then silenced, interrupted by a knock on the door. When Kate opened it, the blank-faced personal assistant was there. He had already been part of this strange day, greeting them with a smooth handshake as they arrived up the gangway, then summoning stewards to take charge of their bags and escort them to their staterooms.

Kate thought him weird, with his white face and pedantic demeanor. His manner had been obsequious to them, and officious to the crew. The stewards were all from the Philippines. Kate wondered what they thought of him.

"Mr. Madden," she said.

"Call me Steve." His smile was tight, as if he had to work at it.

Kate said nothing, but waited.

"There is a problem with your passports."

"Surely not. I know that mine is up to date, and I am sure that Jerry's is, too."

"The ones you gave me are valid, but there is a hitch. The port officials refuse to release the clearance papers, because the passports do not match the guest list."

"Impossible," said Jerry.

"There are no passports for Jerry Jack and Kate Kelly. You gave me the wrong ones."

"Our name is Giacomo, just as the passports say," said Jerry.

"I beg your pardon?"

"I just got so tired of spelling out Giacomo that it's easier to call myself Jack. And Kelly is Kate's writing name. What do you call it? A nom-de-plume?"

A long pause, while Madden looked carefully from one to the other.

"But you are not father and daughter," he said at last.

"But we are," said Jerry blandly. "I adopted Kate when she was small."

He had done it in an ebullient mood, just to foil the Bacchantes.

When Kelly had run away, leaving him with a day-old baby, he would have been in a very pretty pickle, if the Bacchantes had not come to the rescue. But they had — and how! Wow, as he thought now. As extravagant with their hospitality as they were with their grief for the loss of a son, cousin, and brother, they had swept Stefano's widow and both baby girls into the big house on the vineyard, and their warm hearts.

If there had been any hesitation about taking Jerry, too, it had vanished the instant they found his name was Giacomo. The outpouring of Italian had flummoxed him for a while, his father's language being lost to him for so long, but the welcome was unmistakable.

And so the two girls had been raised as twins, attending the same schools and the same church, giving Jerry the freedom to head off to foreign parts to put out yet another fire. When he returned the family tended his wounds and took a lusty part in the big celebrations when the money arrived. He was one of the *famiglia* Bacchante, and had applied for New Zealand citizenship — but when they announced that they intended to adopt Kate, he had rebelled. Kate was his, he said firmly. And he had gone into town and tackled officialdom himself.

"I have my latest work papers, and Kate has her driver's license, if you're so worried about our real identities," he said to this Madden fellow now, and hauled out his latest discharge from a Middle Eastern employer.

Kate found her license, too. Madden nodded and hurried off on his next mission without another word. His expression was as bland as ever, but the flicker of dislike in his eyes had been unmistakable.

Chapter nine

Captain Castellano stood at the foot of the long table in the crew mess room, in bows of the yacht and on the lowest accommodation deck. His audience of stewards, deckhands, and cooks talked quietly amongst themselves as they waited.

When the unpleasant Madden fellow finally bustled in with the clearance papers, Castellano merely nodded. As soon as Mr. Pederson's assistant had gone, he radioed instructions to the bridge. Then, as the deck shivered with the first vibrations from the engines amidships, below and aft of the mess room, he returned his attention to the crew.

The chief officer was on the bridge, of course, along with the helmsman, the lookout, and the pilot, and the two engineers and the bosun were at work. That left ten hands, all watching attentively. Not only was the crew induction a legal formality for the start of every voyage, but on this fancy yacht it was part of the captain's job to familiarize them with the guests, so that the passengers would feel pampered from the very first day. Not only was Captain Castellano the skipper, but he had to be the jovial host of a floating hotel, too.

The crew was a very mixed lot, thrown close together by fate and the small size of the ship. Yet Captain Castellano knew them all very well, having been shipmates with some of them for more than ten years. They lived in cozy quarters, here. From where he stood, alongside a big computer screen, he could see their bunkrooms off to both sides. The deckhands and stewards all slept here, in the bows of the boat, men and women together with not a trace of trouble. They all ate at one big table that was bordered by benches, where most of them were sitting now. The deckhands were Filipino, and so were the room and table stewards, who were deftly managed by the chief steward, Constantia. The bar manager, MJ, was Filipino, too. The captain liked and respected them all.

The head chef and sous chef were French, just as Mr. Pederson always stipulated, and though dismayingly emotional, were very good cooks and didn't stint the crew. The bosun was a New Zealander by the name of Sarah Murray. She had been with the ship for just four months, but the captain had been able to forget his original doubts about taking on a female for the job, as not only had she proved to be firm, polite, and efficient when overseeing the deckhands, but the maintenance and cleanliness of the ship was in perfect order. Constantia had only good reports about her. The engineers liked her, as she was always willing to lend a hand with mechanical repairs, and when a second mate was needed, Captain Castellano found her willing and competent, too.

All of them, except for Castellano himself, lived on this lower deck. The chief officer and the bosun had private cabins, aft of the common crew quarters. The chief engineer and his second, both Scottish, shared another cabin, as did the two chefs. These four cabins all had private bathrooms. There was a small lounge for these petty officers, with a television, a coffee maker, and a minibar, which was set across the other side of the ship from the galley. The launderette, where the room stewards washed, dried and ironed the guests' private laundry as well as all other linen, was between the galley and the engine control room.

Captain Castellano lived on the upper deck, where he had a nice stateroom with a private bathroom, behind the bridge. Most conveniently, there was a passageway from the bridge to the upper deck lounge, so he could check the ship aft. And, if there were no guests, he and the first officer had full use of the lounge for relaxation, or entertaining friends from shore. Mr. Pederson might be a hard taskmaster, and was far too ready to poke his nose into the running of the ship, but he treated his staff well. Captain Castellano considered him a friend.

The engineers had already taken the crew through the first part of the pre-cruise induction, which was the checking of fire doors, fire extinguishers and life vests, plus going through the emergency drill. Now it was Captain Castellano's turn, which was acquainting the crew with the tastes and foibles of the passengers. It was part of the élite service the yacht provided, though he always started with the stern injunction to never socialize with the guests. It should be easy to keep a polite distance, he often thought. They worked hard enough, for God's sake, and had so few hours of sleep that they shouldn't have the energy for sexual hankypanky. But with every chartered cruise there had been problems, always triggered by the guests themselves.

And this voyage was going to be even more taxing. Not only was it very much longer than usual, but the passengers were the owner's wife and daughter, with the two medics who looked after the girl, plus two men and two women who had been personally invited by Mr. Pederson.

It was impossible not to wonder about this last quartet. They all belonged to the *famiglia* Bacchante, and Luigi Castellano, as an Italian, fully understood how complicated family could be. So what were they doing now? Quarrelling already? Playing with their computers? Making the last cellphone calls before the yacht was out of range? Their luggage had been unpacked for them, so they didn't even have that basic job to keep them out of mischief. Hopefully, they were amusing themselves with their minibars, as the lounge bars were closed until the *Odyssey* had sailed the regulation distance from California.

With a hidden sigh, Captain Castellano pushed a button on the remote he held, and an image of Harold Pederson floated up onto the big monitor. Taken years ago, he thought, and overdue for replacement, because Mr. Pederson had aged visibly in the last ten years. It was not a problem, as the crew were all familiar with their employer, but he did remind the bar manager of Mr. Pederson's preference in Scotch whisky.

When it came to Mrs. Pederson's image, he had to consult Constantia's notes, as the owner's wife had not been on board for a very long time, and her tastes could well have changed. It was a surprise, really, that she had come at all, as her two experiences with the yacht had been such bad ones.

He remembered the owner's trial of the *Odyssey* — the gathering storm, and then the chaos of the hurricane. Luigi had been sailing blind, as the superstructure was so damaged that most information was lost. *O Dio* — the storm. He still had nightmares about it, waking up sweating because in his dreams they had not make it to safety. And it had been a very close shave indeed. If the designer, who knew the coast well, had not been on board, they would never have made that little fishing port. And all the time, unknown to everyone on the bridge, Mrs. Pederson was in labor. It was a miracle they had got the yacht secured at all, let alone in time for the baby to be born in a clinic.

When the storm had blown away, Mr. Pederson had carried her triumphantly back on board, along with their little baby. It had been chaotic on board, with the skeleton crew trying to get the ship back to rights, and there had been no time to pamper a mother with a new child. Mrs. Pederson had done her best, but the infant had been fractious, or so he thought. He certainly remembered how glad he had been when they left the yacht at Auckland, to take a plane back to America. And after that, Mrs. Pederson had come back to the yacht only once, for just a short voyage, which had turned out just as unpleasant, though in a different way.

Mrs. Pederson had brought their daughter, Jewel, when the child was about five. And *O Dio*, what a trial it had been, as she was a terror, screaming and demanding, tormenting the stewards, threatening to throw herself overboard, and making all their lives miserable. And yet she had been as pretty as a porcelain doll, and so sweet when she wasn't frenzied. The girl, he was sure, was why something had gone wrong with their marriage, which was a shame. Despite the great difference in their ages, Mr. and Mrs. Pederson had seemed so right for each other, both so disciplined and correct. Perfectionists.

Constantia had listed Mrs. Pederson's preferences in food and drink — fresh fruit for breakfast, salad with olives and European cheeses for lunch, and a single course at night with a particular Californian wine, which the bar manager assured him had been ordered and was aboard. She was living with her husband in the owner's suite, of course, on the main deck, where they were close to the largest living room and the main dining room. Right next to them was a deluxe guest suite, where their daughter would sleep.

But he would talk about the daughter later, Luigi decided. Talking about Jewel Pederson was best left to the end.

Instead, he shifted to the occupants of the VIP suite on the upper deck, Kate Giacomo and Maggie Bacchante. "You will have heard of both," he said optimistically. "Signorina Giacomo has published a popular book under her penname, Kate Kelly, and Signorina Bacchante is a dress designer with the Bellissimo studio."

Judging by his audience's blank faces, his confidence was ill-founded, but there were hums of appreciation when their images flashed onto the screen. Both were very pretty, with large, dark, slightly slanted, feline eyes, and glossy black hair streaked like toffee — beautiful in the vivacious Italian style, or so he liked to think.

"They both prefer to drink wine," he read from Constantia's notes. "A Marlborough sauvignon blanc at lunch, and a Napa Valley syrah at night. Favorites of both varieties have been stocked?"

MJ, the bar manager, smiled and nodded.

"Neither take hard alcohol, or snacks between meals," the captain went on, again referring to Constantia's list. "Nor do they like canapés with their drinks, though they do like olives. Both are very fond of seafood, grilled, not fried, and are particularly partial to sashimi. They both like teppanyaki, too, but prefer a salad for lunch. Fresh fruit with plain Greek yoghurt for breakfast. They have declared no allergies. And, while they may ask you to call them by just their first names, you must not, though signorina may be used instead of miss." Pleased, he saw the stewards nod.

"They are sharing the VIP suite on the upper deck," he said again, then moved onto the other guests, all at the other end of this, the lower deck, aft of the engine control room, and above the engine room and the small hold where the rubber boats and tender were kept. "Mr. Hamilton is a member of the Bacchante family, and it appears that Signor Giacomo — who calls himself Mr. Jack, and prefers to be addressed by that name — is Miss Giacomo's adoptive father. He, too, is a member of the Bacchante family. He is a famous fire-fighter, specializing in oil well fires, mostly in the Middle East."

The deckhands looked alert, sitting up straight as they studied Mr. Jack's picture. Evidently, the fire-fighter was better known than the writer and the dress designer.

Giacomo's image was a casual one, just like the man himself. It had been taken while he was at work, as he was wearing a hard hat and safety vest, and Arabs in robes could be seen in the distance.

"Like Mr. Pederson, Signor Jack enjoys a single malt Scotch, though a different brand, I think. As a nightcap, not before dinner. Is that in hand, MJ?"

The bar manager delivered a wide grin. "Aye indeed, sir. I also ordered three cases of the Italian red wine he likes to have with dinner."

"*Eccellente*," said Captain Castellano, and consulted the notes again. "In the late morning, if they have been working out in the gym, both he and Signor Hamilton relax with a beer, brand and type unstipulated. MJ, will you find out their favorites?" Again the bar manager nodded. "Steak, medium rare, is Signor Jack's preference at night, stuffed with oysters as a treat. He declares no allergies."

"Oysters!" someone exclaimed, and they all laughed. Apparently, oyster-stuffed steak was not part of the Filipino cuisine.

"You have some?" he asked François, the head chef.

"*Oui, si*, yes, sir. Canned. He won't notice the difference, not after a big glass of Italian red wine."

Another laugh. "Thank you," said the captain, and looked again at his notes. "Signor Hamilton also drinks wine with meals — white with lunch, and red with dinner, like the girls. He is very fond of pasta, particularly alla funghi and bolognese."

Captain Castellano had much the same tastes. Aware of his comfortably rounded stomach, he wondered how Mr. Hamilton managed to keep as lean as a rake.

"Mr. Madden you have already met," he went on, as the man's image came up on the screen. "He is Mr. Pederson's new personal assistant." The captain had trouble keeping dislike out of his tone. Madden had already caused trouble by usurping Constantia's position as hotel manager. She had protested to Luigi that it was she who was supposed to have the pleasure of greeting the guests as they came on board, and she should be the one to pass them over to the room stewards who took care of their luggage. But Mr. Madden had elbowed her out of the way and taken over.

Castellano had promised her that he would talk it over with Mr. Pederson, but his efforts had been useless. His personal assistant should be given all the courtesies of a guest, Mr. Pederson repeated — which did not answer the problem, or even make sense. If Madden wanted to take over the duties of a host, he should have been shipped as a supernumerary, and quartered with the crew.

"I am sure that Mr. Madden will inform you of his tastes in food and wine," he said, as there was nothing about his preferences in the notes that Constantia had made for him. When Captain Castellano lifted an eyebrow at the Filipina woman, she merely smiled blandly, confirming that she and Madden were at loggerheads already.

"Dr. Trevor Green and Dr. Florida Sullivan are sharing the fourth lower deck guestroom," he said, and pressed the button on the remote. Images of the busty redheaded woman and an elderly man flashed up on the screen. Both were wearing white laboratory coats, and had stethoscopes hanging around their necks.

"They are medical professionals, which means that — most unusually — this yacht will be carrying two doctors. Unless you are very ill or hurt, however, you should not trouble them, as they are guests, not supernumeraries. Dr. Sullivan is a pediatrician, specializing in children with communication difficulties. Dr. Green is a psychiatrist, and has been treating the owner's daughter ever since she was small. It is at Mrs. Pederson's request that they are on board."

The attentive silence became even more intent. Had they already heard whispers? Captain Castellano paused, and then said deliberately, "I tell you this because you will have to take great care with Miss Jewel Pederson. Be polite, but cautious. Unfortunately, she has been diagnosed with a severe mental illness. I have been warned that she can be violent. As you can see, she is very beautiful, and appears completely normal, but —"

The image on the screen was indeed lovely. Jewel looked elfin, poised on stiletto heels with her waist-long silvery hair blowing, and her skirts lifted in an invisible wind.

Captain Castellano said flatly, "The name of her condition is too technical for you or me to understand. But never forget that she is unpredictable, and can be very dangerous."

Chapter ten

At ten the next morning Chief Officer Beni Boulez headed up to the sun deck to carry out a favorite job. At the start of his first stint on this fancy yacht, four years ago, he had offered to give the guests a tour about the ship on their first day at sea, and Luigi had accepted it as an excellent idea.

And it *was* an excellent idea, Beni thought complacently. On the first morning after departure the passengers were just starting to get accustomed to being pampered, and were still marveling at the extravagant decor. And, while they may have explored the lounges on their own, and had eaten an elaborate dinner at the magnificently set table on the main deck, there was a lot of the ship they had yet to see, such as the bridge, the galley, and the engine control room.

It was a glorious day, with little wind and just a small chop on the water, setting the sea to sparkling, Their pilot had been dropped off in the night, and now their wake ran in a lacy white ribbon towards unseen California. Beni stood with his feet apart and his buttocks tucked in, a stance that he knew set off the muscles of his legs to advantage. The shoulders of his white tailored shirt were embellished with black epaulettes with three gold bars and a fouled anchor, which made him look like a magnificent sea-warrior, or so he believed, and altogether he felt very happy with life.

Beni's four years on the *Odyssey* had been very pleasant, particularly when contrasted with the tedious months of working his way up the ranks on the bridges of container ships. He liked his captain, though he considered Italians rather over-emotional, and he respected the crew, all of whom were loyal and reliable. He spent pleasant off-duty hours gossiping, playing cards, and drinking wine with the two chefs, who were fellow Frenchmen, and he took no notice at all of Captain Castellano's injunction not to socialize with the passengers. At the age of forty he reckoned he should seize all the romantic opportunities that he could. And if marriage to an heiress was a possibility, all the better.

Then his smile faded. Seven people had turned up for the tour, when he had hoped for eight. One was that elderly character with a ponytail, Mr. Two-Names-Jack or Giacomo. He was wearing cut-off jeans and a tank top that showed off a lot of gray chest hair and silvery scars, and had a knowing grin. It was as if he could read Beni's mind, and found it amusing. Next to him was old Dr. Green, apparently still practicing though he looked overripe for retirement. He was hobbling along with a stick, which was a bad sign. Maybe he was at the end of his career, and this was his retirement cruise. Beni hoped that he wouldn't need the old codger's medical attention.

The woman holding him up with a hand under one elbow was the other doctor, some sort of specialist with children. Named after a state, for God's sake — Florida. She was fifty-something, heading for sixty, but handsome enough, with a fine head of red hair, and big bouncy breasts. She and Dr. Green were sharing a cabin, though according to the passenger list they were not married. Beni could have gone for her, but the way she held Dr. Green's arm and hung onto his every word announced to the world that she was not available.

The owner wasn't there, much to Beni's relief, as he was bound to carp at every word Beni said, and probably take over. His wife had come, though. Beni felt a little surprised that she was on the tour, but then remembered that Luigi had told him that it was fifteen years since she had last been on the yacht. Perhaps, he thought, she needed to get reacquainted. Then there were the two girls, who were conferring in low tones with their heads close together. They were both very pretty, very Italian-looking, he thought, dressed in long silk shifts in flowing colors — the product of the one who was a dress designer, he supposed. Privately, however, he preferred Nordic blondes.

The owner's personal assistant was not present, which was another reason to be thankful. Mr. Madden was sticking his interfering nose somewhere else, *Dieu merci*. But where was the owner's daughter, the luscious young Jewel? When Beni had passed her in the main deck living room last evening, she had thrown him an unmistakably flirtatious glance. Then, with a teasing flick of her long pale hair, she had sauntered on before he had a chance to introduce himself.

Never mind — *ça ne fait rien*. There were weeks of voyage ahead, and it was a beautiful day. Beni Boulez gathered his audience of seven together, and then, after welcoming them and introducing himself, he started his patter about this lovely old yacht.

"Technically," he said, with a conspiratorial grin, "*Odyssey* is a tri-deck motor yacht. You may already have noticed that she does not have sails. However, she does have two very efficient Caterpillar diesel electric engines." Smiles, and some laughter, which pleased him. "This," he said, gesturing, "is the sun deck." There were lounging chairs, and a small gym with glass walls, and a bar at the after end, manned by MJ, the bar manager. Seeing them look his way, the Filipino waved a hand over the glasses of tropical juice he'd lined up on the counter.

When the party arrived, MJ greeted them all by name, without a single mistake or mispronouncement. He even remembered to call

Mr. Two-names by the name he preferred, Signor Jack. To Beni's surprise, he heard Mr. Two-names say, "*Kamusta,*" as he took his glass of juice. When MJ laughed with surprise and replied, the old ponytailed fellow said, "*Mabuti na ako, salamat.*" To which MJ smiled, shook his hand, and said, "*Salamat,*" in return.

So under that aging beach boy exterior, Mr. Two-names was a cosmopolitan fellow. But then, Mr. Two-names was a famous fire-fighter, and had spent a lot of time in the East. He probably spoke Arabic like a native. Beni smirked to himself. It was a wonder that he drank wine and hadn't brought four wives.

One level down, in the upper deck lounge, Beni turned and smiled at the gathering, returning to his spiel. "The *Odyssey* is not huge, by luxury yacht standards," he said. "Just one thousand tonnes gross, and sixty meters long. But she is very impressive, all the same."

Beni was very happy with the comparative smallness of the *Odyssey*. The ship did not have a helicopter pad, nor a companion boat carrying all the so-called toys that playboys and playgirls liked, but in his experience the mega-mega-mega yachts were apt to be owned by Asian billionaires or South American drug lords or Russian oligarchs, all of whom were liable to order the skipper to go dark — which meant turning off the AIS, and vanishing like mist into unknown seas, chased at the same time by the authorities of a dozen lands.

He said, "While other yachts are bigger, here meticulous design, both exterior and interior, makes *Odyssey* a stand-out in her class. Every year, she has been updated with the latest technics, and the furnishings renewed." To his pleasure he saw that his guests were impressed with what they saw. Even the owner's wife was smiling.

The upper deck lounge was bathed with sunlight that washed through large oblong portholes and a skylight. There was a table for card games, and a square marble-topped coffee table with comfortable couches on three sides. Glass doors at the after end led to the star deck, which had an informal dining table that was shaded with an awning. Inside, lockers held board games, and tall cases with glass doors were filled with books.

Rather to Beni's annoyance, the games table was cluttered with sketches of garments, and chalks and pencils were scattered on top. This ship deserved to be kept tidy, he thought, and he wondered why the designer girl – Maggie? – wasn't using the perfectly good desk in the VIP suite.

The door to the VIP suite was in the after bulkhead, along with a door to the guest lavatory, which could also be accessed from inside. The two girls were sharing, but it was the designer girl – the slightly smaller one, Signorina Maggie – who flung open a door to show them where they lived.

It was a stunning room, hung with cream slubbed silk, but like the lounge it was not at all tidy. The small breakfast table was covered with books and notepads, and the computer screen on the equally cluttered deck was busy. So this was why the designer girl was sketching in the lounge, he saw; the writer girl, Signorina Kate, had taken over all the available work space. The great bed was a double one, and evidently the girls shared it. Beni pursed his lips, but then remembered that they had been raised in the same family – as twins, or so Luigi had said. Apparently, they had been born on the same day.

The bridge was forward of this upper deck lounge, but the door that led there was firmly shut, and carried a sign saying, *Crew only*. So Beni led the way down a curving stairway to the main deck, where the view was even more stupendous, as both sides of the main deck lounge were lined with windows, rather than portholes.

Two great settees ran fore and aft, with a long coffee table between them, and there was a bureau with a bar and coffee maker at one end. The formal dining room was at the after end of this living room, reached by folding doors that could be fastened back to turn the two areas into one. In there, the space was dominated by a long mahogany table with seating for ten — the limit of the number of guests the ship was certified to carry. At the moment, it held just a huge bowl of fresh flowers, but if the passengers opted to have dinner there tonight, a cloth would be laid, and then an impressive array of cutlery and crystalware.

At the sternward end of this dining room there was a stairway down to the lower deck and the galley and engine room amidships, but Helen Pederson stopped Beni with a hand on his arm, and murmured that he was welcome to show off the owner's suite.

Bon dieu, she was a good-looking woman, and must have been amazing twenty years or so ago, when Harold Pederson had married her. Tall, lissome, elegant, and with smoothly coifed silver-blonde hair, she was perfect. She was scented, just faintly, of something clean and woody. When she opened the door and smiled as the others filed through, her bearing was perfect, too.

Beni was surprised when he arrived in the huge stateroom, as there was an alteration in the arrangements since he had seen them last. Instead of one enormous bed, there were two large ones. Why? Because Harold Peterson was now too old for marital relations? *Quel idiot,* he thought. Because of this different furniture setting, the wall hangings had been changed, though they were still richly patterned silk, and the lounge and chairs had been re-upholstered to match.

The headroom was so generous that there were clerestory windows above the oblong portholes. A lavishly appointed marble bathroom led off to the right, and next to this was the door to the owner's guest suite. Beni usually liked to joke that this adjoining suite had been designed for the owner's bodyguard, but this time had the sense to keep his mouth shut. Now, it was where the owner's daughter slept. To his disappointment, that door was shut, and there was no sound at all from the other side. There was another door from that suite to the lounge, and perhaps the sexy Pederson girl had gone there, he thought.

Between the guest suite and the master bedroom there was a settee with two armchairs, and a table with chairs for six. A buffet displayed a range of select brandies and whiskies, along with a coffee-maker. Next to the buffet, a flight of shallow steps led to a mezzanine, where Mr. Pederson had his office, set immediately above the two beds. To Beni's surprise, Mrs. Pederson gestured for him to take the party through. Then, as he arrived on the mezzanine, Beni's initial hesitation turned into alarm, as Mr. Pederson was there.

The yacht's owner was seated in a revolving chair, and hunched over a long computer desk, which held not just a computer monitor, but a telltale screen with a mosaic of images that repeated all the electronic information on the monitors in the bridge — the GPS, AIS, gyro-compass, speed log and depth sounder. Windows on three sides of this balcony area offered an expansive view of the sea, including any traffic that might or might not be ahead, so Mr. Pederson was supremely aware of their surroundings. He even had a private stairway to the bridge, and liked to materialize by the chart table and make comments and suggestions, which Beni thoroughly hated when he was the officer on watch. Beni often wondered how Captain Castellano felt about this arrogance. Surely he felt resentful, too?

Then he noticed that the two Bacchante girls had moved closer together, and were watching Mr. Pederson warily. They were nervous of him, he thought, and wondered why. Mr. Pederson was staring back at them, frowning, his small blue eyes moving from one girl to another, almost as if he were assessing them for some important job.

Finally, his eyes moved back to the first officer. "Beni," he said briskly, "do you want to use my stairs to take the party to the bridge?"

"Thank you, I would like that," said Beni, and nodded, as what else could he say?

"But Mr. Hamilton has to stay behind. There are papers to check before I sign them. And some spreadsheets, too."

Beni winced, thinking that Hamilton had to cope with arrogance, too. When he issued the order, Mr. Pederson did not even bother to look at the man, but Hamilton simply nodded, his tanned face expressionless.

Captain Castellano, in contrast to his employer, straightened up to welcome them onto his bridge, though he had been busy conferring with the bosun, Sarah Murray. He greeted the party first in English, and then, with a conspiratorial smile at Mr. Two-names, in Italian. When the girls answered him in his own language, he exclaimed in delight, and bestowed smacking kisses on their cheeks. That was one good thing that could be said of Italians, Beni thought — they were very good hosts. Then, after introducing the bosun and the helmsman, the captain sent a deckhand down to the galley to fetch coffee.

The deckhand had been scanning the horizon with binoculars, a task that was made redundant by the rows of monitors and dials that related every little detail of the sea around and below them. But, though unnecessary, it was traditional. And the bridge was certainly big enough to accommodate extra hands. Even now, with Beni and his six guests, as well as the captain, the helmsman, and Sarah Murray, there was enough room for them to stand without being crowded. Sarah was generously sized, too, though with a tiny, tightly belted waist. As Beni often mused with an internal grin, she was hourglass-shaped from every direction. He had tried his luck when she had first arrived on board, and though she had firmly rejected his advances, he still liked her.

They gathered around the chart table, and sipped coffee while

Captain Castellano showed them the charts. And talked. And talked. As Beni thought wryly, Italians were garrulous. Finally, however, Luigi ran to a stop, and Beni was able to lead his party on a reverse course through Mr. Pederson's office and stateroom, on the way to the foyer stairs, the lower deck, the galley, and the engine room.

To his disappointment, the door to the owner's guest suite was still shut, and Jewel Pederson was nowhere to be seen.

Back on the bridge, there was an unusual silence. The helmsman stared ahead, the deckhand scanned the horizon, and Sarah Murray waited to be dismissed. Captain Castellano looked down at the charts, rolling a pencil back and forth idly, lost in thought. They were headed southwest, in the direction of the Marquesas — and also the Tuamotus, Sarah saw. In historic times they were known to mariners as the Dangerous Isles. Low-lying, and surrounded by extensive reefs, the atolls could materialize in front of your bows without warning, if you were careless or unlucky.

Finally, Luigi said, "An interesting family."

She said, "The Bacchantes?"

"*Si*. They have vineyards, great wineries. They were pioneers in your country."

So that was why MJ had been so particular about the ordering of wine. Sarah wondered if she had ever sampled any of their products at home. She knew the name of the firm, but not the names of their wines. Probably too expensive, she thought.

She said, "Mr. Hamilton is one of the family?" She fancied Skye Hamilton, she really did. Lean and dark, pale-eyed like a wolf. And the right age, too.

The captain said again, "*Si*. They adopted him into the family when he was small, or so he told me."

She wondered if he spoke Italian, too — and whether he was as expert in bed as Italians were supposed to be. She said, "And Mr. Jack?"

"Giacomo," Captain Castellano corrected, sounding prim. Obviously, he did not like the Italian name being shortened.

"He's a rogue, a likeable rogue. He had the sauce to pinch my bottom!"

Captain Castellano laughed. Sexual harassment of the crew by the passengers was a constant annoyance, but with these guests it was merely amusing. Then he sobered, and shook his head.

"If we are ever in big, big trouble," he said, "you may find that he is the most valuable person on this ship."

Chapter eleven

Kate and Maggie were both eating a late breakfast in their stateroom. Kate was in bed, scribbling notes as she mulled over the next chapter, and Maggie was sitting at the desk. She was eating fresh strawberries with Greek yoghurt, while Kate was nibbling sashimi on fingers of toast.

Maggie said, "That looks good."

"It is good. The tuna is very fresh. Want some?"

"Yes, if there is any."

"With wasabi?"

"Why not?" But when Maggie bit into the morsel that Kate handed over, her eyes ran. "Do grow up," she said when she had stopped coughing, and Kate laughed.

"Kate," Maggie said then, "I still wonder how — and why — you persuaded Jerry to go along with Mr. Pederson's weird scheme. It's so crazy — and we both have so much to do in New York. What did you whisper into his ear?"

Kate pushed her tray aside, and without looking up she said very quietly, "It's a chance to find my mother."

Maggie's eyes narrowed. "You said that?"

"Yes."

"And what did Jerry say?"

"Nothing, just nodded."

"Does he want to see her again?"

"I don't think so, though he says he liked her a lot. For him, it was just a fling, and he says it was the same for her. He doesn't have any photos of her, even though he tells me she was very good-looking. A smasher, he said. But I have no idea what my mother looks like!"

"Why do you care? She ran away when you were just one day old, for heavens' sake!"

"Jerry said there was something wrong with her, and that she probably didn't know what she was doing."

"What does Skye say? After all, he was at the hospital, too."

"No, he never saw her. They needed the operating theatre and all the beds, so they took Kelly away to a nearby house — belonging to one of the nurses, perhaps. And then the storm came back. Who knows what happened after that? When Jerry checked, they told him she had gone. She could have been hurt — hit on the head — lost her memory."

Kate was clutching at straws, Maggie thought.

She said, "But Jerry told me she was English — from London, the East End of London. Don't you think she might have gone home?"

"But she had no money."

And that was true. According to Jerry's story, he had arrived in London after a big assignment in Saudi Arabia, and a magnificent sum of money had been deposited into his account. It was enough for a four-month vacation, preferably as far from the Middle East as it was possible to go, and so he had bought two tickets to New Zealand. And, on impulse, he had paid a go-go dancer to be his escort on this jaunt.

But this was what Maggie knew. She was not sure how much of the story Kate had been told, because it did not reflect well on her mother.

She hesitated, and then said, "What about your father?"

"Jerry said that I really and truly do not want to know — not that he knew much himself. But Kelly — my mother — said she needed to escape, and when she gave him a few details Jerry believed her. And so he offered her the perfect way to do it. Not," Kate added reluctantly, "that they knew she was pregnant at the time. It made no difference to him — he still liked her and wanted to protect her — but there is no way that Jerry is my biological father. He was just happy that he had helped her get away."

All of which meant that Kelly was not likely to want to go back to London. Maggie paused yet again, and then said, "But Kate, you do know you are a Bacchante. One of us, whatever name you are using. You are a member of our family — the *famiglia* Bacchante. We all love you like a daughter, a cousin, a niece, a sister. You are my sister, Kate. My twin."

"I know," said Kate, and to Maggie's distress tears were running down her cheeks. "But what will happen if Mr. Pederson makes up his mind that I'm the one he wants to be his real daughter?"

"Sweetie, you are not alone in this. I have nightmares, too, because it could just as easily be me. And we have to face the fact that if he argues that the three babies were muddled up, we will have a job to prove him wrong."

The Bacchantes often marveled that Maggie's gift for design had come out of nowhere, and her mother, Rachel, had never painted a picture in her life. She made beautiful quilts, but to them this was not significant. And Stefano? Draw pictures, and follow fashion? What a laugh. He was a talented gardener, and the progenitor of wonderfully grape-bearing vines, and the best company in the world, but that was all. And Helen Pederson was famous for her fashion sense, which was enough to give Maggie dark thoughts in the night. The prospect that she might not be a Bacchante was utterly, totally horrifying.

But then she was distracted.

She frowned and said, "Listen."

"What? I can't hear anything."

"That's it. The engines have stopped."

The noise of the yacht's two engines was never more than a half-heard rumble, but now the silence seemed solid. The vessel was moving uneasily, too, wallowing in the water. Then that silence was broken by an enraged shout. It was in Italian, and came from the bridge.

Kate said, "Something has happened," and scrambled out of bed. Hastily, the two girls pulled on shorts and tops, and opened the door to the lounge.

Jerry came running up the stairs from the lower deck. He was wearing his usual cut-off jeans and tank top, but he looked unusually serious. He said, "We have visitors." Then he led the way through the lounge to the open deck at the back.

The bright sun unsighted Kate for a moment, and they were at the rail before her eyes focused. Then she saw the sailing ship that lay about two hundred yards away. It was a big craft with a lot of sails, some square and some triangular, all of them set but hanging slack, like wet laundry on a line. There were a lot of loose ropes dangling over the sides, along with streaks of rust. There were just two masts, but they were so tall that they seemed like a lot. And there did not appear to be anyone on board. No one was on the deck. It was like a scene in a film.

Looking down, over the taffrail, she saw a rubber boat tied up to the platform that came off the stern of the *Odyssey*, at the back of the lower deck, two decks below. That was what the chief officer had called the Beach Club. There, the platform could be tilted down to make a ramp, so that guests could slide into the water to swim or snorkel, and small boats and surf skis could be launched. It was not usual, however, for visitors to board the yacht that way. Apart from the rubber boat, the Beach Club was empty.

She said to Jerry, "What happened?"

"Two of them hailed the *Odyssey* — men, American," Jerry said. "Apparently they worked their way forward to the lower deck entrance, and a deckhand let them in. He was going to call the bosun, but then that Madden guy poked his nose in."

"Oh no," said Maggie.

"Oh yes. Madden. And he took them up to the bridge."

Even Maggie knew that the bridge was sacrosanct territory. So that had been the source of the shout in Italian, she thought. Captain Castellano would have been steaming with rage.

The door marked *Crew only* at the other end of the lounge slammed open. Two strangers barged right through the living room, looking back and forth and all around as they went, as if they were seeking a way out. Then, once they were on the open deck, they pushed past the girls and Jerry to the taffrail. As one, they leaned over, evidently checking that their rubber boat was still there. After that, they turned and stared aggressively.

Jerry pushed back his cap and said, "What the hell do you think you are doing?"

"Making sure we're not stranded," one snapped. He was wearing a cowboy hat and dark glasses, so that most of his face was shadowed, but Kate could see that he had a thin black moustache, which somehow didn't seem American, despite his Yankee accent. The other man had a baseball cap turned backwards, and his forehead was very sunburnt. He was bearded, and the beard was almost as red as the forehead above his dark glasses. They were both wearing tattered shorts and tee shirts, and had flip-flops on their feet.

"How the hell can anyone guess what's going to happen on this crazy yacht?" Cowboy Hat went on angrily. "Are billionaires in their fancy boats too high and mighty to respond to a request for assistance? All we wanted was to borrow a few tools to fix our desalination machine, which has broken down. How would you like to be stuck out here without drinking water, huh? And then a fellow took over, and pushed us up the nearest stairs. We had no idea we would be intruding on the bridge, not until the captain blew a gasket. Just show us the quickest way back to our boat, and we'll look for assistance elsewhere."

More footsteps in the lounge, and the bosun, arrived, along with Mr. Madden, the owner's personal assistant. Sarah Murray was wearing a cap with her brown ponytail sticking out of the hole at the back, and Mr. Madden had a white, peaked hat, as if he fancied himself as an officer. Both of them also had dark glasses.

Sarah said crisply, "You signaled that you are in trouble?"

"How many times do we have to say that we just need to borrow a few tools to fix our water-making gadget?"

"There is no need to shout, sir." Sarah's tone was crisp and professional. She produced a notepad and pen, and said, "Your names, please."

"Why?"

"Just for the record, sir."

Cowboy Hat looked at his friend, and they both shrugged. "Mulligan, me — and Jacobsen, him," he said, so offhand that it was rude.

"Your ship?"

"For God's sake, we gave all the details in the distress signal we sent!"

"Just for the record, sir," she said again.

"*Ratpack*, brig," Mulligan said, still grudging.

"Registered in?"

"Cayman Islands."

"Your last port?"

"Crescent City, California."

"And how long have you been at sea?"

Mulligan shrugged, and turned to his silent companion. "Ten weeks?" he hazarded.

"And your destination?"

"Who knows?" said Cowboy Hat. He grinned, and spread his hands.

"Very well, then," said Sarah. "We will escort you to your boat, so that you can return to your ship. Once we have reported to the authorities, we will send over an engineer and a couple of hands to assess your fresh water problem."

Kate glimpsed something like consternation in their expressions, but then forgot it, because with startling suddenness music rent the air. It was loud, almost deafening, steel drums pulsing, overwhelmingly compulsive. Then Jewel Pederson danced out onto the deck immediately below, revolving with her arms in the air.

Kate heard Jerry suck in a hard breath. The two visitors from the *Ratpack* were watching even more rigidly. It was as if the deck immediately below were a stage, and the men were looking down from an opera box. Jewel was fluttering her hands, undulating her arms, and revolving her hips. Waist-long hair flowed out from her head like a gold and silver waterfall as she spun. She was like a wraith from ancient seafarers' dreams — a mermaid or a syren.

And she was singing, not a song, but a kind of mantra — "Party, party party, time to have a party!" It was only halfway through the morning, yet she behaved as if she were in the middle of a drunken nightlong rave. She was beckoning to the two strangers, her face upturned with an impish smile, her blue eyes brilliant. Kate sensed them move, on the verge of vaulting over the rail and onto the deck, eight feet below.

The scene froze. The music stopped dead.

Kate saw Jewel spin to a stop, her arms still upraised — and Harold Pederson barged out into the deck, shouting, "Jewel, behave yourself!"

And Jewel began to scream. She swore like a guttersnipe at her father, her language violent and foul. She kicked the furniture, and pounded her fists on the glass doors as he pushed her inside. And she screamed. And swore. And screamed.

"Dear God Almighty," said Jerry two hours later. "I had no idea Jewel was as bad as that."

He and Skye Hamilton were on the uppermost deck, the sun deck, perched on bar stools and drinking beer. They were both sweaty, as they had been working out in the little gym, and apart from MJ, the bar manager, they were alone. The noon sun was high and bright, so that the shade of the awning was a blessing, but still it was hot. There was a smell of salt and warm tar in the air, and condensation ran down the sides of their steins. The *Odyssey* was quiet, except for the rustle and tinkle of wavelets along the hull, and the occasional creak of furniture. Every now and then the engines started up, keeping them in the same position, but right now they were silent.

The weatherworn *Ratpack* still lay off their beam, sails set but dangling, and there was still no movement on her decks. After firmly ushering the two visitors to their boat Sarah Murray had gone to the bridge to report to the captain, jerking her head at Madden to follow. Ten minutes later a boat had chugged off from the *Odyssey* with the chief engineer and two hands, their mission to assess the damage to the desalination machine, and fix it, if they could. There had been no sign of them since.

"I had no idea Jewel was so fragile, either," said Skye. It had taken both Florida Sullivan and Dr. Green to calm the frantic girl, while Helen hovered worriedly. Harold Pederson, looking baffled and furious, had gone back inside, and that had settled Jewel more than anything else.

"But let's face it," Skye said. "How would I know? The first time I laid eyes on her was during that very weird meeting in Pasadena, and apart from sharing the dinner table with her just one time, that's it. She struck me as vacant as an unpowered robot, so the tantrum was indeed a shock."

Jerry considered this, while MJ took away his glass and replaced it with another. He nodded and picked it up. "What about as an infant?" he said to Skye. "Did you see her after she was born?"

"Even if I did, I wouldn't remember. I was only nineteen years old at the time, and had just delivered my first baby. My only baby," said Skye. MJ renewed his beer, too, and Skye took a contemplative gulp. "And then poor Rachel — you do know she was holding Stefano's hand when he died? She was in a terrible state, and I was trying to comfort her while the hospital was crashing down about us. So I had my mind taken up with that. According to my very blurred memory," he said, drinking again, "by the time I got around to fetching Rachel's baby for Rachel to nurse, the Pederson couple had taken their baby away."

"Where?"

"To the yacht — this yacht."

"But surely she was a mess?" Jerry cast his eyes around the deck, trying to visualize what the *Odyssey* had looked like back then. Though over two decades old, the yacht was pristine, testament to a hardworking set of stewards and deckhands, and regular updates, too. But there must have been a lot of damage at the time, particularly to the masts and satellite dishes directly overhead. He wondered how the captain had navigated, with so many instruments lost.

"The yacht was safely moored at the wharf, and in a damn sight better state than the hospital. Or the village. Don't you remember what it was like in Homerville, the morning after?"

"Oh boy," said Jerry. It had been a very gray dawn by the time the hurricane had moved on, to wreak its fury further south, and meantime there had been the horror of stumbling to try to save the nurse who had broken her neck. And then he'd found that Kelly had left the hospital. All he could learn was that she had been taken to a nearby house, to make room in the wards. But there was the baby, still in the crib in the bathroom.

Jerry braced himself with another swallow of cold beer. It stung wonderfully as it flowed down his throat. Then he said, "How many babies were in the bathroom when you went to get Rachel's baby?"

"Two, just two. I remember that now. So I didn't see Helen's baby at all."

"You're sure you fetched the right baby for Rachel to nurse?"

"It was the baby I delivered, for God's sake! I was the first person to hold her. Maggie! Stefano's daughter."

Jerry nodded. "And I gave the third one — the baby who turned out to be Kate — to you and Rachel, because I was trying to find Kelly."

A hopeless quest, Jerry thought now, and traced a fingertip around the condensation on his glass. The day after, when he'd finally located the half-ruined house where they had taken Kelly, he was too late. She had gone.

"That's exactly what happened," Skye agreed, his brows arched. He lowered his voice. "Did you know that Rachel nursed both of them?"

"Both at the same time?"

"No, of course not. At least, I don't think so."

"Well," said Jerry. He had seen Rachel nursing, of course he had, but one baby looked much like another when at a woman's breast.

Not that it mattered, because Kate and Maggie had been raised as twins. And it was as if they really were twins, he thought, for it was amazing how alike they were. They even had the same mannerisms. He had noticed it afresh every time he returned to the Bacchante household. He adored them both equally, and was wonderfully happy to be one of the *famiglia* Bacchante. That was why he had taken New Zealand citizenship.

"Why are you asking?" Skye said.

"Maggie and Kate are both *agitato* that Pederson might claim one of them for his own."

"Instead of Jewel?"

"Exactly."

"Well," said Skye, "considering the scene this morning, one can't blame him, even though the poor girl can't help the way she is. But one cannot blame Kate and Maggie, either. What a horrible prospect! Claimed as property by an arrogant billionaire!"

They both laughed, but after Skye had swallowed the last of his beer his tone was serious. "You know, Jerry," he said with his voice lowered, "I envy you."

"You do?" Jerry was astonished.

"It's not just that you are outstandingly fit for a bloke your age."

"Come off it," said Jerry amiably. "I'm only seventy-one, you know."

"And I'm forty, and haven't done any of the things you'd done by my age. I always wanted to be a deepsea diver, or a test pilot, or an acrobat. Or a topnotch fire-fighter."

"It doesn't have a lot to recommend it, that last. Not except for the excitement and the money."

"Both my parents were artists, as you know, and so I should have been an artist of some kind, too. But the Bacchantes had raised me, and so I've never created anything arty in my life. Whatever creative talent I might or might not have inherited never came to light. Instead, I was turned into a business manager."

"I know." Jerry had witnessed it firsthand. After Skye had spent a year helping one of Stefano's brothers work the east coast farm into the beginnings of the fine satellite vineyard that it was now, he had been sent to Melbourne for a graduate degree, and then to Harvard for further qualifications. Then, after graduating *summa cum laude*, he had returned to the main vineyard, to work with the heads of the family.

"I noticed that you didn't put up any kind of real argument."

"How could I? I owed the Bacchantes everything. But it's a reminder of the old argument about nature versus nurture. If I had been artistic, like my parents, it might have been different, but because I was brought up by the practical Bacchantes, I was good at data sheets and adding up figures, and managing profits and futures, instead. The way I was raised trumped the genes."

"And you are bloody good at management, too." Jerry, as a member of the *famiglia* Bacchante, and a shareholder in the business, profited most agreeably from Skye's acumen. Though silently, he did agree that it was odd. Skye even looked like a Bacchante. And the girls, raised as twins, behaved like twins.

"It's a talent that Harold Pederson has found out," Skye said wryly. "I should be devoting all my spare time to the Bacchante business — or as much as I can do, at sea — but instead he's monopolizing me. He calls me up to his office above the bridge for two or three hours every day, to check some spreadsheets. And there's been no mention of payment. Do you reckon I'm working off the cost of this involuntary cruise?"

"That's a thought," agreed Jerry. "He hasn't asked any kind of work from me, though. Thank all the little tin gods," he added, and saluted with his glass.

"Worst of all, it means dealing with Pederson's personal assistant. Madden is such a surreptitious creep that I wonder what he is really up to."

"You reckon he might be a fraudster?"

"Who knows? He is certainly a fraud."

And they laughed.

At last there was movement on the decks of the *Ratpack*. "Thank the good lord," said Jerry, setting down his glass. "With luck we'll be moving again soon."

When the chief engineer and the two hands reported to the bridge, Harold Pederson came up from his office. Madden followed, but merely hovered, and both were uncharacteristically silent. Captain Castellano, who had delivered a barrage of fury at that arrogant thickhead Madden earlier, nodded briefly at the yacht's owner — who was very red in the face, he thought, with veins standing out on his forehead — then returned his attention to the engineer.

"The desalinator really was broken," the Scotsman said. "And a great deal else, as well." He went into technical details while Captain Castellano made notes, ending with the dour prediction, "Their steering gear won't last much longer, either, not without an overhaul. They should've learned before they raised anchor that a job that takes a day in port takes a week at sea."

"Don't they have a competent bosun?"

"No bosun at all, from what I could tell. They all seemed to muck in, when they could raise the energy."

"How many on board?"

"Five who were awake and moving around. There could be others, but they stayed invisible. That one who called himself Mulligan seemed to be in charge — if they had any kind of skipper at all. Bunch of bums," he said, his mouth turned down. "Wouldn't want to eat on that ship, not at that table, and certainly not off any of the plates. There was a cat, but he was as lazy as the crew, as I saw several rats. Dirty ship, very well named."

"Drugs?"

The engineer looked at the two crewmen who had been with him, and they both shrugged. "Recreational, certainly," he said. "Can't say about anything else. Didn't find any suspicious packages, not where we went. Oh, but one thing," he added. "That Mulligan, the one who seemed to be the skipper, I don't reckon that is his real name, not by what the others were calling him."

"I am sure it wasn't," the captain said. He looked down at the charts, rolling a pencil meditatively. "And I do wonder," he murmured, "what they are really up to."

The engines were throbbing gently below, and the *Odyssey* was picking up her heels as they headed southwest. Their departure early in the year was in their favor, as even though the yacht had very little windage it helped that the seasonal trade winds were pushing them along. But, at a cruising speed of 14 knots, it was going to be a week before the *Odyssey* fetched the Marquesas.

Meantime, they were in empty waters — and the trade winds favored a sailing vessel.

Chapter twelve

When Maggie was working at the table in the upper deck lounge, Jewel sashayed into the room, took a chair, and sat down beside her.

"What are you doing?" she said.

Maggie tensed, but Jewel sounded like an ordinary human being, not at all like the syren who had danced to seduce the visitors, then metamorphosed into a wildly screeching harpie. She also seemed genuinely interested in the scattered sheets of paper on the table. The door to the VIP suite was open, and Kate was working at the computer, inside but within earshot.

She said, "I'm sketching ideas."

"Ideas?"

"For dresses. And tunics. Tunics are going to be big this season, I think."

"Oh! Tunics!" Jewel's smile was bright. She looked down at herself, stood up, pirouetted, and said, "What do you think of my outfit?"

Jewel was wearing white shorts and an oversized red knit cotton sweater with long sleeves, nothing special. Maggie was not at all sure what to say, but she smiled and said, "I love your belt."

It was a wide black and white striped belt, slung loosely about Jewel's hips with a couple of stainless steel clips.

"Do you?" Jewel's smile became brilliant. "Really? It's the strap for a shoulder bag I don't like very much, so I took it off and turned it into a belt."

"That's sensational," said Maggie, and made a note. Then, looking at Jewel, she swiftly sketched in a series of long charcoal lines, detailing the belt but not much else.

"Is that me?"

"Yes, but it is not very good."

"Can I see?"

"Yes, of course."

Jewel sat down. "Can I keep it?"

"After I have made a copy, as I like the idea of the belt."

"Do you want to scan it on my father's machine? He is only just down the stairs."

"No need," said Maggie, hiding a shiver of distaste.

She quickly sketched a copy, and Jewel took the first one, but then set it aside. She reached over her shoulder, pulled a handful of long pale hair forward, and said, "Do you like my hair?"

"It's beautiful."

"Do you wish you had hair like mine?"

"That's hard to answer," Maggie said honestly. "Everyone is different."

"My mother has beautiful hair."

"She is a beautiful woman."

"But she has her hair dyed."

"Well, at her age..." Maggie wondered how old Helen was, and thought that she must be in her late forties. And her hair wasn't dyed; it was streaked and toned, as befitted a middle-aged woman of high fashion.

"I don't dye mine."

"Of course not."

"I have trouble with my skin, though. It takes a lot of work to keep it clear. I use a lot of face masks and creams."

"Do you need to do that? You have a lovely complexion."

"No, no, I don't agree. You are just trying to get round me with silly flattery."

"Not at all."

Jewel was looking at the sketches again. She said, "Why do you draw triangles?"

"I always start with a long upright triangle. The base is the floor, and the apex is the neck of my model. Clothes always look best when modeled that way, with the feet wide apart."

"You mean I should stand like that? As if I have wet myself?"

Jewel giggled, and Maggie laughed. "Of course not," she said. "But if you study fashion magazines, you will see that the models are mostly standing akimbo. It's not flattering for the model herself, but it is flattering for the clothes. On the runway at fashion shows, on the other hand —"

"I wish there were shops here," said Jewel.

Taken aback by the sudden change in topic, Maggie said, "But why? You can ask for most things you want on this lovely yacht, and someone will find them for you."

"But I love to shop. I just like shopping. When we are in New York, I shop shop shop all the time."

Maggie was silent, thinking it was lucky that Mr. Pederson was a zillionaire.

"Can I do some drawing?"

"Of course."

Maggie stood up, found her big sketchpad, and tore off some sheets, but when she turned round Jewel had simply taken the pages she had been working on, and turned them over. Now, with her elbow crumpling the pile she had made of these, she was drawing on the back of one.

Maggie's first instinct was to protest that this was thoughtless — selfish, even — but that was impossible. Silently, with her lips pressed together, she took the stack of sheets she had torn off her sketchpad, and rapidly drew on one after another, recreating what she had drawn — after hours of deep thought, in some cases. It was easier than dreaded, and at times new inspiration impelled the new drafts. The last was a pleated tunic with a broad, striped belt draped low and loose on the hips, held in place with a couple of stainless steel clips.

It was the best work she had done since she had boarded this ship. With a deep sigh she straightened, brought back to the present. Belatedly she remembered hearing paper being torn up, and winced, even though she had redone the work. Jewel was still there, but she was scribbling frantically over her latest effort, her expression fraught and furious.

"I can't do it!" she cried.

"Do what? What are you trying to do, Jewel?"

"Draw a cat, stupid, a cat, a cat, the cat I used to have at home — the same cat I loved so much that I have its ashes in a necklace."

"*What?*"

"The pet cat I loved! But something happened to it, and it died."

Maggie swallowed hard. "You have your pet's ashes in a *necklace*?"

"Yes! And when my mother dies I will have her ashes in a necklace, too. Don't you listen, or are you stupid? I want to draw that dead cat, and it won't come right!"

"Can I see?" Wincing inwardly, dreading what was likely to come next, Maggie took a corner of the sheet of paper, and pulled it to her side of the table. It was indeed a drawing of a cat, but not a good one at all. Jewel was displaying all the frustration of an artist who could not replicate what she saw in her head. It was common enough, and Maggie supposed it was understandable enough that Jewel should scribble over it in despair, too. But this furious reaction was beyond comprehension.

"It is fine, just needs a few adjustments," she said, as calmly as she could. "The front paw needs to be made bigger, as it is closer to the front."

"That's no use! I need my mother! I thought I liked you, but I don't, I hate you, because you are just another bossy know-it-all teacher." Jewel jumped to her feet, whirled, and was out of the lounge before Maggie could say another word. As she pulled over the ruined pages, she could hear frantic steps retreating down the stairs, and then a lot of swearing.

Voices echoed, and then Florida Sullivan came into the room. She said crisply, "What happened? What did you do to upset her?"

Maggie exclaimed, "Nothing! We were perfectly happy with our sketching until Jewel suddenly became angry."

Kate, arriving in the doorway, said, "Maggie did nothing wrong. I wondered what was happening when there was a very long silence, but when I checked they were both happily sketching. Maggie could not have been nicer to Jewel."

Florida frowned, but her tone became less aggressive. "She came down in a very bad way. Something must have set her off."

"Nothing I did," Maggie insisted. "She drew a cat, and was unhappy with it. It didn't come out the way she wanted, so I tried to give her a little advice, and it was that which sent her into a spin. I didn't know she hated teachers! Here it is — look!"

She snatched up the scratched-out drawing and thrust it at the psychologist, furious that she should be blamed when she felt absolutely blameless. "I had every excuse to scold her, but I did not! She stole my sketches," she angrily went on. "She just grabbed up the sheets and treated them as if they were worthless. Crumpled them up and drew on the backs and then crumpled them up again. Some she tore up and threw away. Is it right for someone to be so unaware of another person's feelings? Surely she must have realized that when she was treating my work as scribbling paper, she was being disrespectful? But I said nothing! Instead I did my work all over again, and left her to sketch as she wanted. So what did I do wrong?"

Florida winced. She said in a low voice, "I'm sorry that happened to you. I will do my best to make sure it doesn't happen again. But Jewel can't help it — it's a symptom of her condition. We are trying to ameliorate it with counseling, but it will be a long task. There are no known medications, you see."

She walked out with her shoulders slumped, and Maggie suddenly realized that Helen's friend was older than she had realized. Well over fifty, definitely. Perhaps even sixty. Old. And so tired. Grim, determined not to be defeated, but defeated anyway. It made Maggie feel awful.

She began to cry, from guilt as much as the aftermath of anger. "I'm so stupid. Katie," she sobbed. "The truth is that when I did the work over again, I did it so much better. So I am angry for no real reason."

"Oh come," said Kate, with a hug. "You have every reason to be angry. I know I would have hated it if my day's writing was interrupted like that, even if it did need a lot of revising."

"But oh my God," Maggie gasped. She had picked up one of the crumpled drawings Jewel had left behind. "Look at this."

It was a picture of five goldfish in a jar. Their mouths were stretched wide open in soundless screams, their fins held up like pleading arms. A tag tied to the jar had one sad word: 'LOST.'

The silence went on a long time. Then Kate said softly, "Oh, the poor, poor child."

Ever since the first awkward dinner in the main dining room, the four Bacchantes had eaten outside, and kept to themselves. It was very pleasant on the star deck in the light of hanging lanterns, with the awning spread to catch the dew. The trade winds had been soft and gentle all week, and it was relaxing, too. Even though the four of them were family, they still had untold stories to tell.

Their table steward was Agnes, a plump and happy middle-aged Filipina who bragged that she had been a pole dancer in her youth. They didn't believe her for a moment, but enjoyed her laughter and her sparkling eyes. MJ, equally amiable, kept their wine glasses filled.

Tonight, Kate had been unusually quiet. Then she looked up as a plate of grilled tuna was slid on the table, and said, "Agnes, what is the drug policy on this yacht?"

Agnes stilled. Her eyes went quiet. She said, "That's a very hard question, signorina." Then she left.

Jerry said, "Why do you ask?"

"Jewel was so hyped that I wondered if she'd got hold of something."

"But Helen doesn't look the sort to go in for recreational drugs. And Harold?" Skye shook his head and laughed.

"I agree. But the last lot of chartered guests might have left something behind."

"That's a stretch," Jerry objected. "This is the cleanest ship I've ever seen. They must do a deep clean at the end of every charter."

When Agnes came back Constantia, the head steward, was with her. Kate stopped eating, but before she could say anything Jerry greeted Constantia in Tagalog, and then ran on in a few rapid sentences, gesticulating as he talked.

When he silenced Constantia's eyes slid to Kate. "You asked a big question, signorina," she said in English.

"Yes, I know it is difficult. But I would like to know what the policy is here. Not for myself," Kate said hastily. "But because of something else. Have you had any trouble with charterers?"

"We have a zero tolerance policy on this ship, signorina. Mr.

Pederson is very strict, very, *very* strict about it."

"That's good to know."

"All the medicines in the first aid box have doctors' prescriptions attached to them, for fear of close inspection by the officials of any port in the world. And Mr. Pederson has copies of those prescriptions, in case of further questions." Constantia paused, and then said, "But yes, you are right. We have had problems with chartered guests bringing cocaine on board. The instant it is detected by any member of the crew, the yacht sails for the nearest port, and all the guests are sent on shore. All of them, no question, and reports are made by the captain to the local authorities. They forfeit all their charter money, and have to find their own way home. That is in the charter papers that they signed."

"Thank you," said Kate, feeling rather stunned.

"You are very welcome, signorina. And I should add that if any port officials find drugs on board without being warned before-hand, we all lose our seafaring certificates. All of us. The captain, the engineers, the stewards, everyone. We have to go home without a job. And the yacht loses its license, too."

"Oh dear," said Kate. "I can see why you are so careful."

Constantia nodded, and then visibly relaxed. "Signor Jack, his Tagalog is very fluent," she observed.

"That's because his wife is Filipina."

"She is?" Both Constantia and Agnes looked at Jerry in surprise, and Kate saw that MJ's eyebrows were very high, too.

"Was," said Jerry blithely. "She ran off to Manila with the kids when she got tired of me being away all the time."

"But he visits them often," Kate said. He had taken Kate with him when she was in her teens, and Maggie too, because Kate had insisted on it. She and Maggie had fallen in love with Manila and the people, and had been amazed that Jerry's kids were so old. Even his grandchildren were almost as old as they were.

"And I still love her," said Jerry, still very amiable. "In fact, we've had another couple of kids since she ran back to Manila."

Constantia's eyebrows shot up. It was the most amazed the girls had ever seen her. Shaking her head in bemusement, she went away, and after refilling their wine glasses MJ went off too, presumably to do the same at Harold Pederson's table in the owner's suite. Agnes took their emptied salad plates, and headed for the galley, and so for the moment they were alone.

Jerry pushed a bread roll through the meat juice on his plate. "What I can't understand is why Pederson bothers to rent out this yacht," he said. "Surely he can afford to keep her in a convenient marina, ready for the next time he wants to take guests on a cruise."

"It's because he's tight, mean, and cheap, as zillionaires tend to be," said Skye. He twirled a huge forkful of spaghetti, which he chewed lustily. "My God, he's working me like a Greek slave with an abacus, and with absolutely no contract or pay. I should sue!"

"Watch it," said Maggie. She was wearing beige, and Skye was talking with his mouth full.

"And that Madden is up to no good," Skye added.

"How?"

"I keep getting the feeling that he has his own agenda — that he is not really working for Pederson at all."

"That's because you don't like him."

"Nobody likes him, but what I particularly don't like is his focus. Since Madden took over as personal assistant two months ago, he has neglected the cruise ship accounts to concentrate on an enterprise called Pederson Strategic, where a lot of Pederson money has been invested. And when I say a lot, I mean a *lot*."

"Pederson has fifty-one percent of this enterprise?"

"Forty percent. Which means that Pederson has no personal

control, apart from a place on the board. I don't think he likes that, which would be a reason he's getting me to check the records."

"And the other sixty percent?"

"Saudi Oil."

Jerry whistled. "Wow."

"Well," said Skye, "I've been lobbying hard for Pederson to stock Bacchante wines on his fleet of discovery ships. Basically, that's the reason I responded to Pederson's invitation to that meeting in Pasadena. But now I'm not nearly so keen."

Jerry forked up some baked potato, coated it with sour cream, and munched meditatively. Then he said, "Saudi Oil is a huge operator. Are Pederson Strategic and the cruise ship side of his empire linked in any way?"

"Not obviously, and perhaps not at all. I've been looking at the cruise ship records, and haven't found any connection. Yet."

"So, what is your problem?"

Skye looked down at his pasta, and stirred it slowly. Then he lifted his head, and smiled lopsidedly. "Actually, it's just a strong gut feeling. Emotion has taken over from logic. It's a family matter, really."

"What on earth do you mean?" said Maggie.

"Despite being in New Zealand for several generations, Bacchante is Italian in its heart and soul, which is a reason we have succeeded so well. It's the village mentality that the founders brought to New Zealand from Sicily. We rely on seasonal workers, but we don't just expect them to turn up as needed. We know we have to provide decent accommodation and decent food and water, as well as decent pay and a few bottles of wine, along with a big party when the grapes are in. Because of that, the same happy people come along for every harvest. We can rely on them, because they rely on us. And, because of that, we see good figures on the spreadsheet."

"I don't follow, Skye. What are you trying to say?"

"As I said, it is just a gut feeling. But I wonder about the crewing system on Pederson's discovery ships. The passengers are treated well, though I find it disturbing that they are treated as packages, but it is well understood that a cruise is advertised as a dream, and it is a dream that must be fulfilled. Crewing cruise ships is another matter. They are treated as another package. There are agents in Singapore and the Philippines and Indonesia who supply the hotel workers and seamen, and franchises that supply the shops, casinos, and beauty salons. The deck officers seem to all come from Europe, so that is another side of the equation."

"Wow," said Maggie. "So that is why our lovely stewards and deckhands are Filipino? While the cooks are French, and the engineers are Scottish?"

"And the captain is Italian, while the first officer is French," Skye agreed. "So, yes, this yacht is a microcosm of a cruise ship. What I wonder is what it is like for them all when they turn up for work on his ships. Are they treated as well as we treat our seasonal workers? I don't have any way of knowing, and because of that I wonder if we will lose some of our image as socially aware employers if Bacchante wines become standard on board. My instinct is to steer clear in the meantime, and that's what I will be reporting when we get back home."

"Fair enough," said Jerry. He nodded when Agnes came in and carried away his dinner plate. She smiled and picked up Skye's emptied pasta bowl, and left. MJ topped up their glasses and went.

They were alone again. "But the crew of this yacht are treated well," said Maggie.

"Helen said that Constantia is an old friend, that she has always been very, very kind to her," said Kate.

"I'm sure they are treated well, because Pederson understands that following the high standards he sets for them depends on his own good treatment. That's probably the real reason he keeps this yacht running — for entertaining top travel agents, and giving them a great impression of the Pederson way of pampering vacationers. Though it also means that he can write the yacht off as a business expense, which would be thoroughly in character. But on his cruise ships? In a very competitive environment where profit depends on limited outgoings? Are the staff there treated as well as the crew of *Odyssey*?"

Jerry said, "It's more complicated than you think, Skye."

"What do you mean?"

"The people of the Philippines will put up with a lot, and still count their blessings. And they have a connection to the sea that goes back many centuries, mainly because the country is made up of countless islands, so they have low expectations of life on board. Did you know that one third of the seafarers today are Filipino? There are all sorts of reasons for recruiting them. They are self-disciplined and obedient, and will carry out jobs that are not in the original description — even very dangerous jobs in the engine room or the bilges, because they willing to try out another skill. In the fishing fleets and on oil rigs, and on freighters all over the world, Filipinos are given a very bad deal. The contracts they sign before shipping mysteriously disappear, and much less generous contracts take their place. And the conditions can be very bad, dangerous and very unhealthy. For them, working on a cruise ship is a pinnacle, something to be dreamed of, a job they aspire for, and working for Pederson is an enormous bonus."

Kate said, "So they are willing to take less pay?"

"Yes indeed, *piccolo*. They are certainly paid less than their European counterparts. But they are sought-after by the cruise industry for more reasons than thrift. They are fluent in English from childhood, because that is the primary language in schools, are always ready with a smile, and they do not get drunk. They don't want to spend money that way, because most of their money goes back home. Yet they are not tip-hungry, like American crews. It's no wonder that Pederson employs them."

Silence. Then Maggie said, "So Agnes and Constantia and MJ don't get paid what European workers would get?"

"Exactly. And because they are not European, officialdom does not come asking why the situation is so unfair. The tax department doesn't get involved, because they are not on the records. However," Jerry added, "one does have to remember that the dollars they are paid go a very long way in Manila. When they get home, they are considered very rich."

Another long silence. Kate was frowning. "I still feel that they should be paid the same wage I would get if I did any of their jobs."

"As is our policy on the Bacchante vineyards," said Skye, returning to his argument. "If Harold Pederson paid the Filipinos the kind of wage we pay our grape pickers, would it affect his margins? I don't believe so, as the charterers pay hundreds of thousands to book a cruise on this yacht. But it could be a different matter on his cruise ships, where the passengers don't pay that much money."

He silenced, as Agnes came in with their desserts. She smiled at them brilliantly, said, "Happy, happy everyone on board, okay?" and took orders for coffee and tea.

When she had gone, Maggie said, "What was that about?"

Jerry drank the last of his wine. "Who knows? But it does seem that she overheard what we were saying."

"Maybe our voices were raised."

"Perhaps." He shrugged. "But what I really want is to get Pederson to start up a foundation for the welfare of Filipino seafarers everywhere. The seamen on trawlers and freighters are the ones I really worry about."

Skye thought about it, and said, "But what is the point of persuading Pederson to start up a charitable foundation, when he doesn't even have control of his own venture capital company?"

Jerry grimaced. "Is any of the money being siphoned off?"

"It would be the classical outcome, I agree. But I haven't found any evidence."

"Then I suggest you keep looking."

Kate said, "Do you think Madden is working for Saudi Oil?"

"Who knows? It could even be for a government."

Another long silence, and then Maggie asked tentatively, "Will it hurt Bacchante if he doesn't buy our wine?"

"No, no. There are plenty of other avenues. Even if we do nothing, our heads are well above water."

"That's a relief," she said, and silence fell again while they ate their desserts.

"At least Mr. Pederson isn't running drugs," Maggie said as she put down her spoon. "Though drugs would explain a lot about his daughter."

"Jewel was pretty bad today?"

"You have no idea. And I bore the brunt of it."

"That goldfish picture was very grim," said Jerry, who had seen it. "I wouldn't be surprised if they put her on anti-depressants."

"Who knows how it would affect her illness? Maybe it would have the opposite to the intended effect. Florida — Dr. Sullivan — said that there are no known medicines for her condition."

"Has she recovered from that meltdown?"

"I suppose so, because the shouting stopped." Then Maggie said, "I wonder what it's like at their dinner table? What do *they* discuss?"

Kate said nervously, "You don't think Mr. Pederson could hear us? You know how sound carries at sea."

"Impossible," Jerry reassured her. But they all silenced, half-expecting to hear voices from the owner's suite, down one deck, and at the other end of the ship. But the only noises were the lap of water, the quiet throb of the engines, and the rattle of cups and saucers on a tray as Agnes brought up their coffee.

Chapter thirteen

Helen was still awake when Harold came down from his office. Wrapped in a bathrobe, she was curled up on one of the settees, watching television with the sound turned low.

She turned it off, smiled brightly, and said, "Everything going well?"

"As good as can be expected. Steve Madden is finishing up."

He had answered her, which was a plus. She drew a breath and then said quietly, "Harold, you and Mr. Madden seem very close."

"I need a personal assistant, and have always had one. He was a good replacement for the last."

"Yes, but he is more than that, isn't he?"

He turned and scowled at her. "What are you implying?"

"Nothing. But he seems to be very involved in your business affairs."

Business had been the only conversation at the dinner table. Jewel had refused to come out of her room, so Constantia had sent up their room steward, Luiz, with a tray. An hour later, though, the tray had been shoved out of the guest suite door, the food untouched. Helen wondered if Florida had given her a medication that had turned out to be an appetite suppressant. She didn't like to ask, though, as Florida was looking so tired. Was she prone to seasickness? Or merely worried about Trevor Green? The old psychiatrist was not looking well at all.

"Madden does well at all facets of his job," Harold snapped. Then his tone moderated. "He has excellent qualifications, and over the last two months he has given value far beyond what I pay him. I am even thinking of promoting him to a managerial position."

"Where?"

"In Pederson Strategic."

Helen had never heard of it. This troubled her, as Harold was perfectly aware that she had managed a successful business in Washington, and should have told her more — though of course he would never condescend to ask for advice.

She thought over the past two months. Harold hadn't summoned her at all, which was the reason she had never seen Madden or heard his name. The last time she had been called up by Harold, it had been to Dubai, she remembered. It had been just before his last personal assistant resigned.

She said, "Is Pederson Strategic based in the Middle East?"

"The headquarters are in Geneva."

"So it's your own company?"

Harold scowled. "I am a major partner."

But not the most major, she deduced with alarm. He wouldn't be the first ageing billionaire to be defrauded. Her experience in diplomatically fraught Washington came to mind, and she feared that her husband was walking dangerous ground.

As if he sensed it, he changed the subject abruptly, snapping, "Why was Jewel shouting?"

"This afternoon?"

"Of course I mean this afternoon."

Helen paused. "She was upset because she had been trying to draw a cat, and it didn't work out."

"For God's sake! Something so petty?"

"She might be talented. And artists can be emotional."

"So I could draw pictures when I was young, and some were good and some were bad, but I didn't create a scene when I made a mess!"

"You drew?"

"Nothing exceptional, I assure you."

Harold was undressing with abrupt, angry movements. His voice was muffled as he pulled off his shirt. "I need an heir, damn it."

"You have Jewel," she pointed out quietly.

"Bah!" It was a furious grunt, as he jerked his nightshirt over his head. Then he said, "Jewel isn't competent to run a pizza parlor, let alone a business. She needs to marry someone suitable and then get pregnant."

"*What!*"

"You heard me. She is old enough. I need someone to take over, and we need to make sure of a grandchild. A grandson, preferably. And hopefully it will be a normal human being."

Helen was silent, biting down anger. Instead of speaking, she took off her robe and climbed into bed. As she slid between the sheets she winced at the thought of what Harold would say if she informed him of the reality.

Jewel had been uncontrollably promiscuous from the age of fourteen, and so Dr. Green had made sure that it was impossible for her to ever have a child. As he had said, the risk of passing on her mental illness was too great.

Next morning, Constantia arrived at the door of the bridge, accompanied by François, the head chef.

"Captain," she said, "can we have a word?"

"Of course," said Castellano, and they joined him.

"We need to go fishing," said François. He waved an eloquent hand, after wiping it on the side of his regulation gray checked pants. "The men, they are easy. Beef, beef, beef, and when we run out of the vacuum packed, there is more in the freezer. But fish — how the girls love fish!"

"And fish must be fresh," Captain Castellano agreed. This happened a lot, even on the short charters, and was usually fixed by sending a boat to the nearest island, which was not an option in this empty sea. He looked at the chart, and thought about the great improbability of encountering a fishing trawler.

"But," he said, and gestured with his own eloquent hand.

"I know," said François, sympathetically. "Perhaps if we stopped the ship? Put on the brakes for a little while?"

That was another option, and, indeed, the last lot of fresh fish had been caught by deckhands who had fished from the tender while the *Odyssey* was lying still, her course having been interrupted by that business with the brig.

The chef said, "At night, for perhaps some albacore?"

"It would probably be better to make it early in the day, and give the guests the chance to go fishing. We could put out the small boat at the same time, with a couple of deckhands to clean the waterline."

François nodded. "That is sage, Captain, very sagacious. People will eat with enthusiasm what they have caught themselves."

"Good. I will get Sarah to organize it. Anything else?"

"Salad."

Captain Castellano said blankly, "You must be kidding."

Jean-Pierre, the sous-chef, worked a magic with damp cloths and plastic bags that kept washed lettuce crisp and fresh in the cool room for up to two weeks, and they had not been out of port ten days. And there was no way, surely, they could find lettuce in the tropical Pacific.

"The girls, they eat much strawberries."

Fruit salad, Luigi realized. "You don't have frozen strawberries?"

"They like the fresh."

"The chances of finding fresh strawberries at Nuku Hiva are very small," the captain said dryly. "Do you have pineapples? Bananas?"

"*Oui.*"

"Then they will have to get used to tropical fruit. Promise them papaya and mango when we get to Nuku Hiva."

Though Luigi had little idea of what kind of fruit was available in the Marquesan Islands, as he had never been there before. He should ask the crew, he thought vaguely, and then wondered what they would run out of next. He was reminded of the story of the cook of a small freighter who found three days out, when the pantry needed replenishing, that the storeroom was completely empty. The steward who had jumped ship the night before sailing had sold the lot before he absconded. For the rest of the Pacific crossing the poor chef had been forced to devise tasty meals from the dried beans that were part of the ship's cargo. The cook had been French, of course.

Luigi wondered if the story was true, but it was certainly a good one. "We should be able to bargain for fish there, surely," he said, returning his mind to the present.

"*Bien sur*, Captain."

"Any other problems?"

"No, no. We do need lettuce, but this is the easiest party we have carried in a very long time. Not one complaint about the food."

"Well, that is a relief." Just recently a charter party had sent back all the beautifully composed dinners with drunken complaints about fancy food. They had ended up eating cold turkey breast sandwiches, though why anyone would pay many thousands of dollars a day to eat tasteless picnic fodder was beyond Luigi's comprehension.

He nodded, and François left. Constantia, however, stayed behind, just as Captain Castellano had expected. He smiled, and then led her to a bench seat on the starboard side of the bridge. They were old friends, having been recruited at the same time for the *Odyssey*'s maiden voyage. Luigi relied greatly on Constantia.

"And what do *you* think of our guests?" he said.

She sat neatly with her feet together, her skirt pulled over her knees. Sexual harassment was a major problem with the charter parties, and after the girls who waited at the table had been repeatedly tormented with crude comments about Filipina breasts and legs, the *Odyssey* uniform had been altered. Knit polo shirts gave way to tailored shirts, and cut-off shorts were replaced by trousers, skirts, or calf-length pants. Modesty in dress was enforced for the men, too, as bare-chested deckhands had been harassed in the past.

"Mrs. Pederson is unhappy, I think, as perhaps she does not believe her husband loves her any more. It is not like the time long ago when she first came on board, when the yacht was very new, and it was so evident that he adored her. Then, they were happy that they were expecting a child, but since then, much and many changes."

Luigi nodded, as he had come to that conclusion himself.

"But, as François said, as a group they are easy. The signorinas in the VIP suite are untidy, very," Constantia went on, and clicked her tongue. "They even mess up the upperdeck lounge. But Gladys copes well, and is not unhappy, because they speak so nicely." Gladys was their room steward.

"And it is the work they are doing, not just playing around," she added.

"And in the owner's suite?"

"Mr. Pederson, just as usual, he works, works, works. At the computer all day, making radio calls, big business, neglecting his lovely wife. Madden is there, too, but Mr. Pederson makes Signor Hamilton check everything."

"He does?" The captain was surprised. Surely Hamilton was an ordinary guest?

"I don't think Signor Hamilton likes it much, as he would be happier out on deck with the girls and Signor Jack, and I believe he has his own work, but what can he say?"

Luigi pursed his lips, gazing out at the sea. The helmsman perched silently on his stool at the helm, and the deckhand silently scanned the horizon with his binoculars. Beni Boulez was taking a break, as Captain Castellano was nominally in charge of the bridge, but nothing out of the normal was happening.

Finally he said, "I can't help but wonder why Mr. Pederson needs everything checked. Are you certain of this?"

"Oh yes."

Luigi believed her, as Constantia had her sources. Agnes would report what she heard at the table, and MJ would report on Mr. Pederson, as he was often in the owner's suite. His job involved replenishing the minibar, and making sure that Luiz, the room steward, was doing an impeccable job. And Luiz had eyes and ears as well. All the Filipinos, whether deckhands or stewards, knew that they could confide safely in Constantia.

Constantia lowered her voice. "Perhaps it is because of Mr. Madden. Mr. Pederson is getting old, and his thinking is muddled at times, but he is shrewd enough to feel doubts. Yet I do not believe he knows that Mr. Madden copies his data onto his own computer, down in his stateroom."

"Oh my God." If there was industrial espionage on board, the implications were shocking, for the ship as well as the owner. Luigi had visions of officials from justice departments storming on board.

"You think that Mr. Madden might be informing someone about Mr. Pederson's business affairs?"

"All I say is that MJ has seen him copying with a flash drive. Signor Jack likes a nightcap, and MJ brings it to his stateroom himself, as they like to talk, you know, and twice with the sway of the ship Mr. Madden's stateroom door has swung open as MJ passed.

"And," she went on, having still more bad news to impart,

"Signorina Kate was asking Agnes about drugs."

"Oh God." Drugs were a constant nightmare.

"Not for herself. She is very clean. Signor Jack explained to me that she is concerned that Mr. Pederson's daughter might have got hold of some drugs, perhaps left behind by a charter party."

"He told you all this? When?"

"He speaks fluent Tagalog, Captain."

"*Buon Dio*," said the captain. "Surely you are kidding."

"His wife is a Manila woman. His heart is with the Philippines. He would like to campaign for Filipino seafarers to be treated more fairly. Agnes heard him say that."

Captain Castellano paused, absorbing this, then said severely, "English is the language of this ship, Constantia."

"Of course, sir."

He nodded, and did not pursue it. Obviously, if Constantia was addressed in Tagalog, she was forced by courtesy to talk in that language, too.

Instead, he said, "Why was Signorina Kate concerned about drugs?"

"Signorina Jewel became very upset in the afternoon, and Miss Kate wondered if she was high on something."

"Is it possible?"

"We are of course certain that no drugs were left behind by the last charter party, but Dr. Green and Dr. Sullivan do have medical bags."

Captain Castellano was silent. Up to now, he had been grateful that there was a strong medical presence on board, considering Jewel Pederson's history. The possibility that she would steal from their supplies was most unwelcome.

"Was any damage done during the outburst? Anyone hurt?"

"Luiz didn't say so, and I haven't heard anything from anyone else.”

“Well then, let’s just hope that it doesn’t happen again,” said Captain Castellano fervently.

And, having come to the end of the update, Constantia smiled and went away.

Chapter fourteen

The four Bacchantes hailed the idea of going fishing with delight. At the last moment, though, as the rubber boat was about to be launched from the Beach Club ramp at the stern of the yacht, Jewel Pederson arrived at the door from the lower deck. She was wearing her usual white shorts and long-sleeved cotton knit top, but today it was blue, which enhanced the intense blue of her eyes.

Kate looked up and said, "Do you want to come with us?"

Jewel stepped back a pace, and shook her head.

"Are you certain? You would be welcome."

"No, no." She seemed frightened. "I want to draw pictures with Maggie."

In the boat, Kate, Jerry and Skye looked at Maggie, who was trying to hide her dismay. Sarah Murray, the bosun, was at the helm, her abundant curves confined in a blue uniform shirt with epaulettes and calf-length cropped trousers, tightly belted. Her hair was caught in a ponytail that was pushed through the back of her blue baseball cap. Under the shadow of the peak her expression was perfectly bland, but it was obvious she was paying attention.

Kate said to Jewel, "Are you sure you want to stay inside? It will be so nice to be out on the ocean."

"No, I want to draw pictures."

Helen Pederson appeared behind her daughter. She had heard it all, because her expression as she looked at Maggie was pleading.

"It would be wonderful for her," she said.

"Oh God," Maggie muttered, almost unheard by the others. But what could she do? She stood up and eased past their legs, and clambered out of the boat and up onto the ramp. Then, to her horror, she heard Jerry say, "Mrs. Pederson, would you like to come with us?"

Mrs. Pederson said, "Call me Helen." She was wearing navy Capri pants and a white loose knit sweater, with boat shoes on her feet.

Jerry said nothing, while the others stared at him.

The owner's wife then said, "I would love to come. Would that be okay, Sarah?"

Sarah Murray said, "Of course."

Maggie numbly handed over her life vest, and watched Helen Pederson climb into the boat. Then Sarah spun the boat away. They did not go far, just a couple of hundred yards. Then they stopped, putting out hand lines while the boat slowly drifted, carrying its reflection along with it. In the light of the rising sun the dark-blue water had shades of lime green.

"Come on," said Jewel, and led the way along the corridor to the lower deck foyer, then up two flights to the VIP suite. It was as if she had completely forgotten the meltdown that had followed the last drawing session.

Gladys, the room steward, was making the bed. "I will go," she said quickly, when she saw them. "And come back later, no problem."

Maggie said, "No, we don't want to interrupt you, Gladys. Miss Pederson and I will take drawing materials down to the main lounge, if that is okay."

"Of course, very okay," said Gladys with enthusiasm, adding rather meaningfully, "It's a beautiful day outside on the deck."

"I know, I know," said Maggie with a sigh.

Jewel seemed perfectly fine as she helped Maggie collect her big sketchpad, sticks of charcoal and pencils, chattering about her last shopping expedition in New York City before being flown to

California. The complete shopping list was there in her head, it seemed, mostly involving cosmetics. When they arrived down the stairs to the main deck Luiz, the main deck room steward, was polishing the huge table in the dining area, and poking through the big bowl of fresh flowers to remove the wilted ones. He was a handsome young man, with such long eyelashes that Maggie thought there might be a beautiful Indian somewhere back in his family line.

He beamed and said, "Miss Jewel. Signorina Maggie."

"Good morning, Luiz, *kamustá ka*," she said politely. Then, when he had assured her that he was very well, thankyou, she said, "How on earth do you find fresh flowers in the middle of the ocean?"

He had a beautiful smile to match the eyelashes. "Constantia buys them in the bud, you know, so that they do not bloom until they are taken out of the cool room."

"Good heavens," said Maggie, absorbing an interesting fact. She gestured at the sketchpad she was carrying, and said, "We need a surface for drawing, but this table looks too nice for that."

"There is a table in the owner's suite, Signorina Maggie."

"Excellent," said Maggie, following him into the stateroom. The table was set for six, but Luiz swiftly removed the cutlery and crystalware, before heading back to the main dining table and his flowers.

This time, Maggie gave Jewel a few sheets torn from the sketch pad, and did her own work within the pad, so that the girl could not purloin her drafts. Jewel rattled on about her shopping for a while, drawing as she talked, and then she sat back, finished.

Maggie said, "Can I see?"

Jewel pushed the sheet over. It was a sketch of a vase of flowers, all of them drooping sadly. It was very clear, and also evocative.

"That's excellent, really excellent," said Maggie with perfect sincerity, very delighted that it wasn't a badly drawn cat. "You have a natural sense of composition, and it carries lots of emotion. What are you going to call it?"

"Neglect," said Jewel.

"Very good." Maggie wondered if the choice was significant, but the artist's expression was just as usual, sulky but calm.

Jewel said, "Are you drawing another picture of me?"

"No. It is a draft for a snowdrop dress. It's sleeveless, and tight and low in the bodice, but then falls loose from beneath the bust, like an Empire gown, only calf length, not ankle length. In a silky, finely pleated fabric I think it could be a hit."

Maggie quenched a sigh, because she should be in the cutting room at Bellissimo right now. "The current thought is that the cut is more important than the fabric, because it keeps the cost down," she mused on. "But I don't agree. A cheap fabric makes a cheap garment, no matter how good the cut."

She remembered how horrified she had been at the fate of her graffiti dress in the budget department stores. "It is better to have a beautiful fabric as well as a wonderful cut," she said, "and have fewer garments — just garments that make the wearer feel confident and glamorous, whatever the occasion. Clothes that pack well and wear well, and last for years without getting dated. Timeless wonders that are worth whatever they cost."

Jewel wasn't even bothering to look at her, let alone pretend to listen. Having finished meditating to herself, Maggie tore the draft out of the pad, handed it to Jewel and said, "What do you think?"

Jewel merely glanced at it. "But you must have a model, not just a silly triangle. Why not me?"

Maggie had never come across such self-absorption before. Even fashion models were not that egocentric. Deciding that it was best treated lightly, she winked conspiratorially at the steward, who had come in to polish the buffet, and said, "Why don't I draw you, Luiz?"

"Me?" He straightened up with the cloth in his hand, looking most animated. "A drawing of me?" His enthusiasm was a refreshing contrast to Jewel's conceit. Maggie cooperatively penciled a quick sketch, emphasizing the eyelashes to a ridiculous length, and making his beautiful grin split his face almost in two.

It was a cartoon rather than a portrait, but Luiz was delighted. "Oh Signorina Maggie, it is wonderful. Can I keep it?"

"Of course." She scribbled a fancy signature across the bottom, and handed it over. Luiz rushed out with it, evidently to the crew quarters so that he could brag to his messmates. Maggie could hear the clatter of his happy feet as he ran down the stairs.

Jewel's lower lip was pushed out with temper, so that she looked quite startlingly like her father. Maggie almost expected her to stamp her foot.

She said, "Now you *have* to draw me."

"Okay." Maggie sketched her — not as she sat, looking angry and frustrated, but as she had looked when she had danced out onto the open deck, the morning the unwelcome visitors had called. The slim body was in motion, the arms held high, and the long hair fanned out. In the drawing, Jewel was on her tiptoes, about to take flight.

Maggie held it out with her head on one side, studying it critically. It was one of her better efforts, she decided. She had managed to catch the spirit of the moment.

Jewel snatched it away from her, and scowled at it. A long moment went by, and then, to Maggie's relief, she said, "Can I keep it?"

"Of course."

"Will you sign it, the way you did for the servant?"

Maggie wanted to tell her that Luiz was not a servant; he was a shipmate, to be treated with respect. Instead, she silently scrawled her signature.

Jewel took it back, cast it aside without another glance, and then complained, "I should always be your model."

"But my model is nobody. The basic sketch is just a frame for the clothes, like a store mannequin. You've seen me do it. It's usually just a long triangle."

"I think you use Kate as your model."

"Well, she is my sister, so she's around if I desperately need one."

"I bet she models the clothes after they are sewn, so that you can take photographs."

Maggie was silent, because it was true.

"And you should use me, not a silly triangle or your sister."

Maggie kept her mouth shut, starting another sketch instead.

"Is that another picture of me?"

"No, I must do some work. The studio expects me to send in drafts at least once a week."

Jewel had gone red in the face, and her eyes were like intensely blue lasers. "You won't draw me because you think I'm a freak."

"*What?* No, of course I don't."

"People tell me I am a freak."

"Well, that is horribly cruel, because it isn't true." Unpleasant schoolmates, Maggie thought, and hoped that it wasn't closer to home.

"Do you think my mother uses drugs?"

O Dio, thought Maggie, and said very firmly, "Most certainly not. Your mother's complexion is clear, not pitted at all. Her nose does not run, and her teeth are perfectly white. She is a very beautiful, healthy-looking woman."

As usual, Jewel paid no attention; it was as if she were deliberately deaf. "Because I heard the doctors asking her if she took drugs while she was pregnant with me."

"I'm sure that's usual," said Maggie carefully. "People do take medicines for lots of things, and the doctors need to know if they are likely to harm the unborn infant."

"Why don't you listen? Are you stupid? I heard the doctors say that a long time *after* I was born, when I was old enough to understand what they were saying. They meant *bad* drugs, not medicine, which turned me into a freak. Oh, it is no use talking to you!"

Maggie said nothing, feeling utterly helpless. This terrible conversation was going nowhere. When Jewel stormed to her suite and slammed the door, screaming that she was going to complain to her mother, she did not move, not even to remind the little shrew that she wouldn't find her mother there, Mrs. Pederson having usurped Maggie's rightful place in the boat.

She certainly didn't want to tap on Jewel's door, not while she could hear Jewel kicking the furniture in fury. At last the row subsided. Quickly and quietly, Maggie gathered up her drawing materials, noting with stray interest that Jewel had not neglected to take the portrait away. Mostly, though, she was intent on escaping to the VIP suite.

She might even go to the sun deck for a glass of wine, she thought. It was early, but she needed it. But then she was foiled. To her horror, Mr. Pederson thumped down the stairs from his office, and strode over to the table.

He barked, "What was that about?"

She stood straight and looked at him. He towered over her. His face was very flushed, and he had dark circles under his eyes, as if he got too little sleep. She wondered if he drank a lot, because his nose was veined.

She said, "I really don't know, Mr. Pederson. Jewel wanted to do some drawing with me, and she made a very good sketch of some flowers in a vase. But then everything went haywire."

"Haywire? Talk English, girl."

She said with dignity, "My name is Maggie. And 'haywire' means that the conversation stopped making any sense. I didn't know what to say, and Jewel wanted her mother. If you need her, she should be in her suite. Mrs. Pederson is fishing with my family, so Jewel might still be upset."

Harold Pederson stared down at her, standing too close for comfort, his small blue eyes sharp and assessing. Then he said, "Sit down."

It was the last thing Maggie wanted to do. But he was her host, and she was too proud to flounce out. So, after putting down the sketch pad and drawing materials, she perched on the edge of her chair, ready to flee at the very first chance.

He sat down opposite, still studying her face intently. "You are Maggie Bacchante," he stated. It was as if he were holding an interview.

"I am." She nodded defiantly. "The daughter of Stefano and Rachel Bacchante. Granddaughter of Matteo and Francesca Bacchante, and great-granddaughter of Andreo and Eva Bacchante, the founders of the vineyard." As a teenager, just like all the other young Bacchantes, Maggie had been given the job of escorting tourists about the vineyard and the press house on Sunday afternoons, and so she swung easily into her spiel.

"In 1938, just in time to evade the brewing war in Europe, my great-grandfather, Andreo Bacchante, arrived in New Zealand from sunny Sicily, intent on making his fortune. He started out as a laborer on the wharves, which was usual enough, but his ambition was to build a vineyard and found a dynasty. He started to build the vineyard the day after he'd saved enough to buy forty acres of poor flinty soil in some hills south-east of Auckland. Then he sent to his home village for a wife. The matchmakers chose Eva, a girl who was a stranger to him, and his brother Piero came too, and Piero brought his own wife, and so the dynasty got started. And – like the grapes – the *famiglia* Bacchante has grown, bloomed, and prospered."

If Harold was amused or startled at this recital of family history, he did not betray it. Instead he observed, "Your mother is a widow."

"Yes." Maggie's mouth drooped. "My father died the day I was born, so I never got to meet him. A sheet of roofing iron cut off the most of one of his legs, and he lay bleeding in the barn until some Maori farmers found him. They carried him to the hospital, but it was too late; he had lost too much blood. He died while the clinic was being destroyed by the storm.

"But my mother is a Bacchante still," she went on with spirit. "She lives with the family, and runs the gift shop and art gallery. She sponsors artists from all over the district, some from Australia even, and during the winters the Bacchante women make jam to sell in the shop. The jam is famous. We have our own orchard, as well as zillions of grape vines. And my mother creates the most amazing traditional quilts. They sell very fast for big money, but she can only manage about one a year."

"I want to meet her."

Reminded of Mr. Pederson's troubling reason for hauling them along on this cruise, Maggie kept silent.

"And you design clothes."

"I do. With the Bellissimo Studio."

"Which is Italian."

"I am based in New York — as I think you know already, Mr. Pederson."

"Have you ever been a real artist?"

"Dress design is a real art," she informed him coldly.

At last he smiled. He seemed to like her combativeness.

"Did you draw pictures as a child?"

She frowned, thinking back. "I drew caricatures of the nuns at school," she confessed. "And got into terrible trouble."

"I did drawings, too," he said.

"All children do. It's a way of making their world comprehensible."

"You sound like a child psychologist."

She laughed. "No, just an ordinary person who likes to design clothes. What were your drawings like?"

"Ordinary. I was an ordinary child."

"I am sure that is not true."

"You flatter me, Maggie Bacchante," he said, and hoisted himself out of his chair, and headed back to his office. Something she had only half-heard had summoned him. But on the way to the stairs he turned, and said, "If you need to send drafts back to Bellissimo, just ask if you need any help. I would be glad to assist."

"Thank you," she said. And when he had gone Maggie shook her head. Against all the odds, she liked him.

Chapter fifteen

While fish were certainly being caught by the Bacchantes, fishing was not the major event — or so Jerry observed. Kate and Helen Pederson had their heads together, talking fashion, books, and the stalled promotion party in New York. As Jerry noted with great interest, they were getting along like a house on fire.

"I'm sure our absence did not affect sales," Helen assured Kate. "Everyone loves a mystery, and my assistant has been very discreet, letting imaginations roam where they will."

"Is that the Lady Pamela who sent me all those letters?"

"Lady Pamela Phillips, yes indeed. I suppose you have deduced that she is English. But I bet you would never have guessed that she is eighty years old."

"No!"

"She spent years as a hostess on Cunard liners, and has amazing and very amusing stories to tell. That is where I first met her — on one of the trans-Atlantic crossings, a Christmas one, and very elaborate. There were forty-seven Christmas trees! Truly, I counted them. And then I met her, and got to know her. One of the first-class passengers had wooed and married her, which was how she got the title, but her husband had passed away, meantime. When she finally retired from Cunard, at the age of sixty-five, I invited her to become my assistant, and to my great joy she accepted. Sharp as a tack, and I rely on her greatly."

"Why doesn't she write a book?"

"Because I don't give her enough time, my dear," said Helen, and Kate laughed.

Jerry watched them quietly, his eyes narrow, his expression shuttered. Then he was distracted as yet another fish bit. He hauled it in, threw it in the tub with the others, and rebaited his hook. They had found it was best to fish close to the yacht and within its shadow, so the boat was now drifting along the starboard bow. When he looked up, the silhouettes of two men were at a window on the second deck. Pederson and Madden, he thought, and wondered what they were up to.

Skye, reclined in the stern beside Sarah Murray, his fishing tackle held loosely, was looking up at the shadows of the two men, too. He was frowning, as if speculations were turning over in his head. The window above was open to the breeze, but it was impossible to hear voices. The only sounds were the clink and ripple of the water running along the boat, and scrubbing noises from the two deckhands who were working a small dinghy along the waterline. Occasionally they looked up and waved. It was all very peaceful.

Jerry said, "Hold this," and handed his fishing line to Kate. Then he stood, facing away from them all, and undid his pants. "Time to drain the potatoes," he said cheerfully. When he had finished, he rinsed his hands in the sea, sat down, and took back the line.

"You are disgusting," said Sarah.

"I did wash my hands."

"The next fish we take is thrown back. And, signor, the next time you pinch my bottom, I will clock you one that hurts."

Everyone laughed. "He can't help it," said Kate. "It's him."

"Good luck with the clocking," Skye said. "He's fitter than he looks, and very quick on his toes."

"Oil wells can explode unexpectedly, you know," said Kate. "He's used to darting out of the way."

Sarah looked at Jerry, and said, "How do you put out an oil well fire?"

"Just like killing a human," he said blandly. "You starve it of oxygen."

"Oh God," she said, and they all laughed.

Then they were distracted. The deckhands were moving about in the scrubbing boat. The radio had sounded for one of them, and they were packing up their brushes, ready to get back to the ship. Sarah's earpiece sounded as she got the same message. Looking abruptly alert, she started up the motor.

"Summons," she said. "Something has happened, and we have to get back."

Sarah joined the captain on the bridge just ten minutes later. She had left the deckhands stowing the boats in the hold, and François had already collected the tub of fish. As she arrived, the rumble of the yacht's engines was getting louder. The *Odyssey* wallowed a bit, and then straightened up and got back on course.

Beni was there, too — and Mr. Pederson, annoyingly. She hoped he would keep his mouth shut, and not interfere. Worse still, Madden had followed him.

Captain Castellano poked a finger at a monitor, and said, "Look."

Sarah hunkered down to peer at the screen, which was tuned to the marine traffic finder. There was a blob for the *Odyssey*, which, when tapped, identified the craft by name, registration, last port, and number. There was even an image of the yacht. Otherwise, according to the picture, the sea around them was empty. But, when Luigi pointed at the radar screen, there was a second blob — another vessel looming on their starboard horizon and inching nearer, but not registering with the AIS transceiver.

"It is almost possible to see it with the binoculars," Luigi said.

Beni handed them to her. "You have the best eyes in the ship. Tell us what you think."

Sarah had to lean against the window sill to brace herself, and took a moment to get the instrument focused. Then she spied two tiny clouds on the horizon, progressing determinedly towards them. A moment later she glimpsed tiny triangles as the vessel tacked, evidently with the intention of intercepting the course the *Odyssey* was keeping, but staying out of sight.

She gave back the binoculars. "It's the hippie brig," she said. "What was its name?"

"*Ratpack*," said Beni.

"It looks as if they got ahead of us, and are sailing back to keep within range. How the hell did they do that?"

"With a good trade wind, *ils sont plus vite que nous* – they have the heels on us."

"Do we feel stalked?" she mused aloud.

"They seem to feel a need to be our shadow," the chief officer agreed.

Silence. Then someone remarked ironically, "That must be the first time that sail has beaten steam."

When Sarah turned to look, it was Skye Hamilton. He was still dressed in shorts and tank top, and was redolent of fish. Apparently, he had come in as he was, at the bidding of their employer. Madden was still there, as impassive as ever.

"But it can't be right," Sarah objected. "Our cruising speed is 14 knots, and that of a brig is ... what?"

"Eleven, with a fair wind," said Skye, who seemed to be some sort of an expert.

"So the *Odyssey* is faster. How did they overtake us?"

Captain Castellano said slowly, "There must be someone on board who is a much finer seaman than we assumed."

"But they are coming back — as if they didn't intend to get so far ahead, sir."

"We have been still for two hours. That must have fooled them"

Beni said, "And their AIS transceiver has been turned off."

"I didn't know it was possible to turn it off," said Skye.

"The Iranians and Chinese do it all the time — the Iranians to veil exports of oil, and the Chinese because they like to have the stealth fleet. And there are trawlers fishing in banned waters, too. They do the same. It is called Going Dark. The most modern transceivers have no off switch, but they bypass it by pulling the plug. With no power, it does not work, and so they Go Dark."

"How do we know that the brig has a transceiver?"

"Anything over three hundred gross tons has to have one. But how lawful these people are ..." said Beni, and let his voice drift off.

Sarah frowned. "I feel sure John reported that there was a working AIS transceiver on board."

John was the engineer who had gone over to the *Ratpack* to fix their desalinator. "Better get him up to the bridge," said Captain Castellano, and Beni issued the order through the ship's radio.

Harold Pederson was looking impatient, even redder in the face than usual. He said, "Please enlighten me. What the hell is an AIS transceiver?"

They all looked at him, amazed that a shipping tycoon could be so ignorant. Beni said, "It's part of the automatic identification system that uses transceivers on ships to track their position, course, and speed, sir. It's standard on all your cruise ships, sir."

"So it is used to monitor their movements."

"Exactly, sir. It does make it easy for maritime authorities and governments to keep track of them. And business rivals," Beni added thoughtfully.

"So it is easy to guess why certain ships would not want one."

"I agree that some fishing fleets might not want the authorities to know that they are fishing in a prohibited area — but AIS can be critical, sir — to prevent collisions, and to assist navigation. And for help in emergencies. They make search and rescue operations so very much easier. Cruise ships and container ships could not function without one."

The yacht's owner shrugged, and said, "Okay, you've made your point. So why would these people turn theirs off?"

"Because they are doing something illegal, sir."

"They are pirates?"

"Drug running is more likely," Beni said with relish.

Captain Castellano visibly winced.

Pederson said, "What in God's name makes you think that?"

"They are most likely on the way to Suwarrow, Mr. Pederson sir, but need to call for supplies at Papeete first, and cannot risk their illicit cargo being found there."

"Suwarrow? What's that?"

Skye said, "An uninhabited atoll in the Cook Islands. It has been a drop-off for illicit cargoes for well over a century."

Dear lord, thought Sarah. It sounded like a comic book.

"Are you sure of that?"

"Oh, absolutely. Reputedly, a treasure was buried there about the middle of the nineteenth century. There have been several treasure-hunting expeditions, but they found nothing and nobody. And, since then, it has been a noted spot for yachts from the Americas to drop their cargoes for others to carry on to Australia."

"So you think these hippies are doing the same business, but intend to use us as their mules?"

The chief officer spread his hands and shrugged. "All I suggest, sir, is that they want to put their packages on board of us, so that they will get a clean bill at Papeete. Then, somehow, they would retrieve them after we have sailed from Tahiti, perhaps by pretending to need assistance again."

They all looked out the starboard window. The brig was now hull-up on the horizon, but busily tacking away.

Sarah said, "If they are so keen to be invisible, why are they so near?"

"With their AIS turned off, they have to keep close to keep track of us," said Skye. "We don't have much of a profile, being so low on the water."

"You think that they have a lookout at the top of the mast?"

"Exactly," said Skye. "It's their only recourse. They are invisible to our screen, but we are invisible too. Except to the naked eye."

The chief engineer arrived at the door, tapped on the frame, and said, "Captain?"

"That sailing ship out there. Did you see a transceiver on board?"

"Aye, sir, I did. And when I checked, it was in perfect working order."

Skye said dryly, "Well, it ain't working now."

"Then they have turned it off."

"What about radar?"

The engineer snorted. "They don't have the battery power to run radar for long, believe me. I didn't see it, and I doubt it was there. Nope, they have turned off their AIS for reasons of their own, and don't appear to be worried about the possibility of collision."

"So," said Beni with great satisfaction, "they have Gone Dark."

Jerry found Maggie on the sun deck. She was perched on a bar stool with a glass of white wine in front of her, talking to the bar manager.

"Hi MJ," he said. "Hi Mags, this is revolutionary for you."

MJ smiled, poured Jerry his favorite beer, and vanished.

Maggie said, "I needed a drink. How *could* you guys abandon me? You left me all alone with Jewel!"

"Was it that bad?"

"Not so much bad as weird. It gave me a new insight into people. Most of us — almost all of us — can look into a person's eyes, and know how they are feeling. I can look into Jewel's face and see that she is depressed, uncertain, and angry, very angry. But Jewel completely lacks that facility. She has no idea how other people feel, or that what she says and does can affect them greatly — unless, of course, she is trying to manipulate them. She is utterly and totally egocentric."

Jerry drank beer thoughtfully, and then said, "Narcissist?"

"That's a very big word. I don't know the answer."

"There is definitely something wrong with the girl. So, was it bad?"

"She insisted that I thought she was a freak, because people had told her she was a freak — her schoolmates, I imagine. Teenaged girls can be very cruel."

"Oh, Mags, did you have a foul time at school?" he exclaimed. "You could have talked to me and Skye about it."

She shook her head. "I know, Jerry, I know. There was the whole *famiglia* Bacchante if I wanted a shoulder to cry on. And Rachel, of course. She was such a mother to us both. But the school wasn't that terrible, and I had Kate. She was a tower of strength at times. And," she added, draining her glass, "I was the same for her. We are a huge power together. Have you never noticed?"

"Always," said Jerry, and emptied his glass.

MJ materialized, produced two more drinks, smiled, said, "Cheers," and vanished again.

"She said she knew she was a freak because she had overheard the doctors asking her mother if she had taken drugs while she was pregnant. Not medicines, but bad drugs."

Jerry went very still. But before he could say anything, Maggie went on angrily, "Why aren't the two doctors around more often? I have hardly seen them, and yet I was under the impression that they had been co-opted onto this boat to keep an expert eye on Jewel. That's twice I have had to deal with her tantrums, without any help from them at all. And if there are any drugs on this ship, *they* are probably the ones carrying them."

Skye arrived, and slid onto a stool. He had taken off his cap and dark glasses, and his hair stood up in spiky ends. He was still wearing shorts and tank top, and smelled of salt and fish.

He said, "Did I overhear you talking about drugs? If you were, you are prescient."

"Why?"

"Because that hippy brig is dogging us, and the chief officer has the theory that they are drug-runners plotting to plant their cargo on us before we get to Papeete."

Again MJ arrived from nowhere, bearing a foaming glass of Skye's choice of beer. Skye took it, saluted them all, and drank deeply. "God, that's good," he said.

"So what is this about the brig?" said Jerry.

"It is keeping on our tail — but made a mistake this morning, or maybe in the night. They ran ahead of us, and the radar on the bridge caught them as they were beating back."

Jerry frowned. "The radar? What about the AIS?"

"As far as the monitor was concerned, they were invisible. But the radar did pick them up."

"Do they have one of the old receivers? The ones that receive but don't transmit?"

"Apparently not. The engineer swears they had a working transceiver, which does both jobs, so if it is still working they have turned it off. They were also keeping us in sight, which was why

Sarah was able to spy them coming over the horizon. So it looks as if they have a lookout of their own at the top of a mast."

"So they don't have radar?"

"The engineer says not. Radar sucks up a lot of power, and they don't have enough battery."

"Asking for trouble," Jerry said, and shook his head.

"Indeed," said Skye. When MJ lifted an eyebrow, he nodded, and the bar manager went off for another foaming handle.

"Was it hot out there fishing?" Maggie enquired tartly.

"Not particularly — but I have more bad news."

Jerry sighed, and said, "So okay, ruin my day."

"Harold Pederson says that from now on we are to dine with him and his entourage on the main deck. Eight o'clock sharp, he said."

'Oh boy," said Maggie. What were the odds that she would be seated next to Jewel? Pretty high, she thought. But Jerry, she noticed, did not look particularly horrified. Instead, he twirled his glass, looking down at the suds very thoughtfully.

"That could suit me," he said.

"Good lord," said Skye. "How?"

"I'll get you to help me compose a few spreadsheets. That will be my mission, this crazy cruise. I'm determined to make something useful out of it."

"Useful how?"

"My campaign for him to fund a foundation for Filipino seafarers."

"You are going to do that over *dinner?*"

"Yup."

"Oh boy," said Maggie, and shook her head.

They all laughed, and she said, "Really, how did the fishing go? Do tell me there will be lovely fresh fish for dinner, and brighten the day just a little."

"It was great," said Skye. "Don't know if we caught anything edible, but there were a lot of fish hanging around the hull of the yacht, once the *Odyssey* was just drifting on the current. There must be good stuff to eat hanging off the bottom."

"And two of the hands were scrubbing," Jerry agreed. "That could have shaken off a few nibbles."

"Kate and Helen Pederson got along just fine," Skye added. "They seemed to have a lot in common. Not just books, but fashion, too. So maybe Mrs. Pederson is behind this demand that we all dine together."

Maggie frowned, tilted her head on one side, and said, "Wasn't Mrs. Pederson organizing a big promotion for Kate?"

"Yup," said Jerry. "It was interrupted by that crazy summons to Pasadena, which was a shame, as it was supposed to be really big. But I heard her promise to stage it again. She is terrifically enthusiastic about Kate's future."

"I'm beginning to wonder," said Maggie, and stopped.

"What?" said Jerry.

"I might be deluded, but — you know how the gossip sheets and fashion magazines call Kate and me the Cinderella girls?"

"They do?" said Skye.

"They do," Jerry affirmed.

"Good God, you read that stuff?"

"No, but Kate has shown it to me."

"They reckon that Kate and I have a fairy godmother."

"Good lord," said Skye, and drank beer very thoughtfully. "I think I can see where you are going with this."

"Yes. Someone — someone very influential — put good words into the ears of the top people at Bellissimo for me. I know there had been a lot of talk about the graffiti dress and how it was revolutionizing teenaged fashion, but still my hair truly stood on end when I got a request from their top creative designer to go in with my portfolio. It came absolutely out of the blue. I was terrified, but when it happened he was very nice, and very enthusiastic, and I was hired as a cadet designer right there and then. But I still got the feeling that he was doing someone a favor."

Silence. Jerry's eyes were narrow and unfocused, lost in deep thought. Then he said, "You're suggesting that it was Helen Pederson."

"That *she* is your fairy godmother?" said Skye.

"Yes," said Maggie, and finished her wine rather defiantly. "I am."

Chapter sixteen

At two in the afternoon, when all the guests were at their various lunch tables, Constantia tapped on the frame of the bridge doorway. She was carrying a tray with a plate of bread, sliced salami, cheese and pickles, along with a salad and a coffee pot, with mug, sugar and milk.

When Luigi Castellano turned, she said, "Your lunch, Captain."

He nodded, and led her to the bench under the starboard windows, and she sat with the tray between them. As always, her skirt was pulled down primly over her knees. She was now in her fifties, but plump enough to show her age well. Her hair, still mostly black, was pulled back into an old-fashioned chignon in the base of her neck.

He said, "You knew I would be still on the bridge?"

"Of course, Captain. Because of the brig."

"So you know about the brig." He shook his head and smiled, while he helped himself to a pickle.

"Yes, the same brig that hailed us about the machine to make the fresh water. The one that Boulez believes is carrying drugs."

"Aha," he said, and picked up a slice of salami and nibbled at it, thinking about the disdainful way she had named the chief officer.

"But you do not agree with Beni?"

"No, Captain, we do not."

"So what is your theory for this strange shadowing?"

She shrugged. "There must be a reason for them to be following us so secretly, but we have not decided yet."

Not so secretly, Luigi thought. Though the hippies had turned off their AIS transceiver, they had been naïve enough to stay within range of a lookout with binoculars.

"They are amateurs," she said. "So the engineers believe."

"So they do not agree with Mr. Boulez, either?"

"No one agrees with Boulez."

She did not add the word 'ever' but Luigi could hear it in her voice. He himself found Beni Boulez irritating but competent, and so he decided to keep an open mind.

He said, "The fishing went well?"

"Yes, Captain, it was an excellent idea. The guests who were in the boat were very happy with their excursion. Though only Signor Jack and Signor Hamilton did the fishing," she added.

"But they caught fish, these two men?"

"Lots of fish, yes. Some were quite big. Jean-Pierre was very happy with what he received in the galley."

"And the two signorinas?"

"Only Signorina Kate was in the boat. Mrs. Pederson went with her. Signorina Maggie was summoned by Miss Jewel to make pictures with her."

This was fascinating. Captain Castellano placed salami, cheese, and pickle on a slice of bread, and ate meditatively. On the bridge, the helmsman perched stolidly at the helm, keeping the *Odyssey* firmly on course. The lookout with the binoculars watched the horizon intently, focusing on the tiny shape of the *Ratpack* at regular intervals. He seemed enlivened by the discovery that his job was not outdated and redundant, after all.

The yacht was surging along at fourteen knots, and the sea rippled in a regular pattern that was only occasionally interrupted by a flaw in the wind, or a shoal of fish. The breeze that came in the open windows was cool and clean, sparkling with ozone.

He said, "So Mrs. Pederson took the place of Signorina Maggie in the boat?"

Constantia nodded. "Signorina Maggie and Miss Jewel went first to the upper deck. Gladys would have been happy to make way for them to do their drawings in the lounge, but Miss Maggie insisted that the main deck was better. So Luiz cleared the table in the owner's suite for them to work."

Captain Castellano nodded. He expected nothing less than perfect cooperation from this crew. "And?" he prompted.

"Signorina Maggie made a drawing of Luiz, a portrait, and signed it for him. He showed it to us. He is very happy. It is a very good drawing, and he thinks it will make him famous."

It was hard not to laugh. "And Miss Jewel?"

"Luiz was gone, so I do not know precisely, but Luiz says that Signorina Maggie made a picture of her, too."

"And then?

"Signorina Maggie tried to work, but Miss Jewel persisted in talking — about drugs, again. Or so said Luiz."

"Drugs?" Captain Castellano winced.

"Something about the doctors, what they said."

"What did they say?"

"I do not know, Captain. But I also hear that Signorina Maggie is very unhappy that the doctors do not help her when Miss Jewel is difficult. Mrs. Pederson helps her in some ways, and also Signorina Kate, but the doctors do not."

Castellano had seen little of the two medical professionals himself, though Mrs. Pederson seemed to hold them in high regard. This, he thought, was a mystery. Why indeed were they on board?

He said, "Where were they when Signorina Maggie was with Miss Jewel?"

Constantia shrugged. "In their stateroom, I think. But, Captain, I do not know."

He was silent, finishing off the bread and salad. Then he poured a mug of coffee, and set it to one side. "Thank you," he said. "I enjoyed that."

Constantia nodded, stood up, and picked up the tray. Then she turned and said, "François asks about the fruit again."

"Tell him that we will be at Nuku Hiva the day after tomorrow," he said. "He can do his shopping there."

"Not Papeete?"

"Not Papeete," he confirmed. "Not yet."

Even if Jerry had had the time to prepare his campaign for the Filipino foundation, he would have been foiled. When the Bacchantes turned up in the main lounge, to find the formal table set for eight, Harold Pederson was already there, with very firm ideas about where everyone was to be seated. Rosa, the main deck table steward, had been duly instructed, and she ushered guests to seats as they arrived.

Harold sat at the starboard end of the table, which ran across the deck, with his wife at the other end. The two girls sat on either side of him, while Jerry and Skye sat either side of Helen Pederson. The spare chair between Jerry and Maggie was taken up by Madden, when he glided in, as bland and silent, white and watchful as ever. The place between Skye and Kate was intended for Jewel, apparently. She had not arrived yet, and the two doctors were not coming. They had opted to eat in their stateroom, which raised the question yet again of why they were so invisible.

Perhaps Jewel was with them, Skye thought, but the owner's daughter turned up as they were halfway through the first course, her expression sulky. She looked around, and then perched silently at Skye's left elbow. When he spoke to her she ignored him, simply stirring her *poisson cru* about with her chopsticks.

"Too raw," she said when Rosa took the uneaten delicacy away. "And I don't eat leaves," she said, when Rosa returned with a salad. Rosa merely smiled, and took the spurned salad away. Madden, opposite her, made no attempt to speak to anyone. Instead, he ate as if he were filling in time before getting back to the computers.

Skye did not have a chance to talk with Helen Pederson, either. Jerry, as usual with a good-looking woman of any age whatsoever, was flirting with her, and so Skye was forced to be a silent witness. They were talking about Saudi Arabia, exchanging very different reminiscences. It was hard to believe that elegant Helen Pederson had ever been there — but then, for her it would have been banqueting and reception rooms, and top class hotels. Jerry, on the other hand, would have been out in the desert, living in a caravan, drinking water out of a bottle. coping with terrible emergencies, and ordering workers around. Now, as probably back then, Helen Pederson smelled faintly of lemon balm, very clean, and very delicate. And, probably back then, Jerry had smelled of sweat, smoke, and burning grease.

As he listened to the banter, Skye watched the two girls. Kate was quiet, eating her salad with her usual small, tidy movements, but Maggie was vivacious. It was becoming increasingly obvious that Harold Pederson was fascinated by her, asking alert questions, and then listening with total attention. When the main courses arrived, Pederson hardly looked at his grilled fish. Instead, his big head was inclined towards Maggie, his bristling blond eyebrows lowered as he considered what she was saying.

She was telling him about her apprenticeship at Bellissimo, Skye discerned, and meanwhile charming Harold Pederson out of his expensive designer socks. She had all the shipping tycoon's attention, while Kate was being neglected. Why? It was a puzzle, because the two girls were so alike. During that first year, when Skye was helping break in the east coast vineyard, he hadn't even tried to tell them apart. Each time he'd come home both chubby, dark-haired babies had looked the same, cuddly and affectionate, with sparkling brown eyes that were lined thickly with black lashes.

He wondered if Jerry had had the same trouble telling one from the other. Each time he'd come back from another oil fire incident, the two toddlers had run up to him with their arms held up, and he had grabbed up both, and hugged them with equal delight. When they were six or seven, they had jointly decided to be famous ballerinas, and he and Jerry, along with other Bacchante men, had tamely taken them to ballet classes, and watched as they posed and pirouetted. And this was even though the Bacchantes would really have preferred them to be famous opera singers. And then, when the girls were leggy, and wearing the same school uniforms, he remembered them going off to school with their fingers linked, the way they had been since babyhood ... *Damn it*, Skye thought, *they are both Bacchantes, right down to the heart and soul!*

He was nervous for no reason, he realized. But he couldn't help the ominous thought that Harold Pederson was back onto his crazy theory that one of these girls was his daughter, and that Maggie was the one he hoped for. Looking at Jewel, who was moodily pushing her exquisitely cooked fish around her plate, it was hard to blame him. The girl might be twenty-one, but she was behaving like a teenager in the worst of teenaged years. When Skye had tried to start up a conversation, asking her if she was excited about landing on Nuku Hiva, she merely shrugged, making no attempt to answer.

And, after eleven days at sea, many of those hours spent checking the records of Pederson Strategic, Skye knew without doubt that Harold Pederson was a very, very rich man — and very rich men had the power to make things the way they wanted them to be. To hide his discomfort, he turned his attention to Helen Pederson, who was laughing, too, at something Jerry had said.

Anyone who wandered in would think this was a happy party, Skye decided – but was then distracted by a sense of recognition.

Right up to this second he had been almost positive that he had never seen Helen Pederson before, but suddenly there was something about the way she leaned forward, and the way her chin tipped up and her neck lengthened as she bent her head towards Jerry...

He had seen her with her head turned like that before, but back then she had been standing in a doorway with her arms spread, her hands gripping either side of the doorframe, and she was leaning forward to shout at a nurse, who was yelling back. It had happened over twenty years ago, but the memory was startlingly vivid. Everyone had been so panicked. Helen Pederson had been wearing some kind of hospital gown, and her face had been dead white, her hair wild and greasy, and she had been shouting something about babies.

And he had been shouting too, and Jerry had also been yelling, as they tried to make that stupid, stupid *obstinate* nurse see sense. There had been no need to shout, as it was the eye of the storm, and their voices had echoed, which had made it worse. And then Skye remembered *what* he had been shouting at that stupid nurse who had refused to hear, and he slumped in his seat with a huge sense of relief.

Maggie was most definitely a Bacchante.

When Skye went down to the lower deck foyer MJ was there with a tray bearing Jerry's nightcap. Skye followed him into Jerry's stateroom, and when MJ asked if he wanted a nightcap, too, he nodded. He had no idea what it was, but he didn't care.

Jerry was relaxed in the armchair, with his feet up on the table, his ankles crossed. Skye pushed off the feet, drew out a chair, and sat at the table facing him.

He said, "I did not muddle up the two babies."

Jerry didn't even blink. It was as if he had expected this confrontation. He said, "You've remembered?"

"Yes. I finally remembered where I had seen Helen Pederson before. It was in the hospital, and it was the eye of the hurricane — just before the hurricane returned, and that nurse was killed. We were arguing with the nurse, and the door slammed open. Helen was there, looking sick and confused. And we were in a state, too."

"We were both trying to find out what had happened to the babies," Jerry said. "And I was trying to find Kelly," he added. His eyes were sad.

"And Rachel," Skye said. "I was asking about Rachel — and finally found her holding Stefano's hand."

Poor Stefano, he thought. He had loved him; everyone in the family had loved him for his energy and his laughter. He remembered stumbling into the ward as the hurricane roared and the building rocked and fell apart, and finding Rachel clinging to Stefano's hand. He remembered her thin, heartbroken cry as Stefano's spirit fled, and he remembered trying to comfort her. Then she had cried out for her baby.

"Rachel begged me to leave her and find the baby," he said. "And because the woman who had hung onto the doorframe of the suite — Helen Pederson — had been shouting that there were *three* babies in the bathroom, I went there."

"But when you found the bathroom, there were only two," said Jerry. He sipped from his glass, and nodded. He was staring into the distance, his eyes unfocused.

"Yes. Helen had gone, and one of the babies with her. It must have been Jewel. So the others were Maggie — Rachel's baby — and Kate, Kelly's baby, the one you were worried about. They were both screaming their heads off, but I knew which one was Rachel's baby — because she was still wrapped up in my cheesecloth."

"What cheesecloth?" Jerry stared, this time with full attention.

"That wagon where she was born was my first car. It was an old wreck, but I was so proud of it. I was only nineteen," Skye said, in excuse. "I was driving to the east coast farm, to take up my year with Stefano — stupid of me, with the storm raging all around, I should have waited, but —" He shrugged with a sheepish grin. "I was only nineteen and thought myself invincible. Not far from the farm, I found Rachel trudging through the mud, all hunched over, in pain. She was in a dreadful state, poor woman. Even though she was in labor, her main concern was for Stefano, because he was back at the barn, and badly hurt."

Skye paused, his thoughts far back in the past. "But it was impossible to get to the farm, because a tree had fallen across the road. That was why Rachel was walking, as she'd had to leave the car. I got her into my old wagon, and turned around, but hadn't got much further when an axle broke. And we waited ... and waited, but the baby came before anyone found us."

Unexpectedly, Skye smiled. He said softly, "It was the most wonderful moment of my life. They come out pale, you know, but when they let out their first yell, they go all pink. And then they wriggle. Did you know that?"

Jerry shifted uncomfortably, reminded that he had never been present at a birth. If he had been there when Kelly's baby was born, he suddenly thought, none of the current nonsense would be happening.

But Skye was talking again, this time more practically. "When

Maggie was suddenly there in my hands, all wet and waxy, yelling like the devil and kicking like the devil, too, I looked around for some kind of clean wrapping, and I had a whole new roll of cheesecloth that I had bought just a day or so before. It was intended for cleaning the car, wiping the dipstick, that kind of thing, but instead I took it out of the package, unrolled it, and laid the baby on it, and rolled it up again, with the baby safely inside."

"And she was still rolled up in that cheesecloth when you found her in the bathroom?"

"Yes. Disgusting, as they hadn't even bothered with a diaper."

"It was an emergency situation," Jerry observed.

"So, if she was still wrapped in that roll of cheesecloth when I gave her to Rachel to nurse, it was the same baby I delivered. So Maggie," concluded Skye with huge relief, "is a Bacchante."

A long silence. There was a tap at the door, and MJ came in with Skye's nightcap, then smiled and retreated.

Skye lifted the glass in a salute and then sipped. It was a very peaty single malt Scotch whisky. Not exactly his usual choice, but he didn't care. Jerry's eyes had gone unfocused again. He sipped Scotch himself, then sighed and said, "I believe you, Skye, I most surely believe you. But please don't tell anyone else."

Skye stared at him. "Kate. You are scared that we might lose Kate."

"Exactly. If Maggie is out of the equation, Kate is the only one left."

"But Kate doesn't look the slightest like Helen Pederson."

"Are you sure?"

"Yes! There is a huge difference between blonde and brunette and brown eyes and blue, you know. I don't even know if one can be inherited from the other."

Jerry shrugged, and sipped more whisky.

"And Harold Pederson is blue-eyed and blond, really Nordic. Like Jewel."

"That is very true."

"He couldn't possibly be Kate's father, not in anyone's wildest imagination. Are you suggesting that Helen cheated on him?"

"Not at all — though it could be another factor in the equation. But it's immaterial. Admit it, you were worried that he might claim Maggie as his daughter. By your argument, the same could apply to Kate, so I am entitled to my worry, too."

Skye paused. His thoughts were whirling. Then he said, "You're so right. But it's just as unlikely that Kate is theirs as it is that Maggie is theirs."

Silence, as Jerry finished his Scotch. Then he said, "Skye, I know I can rely on your absolute discretion."

"Of course." Skye was puzzled.

"You must *not* let this get out to anyone, certainly not the girls, and definitely not the Pedersons."

"This?"

"Wait." Skye waited. Jerry levered himself up out of the armchair, and went over to the desk. He fossicked around until he found his wallet, then took a folded paper out of it, came over, and handed it to Skye.

Unfolded, it turned out to be a small poster advertising a bar. The picture was of a young dancer, slim and lithe, her arms flung out, her long blonde hair spinning, her hips akimbo, and her smile brilliant.

Skye frowned. "That looks like Jewel. Where did you find it?"

Jerry shook his head. "It isn't Jewel. It's Kelly."

Chapter seventeen

When Captain Castellano came onto the bridge, Beni Boulez said, "The brig has vanished, sir. It's now out of sight."

"Have they turned their transceiver back on?"

"No, sir."

"Idiots." The bluffs of Nuku Hiva were looming on the horizon, and though the islands of the Marquesas were steep-to, with no reefs, there was a big swell around here even in the calmest weather, and the crew of the *Ratpack* were taking a terrible risk.

"They must be keeping on for Tahiti."

Which was even more dangerous, with many hazards along the way. The Tuamotus, for a start. Known to old mariners as the Dangerous Isles, the group was a wide scatter of low atolls ridden with shoals and reefs. Captain Castellano shrugged, forgot it, and applied himself to the charts.

Taiohae, the harbor of Nuku Hiva where he was headed, was on the southern coast of the small island, just about right in the middle. Entry looked easy, apart from the swell that developed between the two sheltering capes, though he was warned that the only navigational aids were beacons. However, the anchorage itself was full of hazards. Quite apart from a large no-mooring zone, there was an underwater cable that must be avoided at all costs. He would drop anchor as soon as possible after entering the bay, he decided. It would make a long boat ride from the yacht to the town quay, but that should not be a problem.

There were the formalities of making his first call at French Polynesia, too. According to the regulations, it was no longer necessary to drop anchor first at Papeete in Tahiti. Thank God, too, he had a French-speaking chief officer. The customs police at the Gendarmerie Nationale in Nuku Hiva were unlikely to be familiar with the complications of entering a mega-yacht, which was basically a mini-cruiseship.

He beckoned Beni over, and informed him that he had the lovely job of calling at the gendarmerie with the crew list, guest list, passports, visas, customs declarations, and a health certificate, plus copies of everything. The rules also stipulated that the ship's representative should have either the owner and the skipper with him, but as Captain Castellano would keep the bridge while he was away, Harold Pederson was the one who had to go.

This was not a message that either Captain Castellano or Chief Officer Boulez wanted to convey to Mr. Pederson. So Beni sent for their stalwart go-between, Constantia. She arrived looking as sedate as ever, her hair coiled neatly into the nape of her neck. And, just as Captain Castellano fully expected, she didn't betray her wince when he asked her to go and fetch Mr. Madden.

After she had gone, he called Sarah Murray up to the bridge, as she would have to be the one to ferry the guests from the yacht to the landing place. And, as efficient and as tightly belted as ever, she arrived before Constantia had returned.

Beni was saying to the captain, "There is also a note that all shipping in the port of Taiohae is inspected with care. Once we have entered the yacht, they are likely to come calling at any time. Can we be sure that nothing to embarrass us will turn up?"

"What are they looking for?"

"Illegal drugs, including strong medicines, and any kinds of guns. And pearls."

"Pearls?" Luigi exclaimed. Visions of pearl necklaces and pearl earrings ran through his mind. He was trying to remember if any of the women on board had been wearing anything like that.

"It would be black pearls," Sarah explained. "They are very protective of their pearl industry, and insist on absolute quality."

"So?"

"I know, it does seem odd, sir. Perhaps they think people will smuggle inferior pearls, and pass them off as Tahitian pearls when they get to other countries."

"Good God," said the captain. He gazed out the windows. The island of Nuku Hiva was tall on the horizon, as steep and jagged as a crown. The sea rippled with a heavy swell, a dark blue in color, with gilt tips on the waves, and fluorescent green in their depths.

Finally, he said, "We can't do much about any pearls our guests might own, but Sarah, could you organize a discreet check for drugs and arms? One or other of the men just might have a hand gun, so be tactful as you take it away. And Beni, it would be a good idea to take copies of the prescriptions in the first aid cabinet with you."

Then, just as Luigi was starting to wonder why Constantia was taking so long, she finally arrived with Madden, the personal assistant. Evidently he had been difficult. The captain frowned, annoyed, but Madden's face as smoothly uncommunicative as always.

Without bothering with a greeting, Luigi said abruptly to him, "We need all the guests' passports and customs declarations. Can you provide these, please?"

"Of course."

"All passports must have an expiry date more than six months."

"I know."

"We have to testify that there are no arms or illegal drugs on board. And we need a medical certificate to attest that everyone is healthy. Could you obtain this from Dr. Green?"

Madden hesitated, but Captain Castellano carried on, saying, "And, according to regulations, Mr. Pederson has to accompany Chief Officer Boulez to the Gendarmerie Nationale."

Madden pursed his lips. "I am not sure that that is possible."

"I'm sorry, but it is a legal requirement. Please convey that to Mr. Pederson."

Madden opened his mouth, but Beni lifted a hand to get his attention. "There is the matter of visas," he said. "This is no problem for the captain and myself, as we both have Schengen visas. There is also no problem for the bosun or the Bacchantes, as New Zealanders can enter French Polynesia without a visa. Also, we applied online for visas for our crew from the Philippines, so those are all in hand. However, for Americans, while visas are dispensed with for stays of less than three months, there is a condition — *une autorisation de travail est exigée par la réglementation de la Polynésie française pour exercer cette activité.*"

Madden shifted from one foot to the other, looking uncharacteristically at a loss. Ben smiled, and said, "In a nutshell, you have to certify that your employer will be conducting no moneymaking activity while this yacht is in the islands. If he is conducting a business here, he needs a permit."

Madden coughed. "I will appraise him of this, though I am sure there will not be a problem. However, I have a complication of my own."

Captain Castellano waited.

"The two doctors have requested that they be taken on shore as soon as possible, as they need to call at the hospital. I assume the Chief Officer will be the first to take a boat?"

"With the papers and Mr. Pederson to the Gendarmerie Nationale," Beni agreed.

"If possible, please take them with you. They say it is urgent."

The captain still waited, expecting an explanation, but none came. Instead, Madden nodded at them all, and took his leave without another word.

Captain Castellano puffed out his lips, and said, "I wonder what that was about."

"More drugs for Miss Jewel, perhaps," Constantia suggested.

Captain Castellano shrugged, remembering the tantrums he had overheard. The girl certainly needed something.

Beni was still reading the regulations, his lips moving with the French words. He looked up and said, "Flags. We have to fly the yellow flag, *naturellement*. And the flag of France. Do we have a Marquesan flag?"

"I didn't know there was one," said Luigi, astonished.

"It says here that flying the flag of the Marquesas is an excellent diplomatic move."

"*Buon Dio*," said Luigi. "What does it look like?"

Beni consulted his computer and some books, and then said, "It is horizontally divided into red and yellow, with a big white triangle at the hoist, reaching halfway across the flag with a black tiki in its middle."

Luigi blinked, shook his head, and said, "What is a tiki?"

"Here it is a tattooed face, sir."

Beni showed them a picture, and both Captain Castellano and Sarah hunkered down to look.

"Very smart," said Luigi. "Undoubtedly, very appropriate."

Sarah said, "I am pretty sure we don't have one in the signal locker, sir."

"Well then, Beni, you can buy one on the way back from the gendarmerie. The souvenir shops will doubtless have one."

"I may have to wait for the doctors," he said.

"Then wait. They are guests, so you have to bend to their bidding. But surely you can buy a flag while you are doing the waiting? Sarah, you can take over the tendering of the guests who want to go on shore. But first you must take François to do his shopping." Luigi grinned, and said, "If miracles happen, he might even find lettuce."

Then the captain went back to the charts and the screens and to conning the horizon. The entrance to the bay was dead ahead, guarded by massive rocks, with a dark, cloud-capped profile beyond. There was a heavy swell, which involved constant adjustments to keep a straight course. A small yacht crossed their bows with only about fifty yards to spare, as swift and ephemeral as a butterfly, gone before they could react.

Then they were through the passage. Beni whistled. The bay was beyond spectacular, circled with green, plunging cliffs, and with mountains rearing behind. They were entering a huge, ancient volcanic crater. The little town was crouched about the beach, and about fifty sailing yachts were scattered over the water. It was going to be like sailing through a minefield, one that Captain Castellano was determined to avoid by dropping anchor as soon as possible. He was barking orders when he was interrupted by none other than the silent helmsman.

"What the hell?" the Filipino exclaimed.

And then they all saw it.

The brig *Ratpack* lying at anchor.

Kate saw the brig as the rubber boat, skippered by the bosun, puttered through the crowded bay towards the sprinkling of shops and houses on the beach. Jerry, Skye, and Maggie were also perched in the thwarts, but everyone else had missed the unexpected sight of the *Ratpack*, as the view of steep green cliffs lifting to the backdrop of towering mountains was so gripping.

Kate said, "Look at that!"

They looked. Jerry said, "Good God, where did they come from?"

"Exactly," said Kate. "I thought they had been bobbing about on the horizon since that fishing expedition. So how did they get here so fast?"

"They must have veered off while we weren't looking," Skye said, then added thoughtfully, "I judged those two who blundered on board of the *Odyssey* to be just a couple of spaced-out hippies, but there must be one or two good seamen on board."

"Maybe they have an engine."

"That's for sure. But whether they carry enough fuel is another matter."

"Could be a good reason for coming in here — to refuel," said Jerry.

"Oddly," said Maggie, "I had the distinct impression that they were shadowing us."

"Like stalking?" said Jerry.

"But why?" said Kate.

"Didn't you see their faces when Jewel came out on the deck to dance?" said Maggie. "So it could be ordinary and common lust. And then there is the attraction of a boat that's worth several zillion. Do you think they are pirates lying in wait?"

"But we didn't know ourselves that we were coming to Nuku Hiva, not until we were told at dinner," Kate objected. "It's impossible for them to have known that we were headed here."

"True," said Jerry, and shrugged.

The motor cut out. They had arrived at the long jetty that served as the wharf for the little town of Taiohae. It was concrete, and it was high, and the constant waves had hollowed it out, so that climbing the iron ladder was going to be an athletic feat.

"How did the doctors manage it?" wondered Kate.

"Not to mention Mr. Pederson, who doesn't look all that spry," mused Maggie.

Sarah grinned. She said, "Look." A couple of hugely muscular Marquesan men had stepped up to lift the girls onto dry land.

"Wow," said Kate, willingly putting up her hands.

"Wow and my, aren't they into tattoos!" said Maggie, arriving equally lightly. The Marquesans were tattooed from neck to ankle. "I would like to draw them," she declared. The young men grinned, and went off to help a trio of yachties who had just arrived. Jerry and Skye clambered up onto the quay under their own steam, and Sarah bounced the rubber boat away.

"Wow," said Maggie again, looking around.

Tall hills, steep slopes, green, red, black everywhere, a long road that curved round the bay, boys galloping by on horses with no saddles, families on bicycles, and four-wheel drives kicking up the red dirt. Except for the clouds that clung about the mountain tops, the sky was an ethereal blue. The air smelled of fish, salt, fried chicken and vanilla, and echoed with invisible drums. There were fiberglass outrigger canoes everywhere, in the surf, on grass under trees, stacked on stands. Muscular heavily tattooed men strode by on pillar-like legs, their hips bound in bright sarongs, and stout women in equally colorful *pareu* had coronets of flowers in their hair.

"Which way?" said Skye.

"Town, of course," said Maggie. "Shopping!"

"You sound like Jewel," said Kate, and wondered vaguely where Jewel might be. She had not been visible since dinner the night before — but surely Jewel could not resist the chance of shopping, even if it did happen to be in one of the remotest villages of the world? Mr. and Mrs. Pederson had gone on shore with the Chief Officer and the two doctors, so Jewel must be with them.

Fish, fruit and vegetable markets beckoned, along with craft shops. Kate and Maggie headed that way, calling out when they saw François, the head chef. Skye and Jerry broke off, disappearing with intent under an awning with an inviting Hinano sign.

"Local beer," said Jerry. "It's good."

"It is?" said Skye, and pushed his dark glasses up onto his head. He'd had no idea that Jerry had been in French Polynesia before.

"Cheap, too," said Jerry. "Though it might not be as cheap as in Tahiti."

They were served by a large, dark-eyed woman who was wearing a brightly patterned *pareu* and an enormous flower crown. She pushed a bowl of unidentifiable nuts in front of them, and they drank out of the bottles.

It wasn't bad, a light lager where Skye preferred a darker beer, but it was cold and refreshing. They sat at a metal table covered with a plastic cloth, and with the inevitable bowl of flowers in the middle. On the other side of the road waves washed up the black sand, sending canoes bobbing, and dashed up the concrete quay, setting dinghies that had been imprudently moored there crashing against each other, and slamming into the pier. Yachts swayed on the gentle swell in the spectacular bay, and the mountains all around waited for the end of the world.

It was pleasantly shadowy under the thatched awning of the cafe. Two grizzled Frenchmen were smoking Gitanes at another table, and they saluted Jerry with their little glasses of Pernod, and he saluted back. A mottled gray cat prowled around the table legs, and outside a garish rooster stalked among the stems of tropical plants, herding a small flock of browbeaten hens and five cheeping chickens, and keeping a glittering eye on the cat. The trio of yachties came in and tried to ask questions in terrible French and an insulting form of pidgin English, shouting loudly in the belief it would make it more intelligible. The large woman in the flower tiara answered in what appeared to be the local version of English. They wanted coffee and the free WiFi that came with it. Then they settled down and became engrossed in their phones and iPads.

Kate and Maggie came out of a craft shop just a few yards away. They were carrying bags, and had somehow acquired floral tiaras. Leggy in their short sundresses, they looked twelve years old again as they headed off on their shopping excursion with their fingers linked together, just the way they had gone to school.

Skye, like Jerry, was watching them with that old warm affection inside. "It was an understandable mistake," he said. "But what a mistake it turned out to be!"

"What the devil are you talking about?"

"Helen Pederson, taking the wrong baby. Oh God, how lucky, lucky we Bacchantes were, and how disastrous it was for her."

Jerry's grin vanished. "I thought we weren't going to talk about that."

"There was the hurricane, and the hospital was falling apart around her. So when her husband arrived to rush her to com-parative safety on the yacht, she would have taken what seemed like the right baby."

"Skye." Jerry's tone was dangerous.

Skye shut up. Sarah Murray had arrived, light and silent on her feet like many abundantly built people. She smiled and said, "Am I interrupting something?"

"Absolutely not," said Jerry.

Sarah sat down, and the large woman brought her a beer without being asked. Then, when she had gone, Sarah pushed the bottle over to Jerry and said, "It's as much as my job is worth if I get back to the yacht smelling of beer."

"That bad?"

"We have a little crew bar, but only after work, and in moderation. We can get drunk between charters, but not even then if the owner is likely to notice." She looked at Skye, and said with a grin, "Though *you* manage to get away with it, Signor Skye."

He blinked, puzzled.

"Working for Mr. Pederson, and yet indulging in beer and wine."

"I do not indulge, I merely sip," Skye said with dignity. "And anyway, I am not employed by Mr. Pederson. He just uses me. Disgracefully so."

"I thought you were a supernumerary?"

"He seems to think so, too. But when I boarded that yacht it was under the impression that I was an impressed guest."

Sarah looked at him with interest, her brows high as she nibbled at one of the nuts. "So you have no idea why he feels this need to co-opt you?"

Skye paused for thought. "Perhaps it's his age, but he likes me to check a lot of what is coming in. And going out. Perhaps he really is very worried. I don't know him well enough to know."

"But you enjoy working with Mr. Madden?"

Skye snorted. "That's not exactly the word I would use."

Jerry set down the second beer bottle, having emptied it in record time. "Where is Madden, anyway?"

"Still on the yacht, unless he has chartered a canoe," said Sarah. "Though I didn't see him when I called, so he could be anywhere."

"So one wonders what he is up to." Jerry let his voice drift away.

"You've seen nothing to make you doubt his honesty?"

Sarah's question was directed at Skye. He shook his head.

Kate and Maggie came racing in, flushed, and moist with perspiration, looking very pleased with themselves. "Found you," said Kate, and plumped down by Jerry.

"And we found François," said Maggie, taking the opposite chair.

"Rosa and Agnes are here, too, so they can help carry his groceries. He is so happy! He has found lettuce and tomatoes and a huge bonito. *Mais il est désolé, parce'que ils n'y a pas de fraises.*"

"But he did find mangoes," said Kate. "And the most amazing bananas, in all colors of red. Maggie bought some, too, so she can photograph and paint them."

Sarah stood up. "Well, it has been a pleasure, folks, but if François has done his shopping, he'll be looking for his ride home." They watched her as she went, and saw her hail the chef and the galley staff. Then they had all jumped down into the boat. The two huge Marquesan men had vanished, but they managed on their own.

"We talked to Beni, too," said Kate. "He is furious. He has to wait for the two doctors, but they have not come back from the hospital. Helen is with them."

"What about Mr. Pederson?"

"Oh, he is back at the yacht. He made Sarah take him back as soon as the business with the gendarmerie was finished. He was in too big a hurry to get on board to want to stay ashore and be a tourist. And Beni had to stay here to wait for the others."

So Madden had not been left alone with the computers and the files for very long. Did Pederson feel uncomfortable about leaving him unsupervised? This, Skye thought, made Sarah Murray's comment about Madden's honesty even more interesting. Then they were interrupted yet again, as Beni arrived, looking hot and annoyed. His glance at the beer bottles was definitely envious.

He said, "We can go. *Nous allons.* The doctors are still detained at the hospital, and Mrs. Pederson said she would phone when they are ready to be picked up."

He had the yacht's tender, which was higher in the water than the rubber boat that Sarah had skippered, and so it was an easier jump into it. Kate sat in the bows, enraptured by the ripple and light of the water, descriptive sentences running through her head. It was no wonder, she thought, that Tahiti and her islands had inspired great artists and writers. The boat was bouncing along fast, driven by the chief officer's exasperation, and so they overtook Sarah's rubber boat with a lot of shouting and waving. Then they were thrashing past the *Ratpack*, and Kate let out a yell.

"My God!" she exclaimed. "Look!"

Jewel Pederson was standing on the deck. She even had the sauce to wave — and the men clustered around her waved, too.

At the hospital, Helen Pederson said to Florida, "Please, are you sure?"

"The ambulance is being organized already." Florida looked terrible, her gray-streaked red hair greasy and messed, black circles under her eyes. She said, "He is in a state of emergency. An operation is being scheduled in Papeete, and there will be an ambulance waiting when the plane arrives at the airport in Fa'aa."

Helen Pederson shut her eyes and took a deep breath. Trevor Green had been ill for some days, and Florida had been trying to treat him by herself. Obviously, she had managed to keep him alive, but she did not have the resources to counter anything so grave. As a sign that she had recognized this, she had packed bags for them both before they had boarded the tender to the shore.

She said, "And you are going with him."

"I must — Helen, I must." Tears were streaming down Florida's sagging cheeks. "You know what it has been like for us for the past twenty-five years. Twenty-five!"

"Yes." Helen knew it well. All those years ago, when she had first met Florida and they had shared an apartment in New York city, Florida had already been obsessively in love with Trevor Green, despite the great difference in their ages. His wife had been institutionalized with early onset dementia, and so it had been impossible to divorce her, but he and Florida had lived and worked together as a devoted couple for over two decades. It was painfully obvious that Florida had to go with Trevor in the ambulance aircraft to Tahiti, but that left Helen with a major problem.

"What will I do about Jewel?" she wailed. "I have relied on you — you have been my rock! — for so long."

"You'll cope," Florida soothed, but Helen could see that most of her friend's attention was on the noises in the hospital, where they were preparing Trevor for the flight to Papeete. The flight would be a long one, and the drive to the airport here took well over an hour, over rough roads. They had to move fast.

"Oh Florida," Helen whispered.

"You'll be fine. You know you can rely on Constantia — and I will see you in Papeete."

The chief officer had said it would take five days to sail to Papeete, maybe more. Helen shut her eyes, but said nothing.

"And Jewel will be fine, too. She's twenty-one now, and should be in charge of her own destiny, for better or worse. You can't keep on carrying the burden for her."

"I know," Helen whispered as she saw the wagon with Trevor Green's stretcher move away. She waved, but Florida's silhouette in the back window was obliviously bent.

Chapter eighteen

Jerry said, "So that's how the brig's crew knew we were coming to Nuku Hiva. Jewel let them know — with her phone, her bloody phone. Once they knew exactly where we were headed they were able to sail out of sight and motor here. Why didn't we think of it?"

Skye said, "Because it was so unlikely."

"What do you mean?"

"The engineer's report strongly indicated that the brig is crewed by a gang of slack amateurs — and we jumped to the same conclusion. We called it the *hippie* brig, remember. So it seemed highly unlikely that they would have internet, let alone satellite cellphone coverage. Both are expensive, and need an onboard expert. Remember how keen those yachties in Taiohae were to get the free WiFi, so they could catch up on mail? But, if the so-called hippies communicated with Jewel at sea, they must have internet on board, and perhaps satellite coverage, too. That takes money and expertise. We have underestimated them, Jerry."

It was the next morning, and Jerry and Skye were drinking their usual beers at the sun deck bar, after working out in the gym. The *Odyssey* was motoring along at fourteen knots on a sea that had become sapphire now they were out of the indigo shadow of the island. Sternwards, the silhouette of Nuku Hiva was a like an ancient thorny beast, a stegosaurus perhaps, crouching on the horizon.

Jerry said, "How the devil did Jewel get their phone number?"

"Maybe it's the other way round — that they found her number.

She is probably on Facebook, or whatever."

"So are they just toying with the wild and beautiful girl, or do they have other things in mind?"

"The chief officer reckoned they are drug runners."

Jerry shook his head. "The customs inspectors at Taiohae are notorious. They wouldn't hope to get away with it."

"He also wondered if they intended to use us as mules by sneaking their cargo on board the yacht until we were clear of the Tahitian islands."

"But how would they get it back?"

Skye shrugged, and drank beer.

"Did we have a customs inspection?"

"I don't know." Skye looked at the bar manager, and said, "MJ?"

MJ shook his head. "We left too early. The forms were filled in but the officers did not arrive. There were many, many yachts at Taiohae, and the inspections are slow and careful."

"True," said Jerry. "But I bet they took notice of our hasty departure, and they'll be waiting in ambush at Papeete."

They certainly had made a hurried departure. Mrs. Pederson, after conveying her grave news, had demanded that they should sail to Tahiti as quickly as possible. The doctors had left the yacht because Dr. Green needed urgent major heart surgery, as she informed the captain and her husband, and only the main hospital at Papeete had the facilities. The ambulance plane had flown him there, with Dr. Sullivan in attendance, and Mrs. Pederson was anxious to join them in Tahiti.

And so the yacht had prepared for sea as soon as Jewel had been retrieved from the brig by the firm and very unsympathetic bosun of the yacht. Refueling had been a quick and hasty matter, and they had sailed on the dawn tide.

"Was Jewel carrying anything when she came back?" asked Skye.

Both MJ and Jerry shook their heads and shrugged.

"Sarah will know," Skye decided. "I'll ask her."

MJ went away, and Jerry said, "I don't think that Jewel or even drugs is our major problem. You have to think about any industrial sharks who might be looking at Pederson Strategic, because that could be even bigger. Stranger things have happened than a load of grubby hippies turning out to be commercial spies. Can you think of any reason anyone might be hired to carry out surveillance on Pederson's affairs?"

Skye paused, running a finger around a circle of condensation on the bar top. "There is a lot of money coming in and going out."

"Where is it coming from? And going out where? What is it being spent on? Luxury cars? Impressionist artworks? Prime real estate? Gold?"

"Oddly enough, the business is weighted towards environmental organizations, some of them longstanding, many of them start-up. Wind farms, tide generators, electric cars, solar panels, that kind of thing."

Jerry frowned. "That's indeed very odd, considering the major shareholder."

"Saudi Oil?"

"Yes."

"I am not sure that they are still the major shareholder. There has been a lot of movement in the shareholdings, too."

"Saudi Oil is selling out?"

"It looks like it — unless it's going to shell companies."

"And the money coming in?"

"A lot from a private bank that is registered in Cyprus, labeled as loans. The rest from organizations, mostly acronyms I've never heard before. Nothing from individuals, as far as I can tell. There is some kind of agenda, but I'm damned if I can work out what it is."

Jerry rubbed his grizzled chin, the way he did when thinking hard. "In that case, it's little wonder that Pederson is worried."

"Then he should be hiring proper auditors, and not be using me," Skye stated with passion, and swallowed the last of his beer.

MJ materialized, but when he lifted an eyebrow, Skye shook his head. "Almost lunch," he said. "I want to save room for a glass of wine."

The Filipino smiled, and then said quietly, "I found this in the lower deck foyer, Signor Skye. And I believe it is yours."

He took a hand out of his pocket and slid a brightly colored plastic flash drive onto the bar top.

Skye looked it, frowned, and then said, "It's not —"

Jerry's broad palm came out, and covered the little memory stick.

"I'll take it," he said, and closed his hand.

In the dining room of the main deck, Luiz winced as he hurried with the polishing of the table, and the arrangement of the flowers. Then, with just a speedy rub of the buffet, he whisked away downstairs. He didn't dare go into the owner's quarters, even though the beds had not been made. Mr. Pederson and Mrs. Pederson were having a blazing row in there, and Jewel Pederson was screaming and throwing things in her suite. That would have to be cleaned up later, and what a mess it was going to be!

In the owner's suite Helen swept tears from her cheeks, and gazed imploringly at her husband. Doggedly, for at least the third time, she said, "There was no need to confiscate her phone."

"Don't be ridiculous."

"But it was bound to set her off."

"Of course I had to take her bloody phone. The girl is an idiot, like an animal on heat. How the hell did she and those whackos get each other's phone numbers?"

"Facebook," Helen admitted, looking down at her twisting hands. "They were messaging each other."

There was the shattering sound of glass as yet another piece of crystal was thrown in Jewel's room. Harold held his head in his hands. "Can't you put a stop to that?" he pleaded. "For God's sake, Helen, she's tearing the room apart."

"I can't, Harold, I really can't. You set her off when you took her phone, and these episodes are truly uncontrollable. Even Florida would not be able to manage her now."

"She's twenty-one, for God's sake, an adult, but she acts like a toddler out of control. All those years you lived just for her, couldn't you have done a better job?"

"Harold!" she cried, shocked and hurt. "I always did my best."

"You damn well ruined that girl."

"I did my best!" She was shaking with rage, disappointment, and grief. Her voice came out humiliatingly small as she whispered, "No one can do more than that, Harold."

"You pampered her, gave into her whims. She had free run of the house from the day she could walk, day and night. You didn't force her to keep to a strict routine."

"You don't understand, Harold, you never tried to understand. Keeping her to any kind of routine was impossible. Don't you remember how many times she ran away? The times she attacked other children? How she threatened to harm herself? All those deliberate cuts along her arms?"

"You and those two doctors with their fancy ideas ruined her," he repeated. "You ruined her, just the way you ruined our marriage. I loved you, Helen, I was madly in love with you, and we were good together, Helen, so very good. I loved you so much, and when you turned from me to focus on Jewel, you broke my heart. The marriage worked, it really worked; we were a team, a terrific team. But then you had Jewel, and you put me out of your life. Every thought, every occasion, every decision had the label *Jewel* on it. There was nothing left over for me. I'm not a fool, Helen, I know *exactly* what happened."

Guilt tore at her with cruel claws. He was jealous; all these years he had been wracked with jealousy because of her obsession with trying to fix Jewel, and turn her into an ordinary person.

"I was always there when you needed me," she protested weakly. She remembered the flights that had been booked at a moment's notice, the hotels, the formal greetings, the stiff, uncomfortable banquets, the oily smiles on the faces of the tycoons, oligarchs, sheiks, and minor dignitaries; she remembered escorting their simpering, whispering wives around glittering shops, getting them invitations to top-end fashion shows. Barcelona, Paris, Dubai ...

"And you had to be bloody summoned, didn't you? Dear God, when I think of the contrast with those two Bacchante girls! I can't help but wonder what it would have been like if one of them was our daughter, and not that mad virago in there."

"Please, don't start that again, *please*. Kate and Maggie are wonderful young women, but they are Bacchantes — they belong to a big, loving family. The best we can hope for is to make them our friends. To persist in trying to change what is, is not just pointless, it's cruel."

"So why have you been sponsoring them? To make them your friends? And why them, in particular?"

"Sponsoring?" She tried to sound defiant, but her voice was faint. "What do you mean?"

"God, woman, do you think I am blind, dumb and deaf? That I haven't kept track of my money that you have been spending so freely? I know you have given them huge boosts in their careers, and you can't tell me they were a random choice."

Oh, dear God in heaven, she thought. Had he really been tracking her spending? It was as if she were trapped in a golden web. She forced herself to put strength in her voice.

"They were born in the same place in the same hurricane — like Jewel, they are daughters of the storm. I felt a natural affinity — particularly when Maggie Bacchante turned out to be a gifted designer, and it looked as if Jewel could be a good artist, with the right encouragement. There was so much in common. And when they came to New York, and their names started to appear in the papers, of course I took an interest. Particularly in Maggie, but now that I have met Kate, she feels like a kindred spirit, too."

"Jewel? An artist?" Harold snorted.

"Yes! Haven't you seen her drawings?"

"I have, and I don't believe for an instant that Jewel could ever manage the hard grind of developing any talent that she just might have."

"But there was always hope, Harold." Helen looked down at her twisting hands again, and whispered, "There was always hope."

"Are you are sure that chasing talent was the only reason you backed the Bacchante girls?"

His words were followed by more crashing from inside Jewel's suite, and when Harold winced and swore, Helen's tears began to run down her cheeks again.

"Please, Harold, don't torture me like this," she pleaded. "Please, please, face the fact that I am Jewel's mother, whatever the circumstances. I fed her at my breast; I got up to her at night. I was the one who struggled to toilet-train her; I was the one who cried with delight when she produced her first words. I was the one who chose her nannies, and replaced them when they left the job — as you know they did, constantly, often just after a week. It was like a revolving door, Harold, but I coped. I agitated about kindergartens, schools, diets, medical advice, getting her to specialists, trying out medications, while all the time you were busy with your empire. I did love you, I really did, and I am so very, very sorry that you feel as if I neglected you. But that is my fault, not Jewel's, and I don't know how to make up for it."

She was shaking with grief, her eyes shut as the tears ran faster, and the screams and crashing from Jewel's room seemed even more frantic. She heard Harold sigh rackingly, and then his arms came around her. For the first time for years, she rested her head against his solid chest as she wept, and felt his cheek on the top of her head.

He said, "I love you, Helen."

She whispered, "Harold, I love you too, I never stopped loving you. I thought I was everything you needed, but was obviously so very wrong. You wanted more than a hostess?"

"That's what I'm trying to say." His voice was low and rough.

She reached up and kissed him, and he held her hard. Then he pushed her away again. "We have to make a decision. We have to do something about it."

"But we — I — have done so much already. What else can we do?"

"It's simple," he said, and stared down at her as he held her out at the length of his arms. "We either put her in an institution, or she marries someone suitable. There are demands on me and my business, Helen, and they are urgent. For the first time in my life, I can't cope. Something is very wrong, but I can't work out what, or what I can do about it. To be absolutely honest, if it is going to turn out as wrong as I fear it is, I could end up bankrupt, or even in prison."

"Oh God, Harold," she gasped. He had always been so strong, resourceful, and competent. So that was why he had arranged this weird cruise, she realized; it was because he was so afraid for the future that he'd felt a driving need to do something about it.

She said, "You know I'll stand with you all the way."

"Thank you."

"But surely you are mistaken?"

"Unfortunately, I'm not," he said. "I need someone very competent to take over and put things right, and a son-in-law with the right qualifications could be perfect."

Oh God. Something else became abruptly clear. So that was why he was so cozy with that ghastly Madden creature!

But she couldn't help expostulating, "Not Madden, surely?"

"Why not?" he said. "He would be perfect."

The Bacchantes were the only ones eating lunch, so Agnes ushered them to their favorite table, under the awning on the star deck. The white wine they all liked was served, and amazingly fresh fish arrived for the girls and Skye, while Jerry had his usual hamburger. Salads came too, and glasses were topped up, and then Agnes and MJ departed in their usual silent fashion. Like the Cheshire cat, as Kate liked to meditate, they vanished, leaving their smiles behind.

Jerry said, "I ran the flash drive, and found Strategic Pederson files, but nothing else. So, who would want to copy them? And why?"

"What flash drive?" demanded Maggie.

"MJ found it in the lower deck foyer, and handed it to me, as apparently he thought it was mine," said Skye.

"*MJ* gave it to you?"

"He did."

"But why?"

"Well, he knows that I'm working all those hours for Pederson, checking his files."

"So he knows what is on the flash drive?"

Both Jerry and Skye stared at her, startled. Skye said, "Why would he run it?"

"To check the ownership, for a start," Maggie said. "If he found it in the lower deck foyer, it could have belonged to any of the crew."

"I hadn't thought of that," Skye said.

Jerry shook his head. Neither had he.

"Where is it now?" she asked Jerry then.

"I copied the contents onto my own laptop, and will give it back to Madden when — and if — he asks around for his missing flash drive."

"So you're sure it's Madden's?"

"That's the conclusion I've come to, certainly. Obviously, it wasn't Skye's. The only other contender is Jewel, or one of her *Ratpack* boyfriends."

"Or Pederson himself?" suggested Skye. "He had to pass through the foyer to get to the tender, yesterday morning. It could have fallen out of his pocket."

"But why would he copy his own files?"

"He's worried. It's as if he feels that something has gone very wrong. I sense it all the time. It was just the Pederson Strategic files? Nothing else?"

"Nothing else," Jerry confirmed. He chewed on the last of his hamburger, staring meditatively into space.

"Ws it encrypted?"

Jerry snorted. "Of course not, or I would have been stymied. You would know better, but it looked as if at least one of the files was tagged. The one with the records of that bank in Cyprus."

"So it could be tracked through the system?"

"Have a look when you get a chance, and see what you think."

"I certainly will have a look," said Skye. "Because the tagging makes it logical that Pederson made that copy."

"Because he doesn't trust Madden?"

"I don't know anyone who does trust Madden, though Pederson himself hasn't given any sign of feeling suspicious. Yet. He's creepy, like a silent snake, always there, always listening."

Agnes came to take away their plates, and MJ arrived with the wine bottle. When Agnes returned she brought a large dish of fresh fruit. Kate and Maggie leapt forward to snap up pieces of mango, and then fought over the last slice. Smiling indulgently, Agnes and MJ departed.

Skye said, "There is always the chance that it was Jewel."

"What? Who copied the files onto the flash drive?"

"Yes — which takes us back to the idea that the *Ratpack* crowd are commercial spies."

"But would Jewel be capable of it?"

"She appears to be suggestible."

But Maggie was shaking her head. "She could be a talented artist, if only she had the commitment and energy, and I am sure she can operate a smart phone like magic. But anything as complicated as an accounting program would be beyond her. "

"You've spent the most time with her. What is she really like?"

Maggie shrugged. "I'm no expert. I don't want to put a name to what she is like. But she is incredibly self-absorbed, and obsessed with her appearance. Half the time, she seems to believe she is ugly, and the rest she is flaunting herself, and is anxious to know what you think. She has no idea of how other people feel, or the effect she has on them. It makes her unthinkingly cruel. She can't help it, poor girl, but it is very hard on other people."

"But she's not cruel enough to sabotage her father's business?"

"She has no idea of consequences, so I don't think she would reason that way, no matter how much she hated him."

"But she could be talked into it, perhaps," suggested Kate.

Skye shook his head. "Even if she was eager to do it, according to what Maggie says she wouldn't know how to copy the files."

"I agree," said Maggie. "Which takes us back to the original question. Why did MJ give the flash drive to you at the bar, instead of simply delivering it to Mr. Pederson's office?"

Silence. Both men looked at each other and then stared at Maggie.

"My God," said Skye.

"Yes, we were talking about Pederson Strategic. MJ was not in the bar, but ..."

"The walls have ears," murmured Skye. His brows were slanted high.

"And sound travels at sea. Should we be talking in Italian?"

The Bacchantes had their own fractured version of the language, used about the table in the big kitchen of the stone house at the vineyard. If anyone could not think of a word in one language, he or she substituted one from the other. It was guaranteed to confuse any listener, whether English or Italian, but the Bacchantes had no trouble understanding each other.

"It would make *us* look secretive," Skye objected.

"As if we didn't trust the crew — but we do, we really do."

"So we carry on just as before?"

"But be more careful with what we say," said Jerry. And Skye found himself the target of a meaningful look.

Chapter nineteen

Skye wanted to find Sarah Murray, as he had questions to ask her, but was foiled by Harold Pederson, who summoned him to the office right after lunch. The afternoon session was a long one, too. Pederson looked better than he ever had since they had sailed from California, as if he had gained strength and resolution. He worked hard, and worked Skye hard, too, and now that Skye knew what to look for, Pederson was definitely tracking movements from the Cyprus bank.

Madden was exactly the same as always, silent and expression-less, his eyes taking in everything. Skye did not see him use any flash drives at all. The personal assistant did operate the printer, but as far as Skye could tell, all the printed pages were properly filed.

Then at last Skye was released from work. After a vain search of the outside decks, he went down to the crew quarters on the lower deck, where he found Maggie helping François prepare salads in the galley, and chattering away to him in her schoolgirl French, interspersed with Italian when she couldn't think of the right word. Jerry was in the little crew lounge opposite, drinking coffee and talking in Bacchante Italian to the captain, who was looking alternately baffled and entertained.

From what Skye heard as he came through the lower deck corridor, they were exchanging yarns about adventures in foreign parts. Neither the captain nor François seemed to find this intrusion by the guests at all annoying. If anything, they looked indulgent.

He finally found the bosun in the engine room, aft of the galley. Sarah was on all fours on the floor between the two huge glossy engines, talking into her shoulder radio while John, the first engineer, checked dials and buttons. John was in the engine control room, which was above the engine room, and separated from Sarah by a bulkhead with many windows and a single glass door that led to the downward steps. Skye could see that the door had a code lock, though it was unfastened at the moment. Obviously, the arrangement had been designed with preventing sabotage in mind.

Skye paused in the doorway from the corridor, looking around before making his presence known. The *Odyssey* might be old, but to him the engine control room was as alien as the bridge of a space ship. There were telltales and monitors running along the walls above the row of windows that overlooked the engines, and a computer screen on top of a bank of cabinets, which conveyed information from the captain's bridge. This was the engineer's bridge, he realized, just as complicated, but with a very different view. On the other side, below the row of windows, the two engines crouched like glossy tigers, pregnant with power.

Sarah looked up, and her squeaky radio voice called out, "Enjoying the view, Signor Hamilton?"

Her rump was indeed rounded. Skye grinned, and said, "I'm not complaining."

When he lifted an eyebrow at John, the engineer nodded, so Skye stepped down into the tigers' lair. There was not the loud roar he had expected, though both tigers were growling.

Sarah stood up with a grunt and cleaned her hands on a length of cheesecloth. "We have an oil leak somewhere, but I'm damned if I can track it down."

"Is it important?"

"Could be." She crouched down again, and pulled a long wire out of the starboard engine, showed it to Skye, wiped it with the cheesecloth, pushed it back in, and pulled it out again. To his amusement, it was just like a dipstick in a car, only much longer.

She peered at it, and then showed it to him. "Just under maximum, the way it should be." Then she went to the port engine, and did the same. The reading this time was a few millimeters lower. "So," she said, and stood up after pushing the dipstick back into place, "there's a little oil going somewhere, but where and how is a mystery. We changed the oil at Taiohae, but since then — who knows?"

"I am sure you will find it," said Skye. He thought she looked enormously competent.

When they returned to the engine control room, Captain Castellano was conferring with the chief engineer. Both stopped talking, and listened intently while Sarah made her report.

"Filters are clean and secure?"

"Yep."

"And in the scuppers?"

"Tiny puddles of oil under the port engine."

"Only a little oil," the captain said hopefully.

"But, sir, there is a greater danger of fire."

Captain Castellano winced. Fire was a major hazard at sea.

The engineer said, "The oil leak could stem from a crack in a lube oil line, causing excessive wear in a cylinder liner, which is serious. The engines are old, sir, and there has been a lot of wear and tear. They are running rough and not performing as they should. I really would like to anchor somewhere and strip the engine down so I can replace the damaged parts, once we find what's wrong."

"That's a choice of the Disappointment Islands or the Dangerous Isles," Captain Castellano said acidly. "Meaning the Tuamotus. I was planning to head north and give the coral atolls a wide berth."

"Mrs. Pederson is very anxious that we reach Papeete soon."

"I know, Sarah, I know."

Sarah hesitated. "There is good anchorage at Fakareva, sir."

"You've been there?"

"Indeed, sir. There are no chandleries or even shops, as it is a very small atoll, but of course we have spare parts. And it has good holding bottom, and is sheltered from the prevailing winds."

"Perhaps I will consult with you later." Shaking his head, the captain strode away.

The little crew lounge was empty. Sarah said to Skye, "Coffee?"

"You look as if you could do with something stronger."

She laughed. "I count myself fortunate that I can have a glass of wine with my evening meal. That's the advantage of having an Italian captain. Most make the crew go cold turkey all cruise."

Skye found a seat while she did something magical with a coffee machine. Then, after setting down two mugs, milk and sugar, she took the chair opposite.

He said, "You have been this route before?"

"Many times. This isn't my first big motor yacht, you know."

Skye sipped scalding hot, very hot but very good black coffee, smiled, and said, "Tell me."

"How do you know I want to?"

She smiled. She was flirting, he understood. Skye grinned and waited.

"Well, to make a long story short, I was the only girl in a family with five brothers. And a father who owned and ran a petrol station with a workshop attached. All the boys did their apprenticeships as mechanics with him, but I was supposed to stand behind the counter and take money from people who were buying petrol, and sell bags of chippies and warm pies. That just wasn't me. I told my Dad that I wanted to work with engines, and would take my apprenticeship elsewhere if he did not want to put me through it, and he dared me to do it. So I did. I did my apprenticeship at a marine engineering shop in Auckland and got my papers. I came back in triumph, and they *still* wanted me to stand behind the counter. So I ran off to sea."

"That's wonderful. How many companies have you worked for?"

"Oh, I started off on cruise ships, but the Filipinos and Indians, great as they are, edged me out of the market. They were as good as I was, but would accept lower pay, and so I migrated to mega-yachts, and have been with them since. New Zealand crew are highly sought after, as we are a seafaring country with a good seafaring reputation, and we get good conditions and pay."

"But you're a bosun, not an engineer?"

"I've no electrical qualifications, and with diesel-electric you need both. But I'm happy with what I am."

He drank good coffee and nodded, enjoying this. To get her talking again, he observed, "You've chosen an enviable life-style. Any drawbacks?"

"It's certainly a way to see the world. But I tried the northern hemisphere only once — too much competition, too many mega-yachts, too many questionable charters. And the Caribbean is almost as bad. The south Pacific suited me fine."

"You don't get questionable charters in the south Pacific?"

She shrugged. "Sure do. Rich men, particularly young rich men, can be highly objectionable. They pour the free liquor into themselves, and it's surprising how many fancy fat girls. Rich Arabs and Indians are really susceptible."

Skye, who fancied her himself, was far too experienced to fall into the trap of assuring her that she wasn't fat, so simply smiled.

"And of course there were recreational drugs. Lots and lots of recreational drugs. But this yacht is clean, always has been. The *Odyssey* is special. Mr. Pederson is very strict, and Captain Castellano runs a tight ship. He and Constantia have been here since her maiden voyage. Did you know that?"

"No, I did not." Twenty-one years? Good lord, he thought.

"They were both recruited and then flown out to Auckland to take over after her launch. There was a hurricane right after that, and she should have foundered. Captain Castellano did such a brilliant job of saving her that he has been employed ever since."

"On a constantly renewed contract?"

"Salaried. We are all salaried, all of us, no exceptions, with benefits included. Paid holidays, free flights back home and then back to the ship, health and travel insurance, visas, the lot."

Skye thought about what Jerry had been saying. He said, "Very nice — but is that so unusual?"

"My God, yes. Most crew get a contract for four or six months, and are then stood down without pay until the next contract. But this is steady employment. I felt so lucky when they hired me. I've been with Pederson for two years, starting on one of his expedition ships, and they have been very good ones, believe me."

He grinned. "No questionable charters."

"Nope. The slightest hint, and the guests are chucked off. They are warned about it, and it's in the boarding papers they sign."

"But how about this cruise, the one right now?"

She put down her mug, and stared at him. "Are you cross-examining me?"

"I'm curious about that brig."

"You agree with Beni that they are running drugs?"

"There are lots of possibilities," he said, and shifted to his true reason for seeking her out. "Did you see anything interesting when you pried Jewel off the brig?"

She paused, finishing her coffee while she gazed at the poster hanging on the bulkhead above his head. Then she said, "They seemed to be much tidier than John's report indicated. I had expected worse. Three men brought Jewel to the gangway deck. She giggled a lot, but they were perfectly sober. Decently dressed, too, in jeans and t-shirts, and looked fit. They were more professional — more organized — than I had been led to believe. I'm not sure the ones I met were American, though. One blond, the others dark-haired, but European rather than Yankee."

"And Jewel?"

"Just plain silly. I wondered if she was high on something. But she gave in when they persuaded her to come with me. It wasn't until this morning, when her father confiscated her phone, that she went crazy."

"Was she carrying anything when she came back? A bag? A parcel?"

"Nope. Just that phone."

"You have no idea what she might have taken when she boarded the brig?"

"Of course not, just as I have no idea how she got on board in the first place."

Eight bells rang. It was the first time Skye had heard the seaman's timekeeping system on board this ship. Eight in the evening, he calculated. There was a hum of activity in the galley, and Rosa and Agnes were standing by, ready to take dishes up to the table.

Sarah smiled, and said, "Enjoy your dinner. It smells good."

And it did. With a parting grin, Skye headed off upstairs.

There were seven places set at the dining table, but only Harold and Helen Pederson and the four Bacchantes arrived. Jewel was silent but sulking, so was eating in her suite. Madden had chosen to have a tray in his room, too, which made Skye wonder if he was taking the time to transfer files from a flash drive to his laptop. Then, to the Bacchantes' surprise, Captain Castellano materialized, and took the seventh place.

No explanation was offered. Instead, he proved to be relaxed, jovial company, eating salad and pasta with relish, taking a glass of red wine, and exchanging exotic tall stories with Jerry. Skye had the distinct impression that it was a continuation of the lively conversation he had overheard earlier, though in English instead of fractured Italian. But finally, with the coffee and fruit, Captain Castellano got down to his real business, which was to inform Mrs. Pederson that most unfortunately the voyage to Tahiti would take longer than anticipated.

She looked down at her hands and said softly, "I got an email. Dr. Green has had the operation, and has come through it in reasonable shape, but the next few days are critical."

"*Mi dispiace*," he said, lapsing into Italian in his distress, as his eloquent hands gestured in vast regret. "But the Tuamotus intervene, with many shoals and reefs, and the safety of my ship and the souls on board is my first priority. We must proceed with great caution, particularly at night."

Skye said, "We are not dropping anchor at Fakareva?"

"No, no, that would be too great a diversion. Though the bosun tells me there is a very pretty church," he added. "Much beloved of sailors, blue inside and with much mother-of-pearl."

And with this *non sequitur* Captain Castellano left. Without mentioning the oil leak, or so Skye noticed.

It was the start of a new routine. The *Odyssey* glided slowly through peacock waters by day, while atolls appeared and vanished on the horizon, and at night their progress was barely discernible. They drifted, almost as if the engines were not working at all.

By contrast, Harold Pederson worked very hard indeed, and kept

Skye with him all afternoon. It was as if he had come to a decision, and the figurative bit was between his teeth. Then he, like the port engine, closed down at six, when the sudden equatorial sunset happened. Curious about this, Skye made an excuse to go up to the bridge just before six one evening, to see the sun dive into the horizon dead ahead. For a breath held moment it was a molten half-circle, blinding red, sending out ripples of gold, yellow and purple. Then it was gone with just a flicker of fluorescent green, and night shut down, along with the port engine.

The green flash was supposed to be some kind of omen, a warning of dragons, witches, or *taniwha*, but nothing unusual happened. Skye went to his stateroom to shower for dinner, idly speculating about who might be at the table that night. Jewel had continued her sulk, refusing to eat at the table with her parents, and was otherwise as numbly expressionless as a shop window mannequin. Madden, too, took his dinners in his stateroom most nights. Skye wondered what he was doing. Copying files? Or spending hours on his computer, online? And why did Mr. Pederson make no objection?

The officers and petty officers of the ship filled the gap, one by one, no reason given. The Bacchantes wondered if Mr. Pederson was inviting them, one after another, but no one mentioned it, if so. Beni Boulez was the first, and turned out to be as affable as the captain, flirting madly with the two girls, but getting nothing but some teasing in return. The chief engineer was next. Mr. Pederson seemed to know him very well, and talked with him at length, reminiscing about previous cruises. John had been with the yacht for some years, apparently.

On the fourth night, eight places were set, and Skye fully expected to see the two French chefs arrive. It was Jewel who came, however, looking sulky. Evidently either her mother or her father had ordered it — probably Mr. Pederson, as she took a seat at Skye's right hand, making it clear that she wanted to sit as far from her father as possible.

Then Sarah Murray came in with her usual light tread, and took the seat on Skye's other side. She was wearing a crisp white uniform, her waist cinched in with a black belt, black epaulettes set squarely on her shoulders, each with two gold bars and a gold fouled anchor. Freed of her customary baseball cap, her brown hair turned out to be curly. She smelled strongly of soap, and her broad hands were red, as if she'd had to scrub them hard.

She smiled brightly at them all, saluted the table with her glass of red wine, and announced, "You would be glad to know that we are out of the Dangerous Isles."

Helen Pederson said, "The ..?"

"The Tuamotus. So tomorrow we will be heading at a good speed for Tahiti."

"That's so good to hear," Helen said. Dr. Green was still in intensive care, and she was looking pale and worried.

"Just another day or so?" Harold Pederson asked.

"Actually, just a few hours. We should be there by afternoon. Barring accidents, of course, sir."

And, having delivered this caveat, Sarah applied herself with relish to a large bowl of pasta, eating the salad as an afterthought. Jerry, who sat across from her and was eating spaghetti with equal appetite, watched her with huge approval, and the two chatted across the table, swapping travel yarns, and saluting each other with their wine glasses every now and then.

Skye watched them with one eyebrow high. They were flirting, he thought, and found he did not like it. When he lowered that eyebrow at Jerry the old rogue just crinkled up his weather-beaten face, obviously enjoying an internal laugh. The two girls, seated between Jerry and Harold Pederson, had their heads together in lively conversation, with the occasional giggle, and Skye had the distinct impression that they were talking about him. Was it so obvious that he found Jerry annoying?

Maggie, however, mostly talked to Harold Pederson, who liked to have her at his left elbow, and he, as usual, looked remarkably entertained by whatever she was saying. But when the desserts arrived he broke off, to ask, "Jewel, my dear, how did you spend your day?"

It sounded so artificial that the Bacchantes winced. As expected, Jewel merely shrugged. She had pushed her pasta away uneaten, and was toying with her ice-cream, pushing it around and around in the bowl while it melted.

The silence dragged. Then Kate said, "Do you want to go shopping in Papeete?"

"Is there anything to shop for?"

"Oh yes," Sarah said. "There is the market for all kinds of fruit, vegetables, and artwork, but if you head into town, there are clothes shops, shoe shops, and book shops. And you can buy cosmetics."

MJ topped up their wine yet again. It was turning into a party.

Harold turned to Jewel again, evidently determined to make her remember his existence. "Have you done any drawing?"

She lifted one indifferent shoulder. Sarah said, as brightly as ever, "There is a very good art supplies shop, if you like."

Another shrug, and another awkward silence.

This time Jerry filled the difficult pause, asking Sarah how she had found her way into the mega-yacht business? Where had she been? And, fueled by the wine she had drunk, her answers were interesting indeed. In the Mediterranean there were the Arab potentates who cruised in order to drink alcohol out of the sight of the mullahs, though their real goal might be to carry out a great deal of the kind of business that might not be quite legitimate. Harold Pederson became intensely intrigued, and took over the conversation, asking sharp questions that Sarah fielded with ease. Kate and Maggie were wide-eyed with fascination. Helen Pederson was silent and distracted. Jewel showed no reaction whatsoever.

The coffee arrived, along with fruit, nuts and cheese, and it was time for the party to wind up. Skye seized a pause in the ongoing banter between Jerry and Sarah to say, "Have you fixed the problem with the port engine?"

"Not really," she said, and gazed at him with her luminous blue eyes. "Why don't you come down and look?"

"Right now?"

"Why not?"

As they left, Skye looked back to see Jerry's lascivious wink.

Twenty minutes later, they were in Sarah's bunk. It was like a shelf, with lockers above and below, and with a very small porthole at the seaward end. The shelf was just wide enough for the two of them. Skye was very conscious of the bulkhead at his back, which divided Sarah's little stateroom from ... whose? The walls had ears, and sound traveled easily at sea, but somehow the chance of being overheard was a spice.

And she was definitely luscious, this generously built bosun. Afterwards, when Sarah stretched out on her back with Skye curled around, above and about her, her feet meditatively brushed against the wall at the foot of the bunk. Her expression was like none he had seen on her face before, gentler, visibly softened. When she stretched and her feet made that brushing noise, it was like a purring cat.

She said, "You are in terrible danger, you know."

He shook with silent laughter. "I know."

"No, you don't. Mr. Pederson has designs on you."

"Ouch. I have been worried about that."

"He intends you to marry Jewel and take over his business."

"What? Oh God." Skye was shocked. He definitely had not been expecting this.

"You are not delighted at the idea?"

"Oh God, no."

"Madden rejected the proposition, and so you are next in line."

"What? He was approached with the idea?" No wonder Madden wasn't eating with the family any more. "I can't blame him," Skye confessed. It was the first understandable human reaction from the man.

"Mr. Pederson should really focus on Beni," she said with a grin. "Beni is determined to marry an heiress. But you have better qualifications."

"No, no, no, oh God, no, no. Beni can have her, and welcome. How do you know all this, anyway?"

"Someone told us. We all know. Now, who was it who told us?"

"MJ," he said, remembering the flash drive and that he and Jerry had been overheard discussing the Pederson Strategic files.

"Perhaps Agnes or Rosa or MJ or Luiz, but probably Constantia. She keeps Captain Castellano up to date with everything that is happening on board, which is why the *Odyssey* functions so well. She is wonderful."

"She runs a shipboard grapevine?" He was both astonished and appalled.

"She is a living saint. Did you know that she sponsors an orphanage in Manila? That she pays for the keep and education of fifty-seven orphans?"

"Good lord." He supposed it was true, as the American money that Constantia was paid was bound to go a long way in Manila.

"They send letters and cards to her, even the ones who have graduated from the orphanage, and have jobs and have married, and have children. I have seen them. We have all seen them."

"That certainly is wonderful," he said, but was mostly absorbed by unsettling memories of conversations that Constantia's grape-vine might have overheard. Dear God, he thought. He had heard of the 'coconut wireless' that was whispered about on south Pacific islands, but *this*?

"Are you married?"

"Me? No." Which, right now, made him feel vulnerable.

"Ever been married?"

"I never felt the need." There had been girlfriends, and even a couple of partners, but, being a Bacchante, he had a ready-made family.

"I wondered about you and Maggie Bacchante."

"What? Why?"

"You are obviously very fond of each other. So why not?"

"Dear God," he said, scandalized at the very thought. "It would be tantamount to incest — I delivered her as a baby, you know."

"Good lord. You did?"

"I was only nineteen, so it was quite an experience. Her mother, Rachel Bacchante, was driving to the hospital when she was stranded by a terrible storm. I was the first one to find her trudging away from her broken down car, and Maggie was born in my old wagon an hour or so later." He went on very soberly, "It was the most wonderful moment of my life."

In fact, he thought of himself as Maggie's father, which was all he wanted to be. It would be more logical, in fact, to marry Rachel. After all, she was only three or four years older than himself. But he could imagine Rachel's horrified reaction if he ever proposed the idea.

Sarah said, "What are you laughing at?"

"Just a stray thought." To distract her, he stroked a bounteous breast.

Sarah purred, "You like doing that?"

"God, yes." At that moment he found her beautiful, and truly she was delicious.

"Tahiti tomorrow?" he said sleepily at last.

"Papeete, and I will be very busy. We have to strip the port engine and find out what the hell that drip is about."

"So I should go and let you get some sleep."

"Yes," she said, and lifted herself and kissed him, and he gathered himself and his clothes together, and sneaked out.

Chapter twenty

Harold hired a car to take Helen to the hospital. She had argued for a taxi, but he said it was better to be independent. He may have regretted it as he negotiated the mad traffic down the Rue du General de Gaulle, however. It was the afternoon rush hour, and though this might be a small island, everyone drove with mad impatience, as if they had to go hundreds of kilometers before nightfall. But, if Harold was openly wishing he had listened to her, Helen did not notice. She was very pale, fraught with suspense.

Kate and Jerry had come for support. Maggie and Skye would have come too, but there wasn't room, as the rental wasn't large. Cars and small trucks raced past and around them; the multi-lane highway dipped under an overpass and soared up again. Kate noticed that Jerry's hand, as he hung onto a strap over the car door, was white-knuckled. Perhaps this was worse than a big oil rig fire.

Then, with a jerk, they were there. The hospital was shaped like a canoe, and took up half the border of a big roundabout. Finding the parking area was another nightmare, but at last they were able to clamber out onto the tarmac, though Kate's knees were definitely rubbery. The entrance, when they found it, was as clean and expansive as in a major hospital in New Zealand, with the same aura of disinfectant and efficiency.

Luckily, Helen's French was adequate, as the language had completely fled from Kate's mind. The receptionist ushered Helen away, but shook her head when the others tried to follow.

They found three hard plastic seats and sat down. Harold looked beleaguered, but still much stronger and more confident than he had the first time Kate had seen him. He sat with his knees spread, because he was such a large man. His blond eyebrows bristled, and his small blue eyes hunted the foyer constantly as they all waited for Helen to return.

When she finally came back, she was in a terrible state, hunched over with her hands wringing, her pale face now red with weeping, tears still streaming down her face.

She cried, "Harold, Florida's gone! Dear, dear Florida is gone."

"What?" he said. They were all puzzled. Kate saw Jerry frown.

Helen sobbed, "She's dead, Harold. She died here last night; she had a massive stroke."

Harold Pederson stood up, and she fell into his arms. Over her head he said confusedly, "Florida? Not Dr. Green?"

"Florida! She was only fifty-nine, Harold, so young." Her voice was muffled against his chest. "And Trevor Green, he doesn't know about that yet, as he is so very ill. They say he is far too sick to leave the hospital, even to fly to New Zealand. They say he could not stand the flight — four and a half hours, and then the drive to the hospital from the airport. He couldn't take it, so he has to stay in intensive care here."

Harold said numbly, "So what are we supposed to do?"

"There's paperwork — and the funeral. Oh God, Harold, the funeral."

"I'll ask at reception," he said, and eased her into the chair next to Kate. Helen reached out and clung to Kate's hand, and then leaned back with her eyes shut. Tears trickled down her cheeks.

Another long wait followed. Obviously, making arrangements to have the body collected and filling in all the necessary forms was a laborious process. There would be bills to pay, too. Kate had no idea if they would include the mercy flight to and from Taiohae, but thought it was lucky that Mr. Pederson was very rich.

So what about all the other formalities in this French island? She decided that Beni Boulez must be clearing the yacht's papers, as he had done in Nuku Hiva, which now seemed so long ago. And Skye and Maggie were shopping, she supposed, though it was getting very late. Were Sarah and the engineers still stripping the port engine? It sounded very heavy work, and very complicated, so she supposed that it was lucky, in a grim way, that they were to be delayed in Papeete.

At long last Harold returned, and they were able to head back to the ship. Helen had to be assisted to the car, and then insisted that she be seated in the back with Kate. As soon as she was settled she sought Kate's hand again. Her fingers were very thin and cold, like scantily covered bones. Night had fallen, and the stream of car headlights zooming towards them was disorienting. Harold got lost, and finally found that he had to make a great loop about the northern end of the wharf.

It was only then that Kate noticed something. She reached over the front seat to tap Jerry on the shoulder. When he looked around, she pointed.

The brig *Ratpack* was in port.

The next day was Sunday, so the Bacchantes attended Mass at the Cathédrale Notre-Dame in the town square, just a walk from the yacht on a beautiful morning. They had lots of company, because the Filipino crew wanted to come, and the two French chefs were with them. The Filipinos had a small shrine in the crew quarters, but going to a cathedral was much more authentic, they said. The Bacchantes suspected that Jean-Pierre and François simply wanted to go to something that was conducted in French. Outside, the cathedral with its single spire was very yellow, and inside it was very white, with much sunlight coming in the long windows. The service was in French, which undoubtedly pleased the chefs, and the wonderful singing was in Tahitian, the congregation swaying as they belted out the tunes.

The funeral of Florida Sullivan was held there, too, the next day. Helen said that she had no idea of Florida's religion, and had never known her go to church, but Harold had organized it. Though he was not Catholic himself, he had assumed that Tahiti, being French, had only Roman Catholic churches, and so he had chosen the biggest. Sarah Murray told him that there were several churches of other denominations, but by then it was too late.

Sarah attended the funeral, and so too did the Filipino crew. As Constantia said, while they had not known Dr. Sullivan very well, they respected her for the struggle with Miss Jewel's big problems, and, anyway, it was good to go again to church.

The funeral was held in French, and did not last long. The choir sang beautifully, and Helen Pederson cried a lot. When it was over the Filipinos went back to the ship to clean rooms and help the two chefs with their market shopping, and Sarah went back to helping the engineers with the port engine. Helen wanted to follow the coffin, so Harold drove her to Uranie cemetery, on the outskirts of the town.

The Bacchantes, by contrast, wanted a drink.

Jerry found a cafe near the cathedral, in a shady arcade. It was just like Taiohae. They were served by a large, smiling Polynesian woman in a bright *pareu*, with a crown of flowers in her cascading black hair. He could have sworn that the same grizzled Frenchmen were sitting at one of the tables, sipping Pernod and smoking Gitanes. When the bottles of Hinano arrived he saluted them, and they tipped their little glasses in return. There was no cat, and no garish rooster, but there were three tourists, who came in and yelled in English, as if yelling made their words more comprehensible. It was no surprise to find that they wanted coffee and free internet.

Kate said, "Where was Jewel?"

They all stared at her, and she nodded. "She was not at the funeral, and not at church yesterday. In fact, I haven't seen her at all since dinner the night before we got here."

Maggie frowned. "I'm surprised her mother didn't make her go to the funeral."

"Helen's in a terrible state," said Kate, who had spent Sunday afternoon trying to comfort the poor woman. "Probably too distraught to notice."

"Were she and Dr. Sullivan very close friends?"

"I would say so, definitely yes."

"So what is going to happen to Dr. Green?"

"He will probably die, and be buried on a tropical south Pacific island like Robert Louis Stevenson," said Kate. "His tomb will be on a hill, overlooking the sea."

"I don't think Uranie cemetery is on a hill," Maggie objected.

"I was just being romantic. After all, the thought of his grief and despair when he wakes up to find he has lost his soul partner is quite romantic, in a Victorian sort of way. Though he probably isn't Catholic," Kate added.

"Do you think Helen will make her husband keep the yacht here until after Dr. Green is dead and buried?"

"Who knows?" said Kate. "He certainly seems a lot more attentive to her wishes." Which, she thought, was romantic, too. Mr. Pederson had sailed with the crazy idea of finding a daughter, but instead he had rediscovered his wife.

Chapter twenty-one

On the bridge of the *Odyssey*, Captain Castellano was studying the charts and watching an evolving satellite image of the south Pacific. The satellite image came from NOAA — the clumsily but accurately named National Oceanic and Atmospheric Administration — and he relied on it greatly, though without understanding the science. Ducking his head to the radio on his collar, he called, "Sarah, would you come up to the bridge, please?"

There was an affirmative in his ear, and she arrived within minutes, very sweaty and with her t-shirt and jeans smeared with grease. She had not stopped to clean her hands.

He said, "Look at this," and tapped the screen.

She hunkered down to look. It showed a thick band of cloud curving down from the equator, echoing the shape of western South America, and reaching towards Tahiti.

She frowned, and said, "It can't be a hurricane."

"It is the hurricane season," he pointed out.

Twenty-one-year old memories were as distinct as the day the storm had almost wrecked the *Odyssey* on her maiden outing. He had battled tremendous seas and an unbelievable gale to work the yacht to a tiny haven in a crook of the east coast of New Zealand, where the town was called Homerville, and then had battled to get her secured to a frighteningly short quay. The lines had held, the buffers had done their work, and the *Odyssey* was alive today, but it had been a very close shave.

Sarah said, "Yes, but this is just a band of thunderstorms. Tahiti never gets hurricanes."

"There is a low level centre. They reckon it is going to get a lot worse."

"Have they predicted its course?"

"South of Tahiti, and then west along latitude twenty."

She winced, and said, "That's close." It would be like a gigantic comma, curling about the island.

"Too close. I would like to get away. You know the engines, and you know the seas here. What do you recommend?"

This was the most taxing question Sarah had ever been asked, and one she had never expected of a bosun. She regretted telling him that she had sailed south Pacific waters before.

She said slowly, "We've got the engine back together, and replaced a few parts, and stocked up with stuff from shore. But I have to tell you, sir, that a complete overhaul is overdue. The port engine is the one showing wear first, but they are both at the end of their useful life. In my honest opinion, we can't rely on either of them. But you will need to ask John to confirm that, sir."

The captain paused, staring at the satellite image. The tail of the dense cloud bank that curled down from equatorial America looked ominously as if it were on the verge of bursting. Almost to himself, he said, "Going back to California is not an option."

"Not one that I would choose, sir."

"And staying here does not look like an option, either."

"Tahiti does not get hurricanes," she repeated. "The islands are out of the hurricane belt."

"But big storms do happen?"

She nodded.

"Is it possible to start both engines now? And keep them going all the way to New Zealand?"

"I honestly don't know. You will have to check with John, sir."

"Is everyone on board?"

"I don't know that either, sir."

"No, of course not," Luigi said, and realized he had been thinking aloud. "Please ask John to come up to the bridge."

"Sir," she said, and went.

The captain then called Harold Pederson on his private radio, and pointed at the satellite image after the owner arrived up the stairs. The tail of the storm was thickening, he was sure of it.

He said, "They predict that its course will take it south of Tahiti, and then head west. But at the very least, there will be a big storm here. Lots of wind and rain."

Harold studied the screen and then straightened and stared out the side windows. The Bacchantes were coming along the wharf, and as he watched a gust caught Kate's straw hat, and flicked it into the sea.

He said, "That girl has been wonderful. My wife is in a terrible state, and Kate has done so much to comfort her."

"Mrs. Pederson is still sadly bereft?"

"She's ill with grief, has taken to her bed."

"But is she fit to travel? I would like to get away as soon as possible."

Other craft were sailing. Luigi watched the brig *Ratpack* motor through the gap in the reef, and then put on sail. Once under canvas, it was surprising how quickly the brig moved. Within moments it was obvious that the sailing ship was heading northwest, the same direction Luigi wanted to take.

The chief engineer arrived. He ducked his head at the owner, and then said, "Sir?" to Captain Castellano.

They had a discussion about the engines while Pederson listened. John agreed that a big overhaul, including replacement of the engines, was due, but was more optimistic than Sarah about getting to New Zealand.

"Can you prepare for sailing now?"

The tail of the thunder belt was thickening even more, and was definitely headed for Tahiti. The captain pointed at the screen, and said, "I'd very much like to get into calmer waters before the storm gets any further south."

"Of course, sir, and I am sure we can do it. Just give us one hour."

John went, and Beni Boulez came in from conducting ship's business in town. Harold Pederson listened as the chief officer confirmed that the paperwork was in order, the duty-free top-up of the fuel tanks had been paid for, along with the various fees, and that the yacht had been cleared to go.

"Excellent," said the captain, and called for Constantia to come up to the bridge.

The chief stewardess arrived in uniform — because she had been at the funeral that morning, he supposed. Constantia's shirt and pants were crisp and white, and the black epaulettes with the three silver bars and silver crescent moon sat squarely on her shoulders.

He said, "We are leaving in an hour, Constantia. I saw the Bacchantes arrive. Is everyone else on board?"

She looked doubtful. "I will check the crew, though I think they are all here, sir, as they walked back with me after the funeral service. But I am not sure about Miss Jewel."

Harold Pederson said, "I heard the shower running in her suite."

Constantia looked relieved, but said, "I will ask Luiz," before heading down to the lower deck.

The engines started up as the Bacchantes were eating lunch at their favorite table, under the awning on the upper deck. Jerry said, "Surely we're not sailing yet?"

Kate had been into the owner's suite to check on Helen. "Mr. Pederson said the captain is very anxious to get to the north," she told him. "There is a big thunderstorm heading this way."

"Maybe that's why the *Ratpack* left," Maggie meditated. They had all stopped on the wharf to watch the brig set sail, and both she and Kate had found the sight beautiful.

"It's weird, the way those hippies are always somewhere close by," she went on. "Didn't someone say they were shadowing us?"

"Beni," said Skye. "He was convinced that their foul intent was to make us their drug mules."

They all laughed. Maggie said, "I still think it is pure animal lust. I saw their faces when Jewel turned on the music and came out to dance."

Jerry shrugged and said, "It doesn't signify, anyway. The *Ratpack* must be well ahead of us by now."

"Even though we have engines and they have sails?"

"There's a favorable wind and a following sea, and there seems to be at least one good seaman on board. They beat us to Nuku Hiva, remember."

Maggie said, "But they do have a motor? I thought they didn't set their sails until they were well away from the reef."

"Yes, but their engine won't get them very far, while our monster engines can work all the time," said Kate.

Hopefully, thought Skye, but didn't say it. The yacht gave a sudden lurch, and they all grabbed their wine as plates slid about the table.

"It's getting rough," Jerry observed, as Agnes hurried up to clear away.

"We got away from Papeete just in time," she agreed.

Chapter twenty-two

That night the Bacchantes dined on the star deck, just as they had before Mr. Pederson had decreed that they had to eat in the main deck dining area. Agnes had carried the message that Mrs. Pederson did not feel well enough to be good company, so they would have to be alone. They were very happy to comply, but Kate asked Agnes to convey their best wishes to the owner's wife.

"Do you think she will take a long time to get better?" Maggie queried after Agnes had gone.

"Perhaps," said Kate. "She was really most dreadfully fond of Dr. Sullivan. They met twenty-five years ago, when they both needed a housemate to help with the rent. She told me funny stories about when they were two bachelor girls in New York, how they used to share clothes, and take each other's places if one had an invitation she didn't want to accept."

"Good lord," said Maggie. "She's so poised and elegant that it's hard to think of her as being young and silly."

"She said it was because of Dr. Sullivan that she met her first husband."

They all stared at her. Maggie said, "Helen was married before?"

Kate dimpled. "Don't all zillionaires marry at least twice? Mr. Pederson had two marriages before her. Though I think Helen's first husband was some kind of diplomat, and not a mega-millionaire. They lived in Washington, which should have meant that Dr. Sullivan had to find a new housemate, but by that time Dr. Green wanted her to move in with him.”

Good lord, thought Skye, Kate and Helen Pederson surely had been getting on like a house on fire. He couldn’t help asking, “Who was her first husband?”

“I’d never heard of him, but he had the same name as a luxury car. Pierce. Pierce something. Not Pierce Arrow, something else. She said he was very handsome, but Mr. Pederson swept her off her feet.”

“Then she must get over the death of her friend,” said Maggie, comfortably tucking into her sashimi. “She has a devoted husband to fill the space. And I must confess that I am very happy to be spared Jewel’s sulks at the table.”

The next day, the Bacchantes breakfasted on the star deck, but the weather was deteriorating. The sea was choppy, and the skies were gray, with racing clouds. Skye and Jerry worked out in the gym for an hour before lunch, but it was a sweaty business, because the air was so sultry. The beers, when MJ pushed them across the bar, tasted wonderful. They lunched at the big table on the main deck, as a fine rain was misting down. The sea swell was definitely getting heavy, and Jewel and Mrs. Pederson were still invisible, most probably seasick.

They had just started coffee when Harold came in from the owner’s suite to ask Skye to help go over spreadsheets in the afternoon. He seemed preoccupied, not at all his usual businesslike and glowering self. It was a change that he had come personally to ask the favor, instead of sending Madden; he seemed greatly changed altogether, very different from the man who had made the crazy demand that they should sail with him to New Zealand.

Kate said, “How is Helen?”

He grimaced. “Seasick. She got very little sleep last night.”

“Do let me know if I can help.”

"Thank you. She is asleep right now, but I will keep that in mind. You are very kind."

"Not at all," said Kate. "I'm glad to be of use."

He refused coffee when Agnes offered it, and went back through his suite to his office. His retreating steps were very quiet, evidently so he would not disturb his wife.

Skye sighed, finished his coffee, and stood up. "The salt mine," he grumbled, and headed up to the upper deck, where he washed his hands before taking the crew-only door to the bridge and Pederson's office.

"He seems so different," Maggie remarked. The Bacchantes were enjoying a pre-dinner glass of wine in the upper deck lounge.

"Who?"said Skye.

"Your boss. The man who's not paying you for a terrific lot of work."

"He has patched it up with his wife, whatever the original issue was," said Kate.

"Oh, it's more than that," Skye contradicted. "He's a very, very worried man. Something very strange is happening with Pederson Strategic, and he is as puzzled as I am. On the surface, it looks almost like a charitable foundation. All the money coming openly out of Pederson Strategic is headed for eco-friendly stuff. Wind farms, fish farms, shellfish farms, solar power, electric vehicles, saving coral reefs, buying up palm oil plantations to return the land to the jungle, designs for mini-water mills, that kind of thing. Some of this is simply a faucet for losing money, but other start-ups are going to be big earners, I'm sure. It's like the latest investment craze. Money is pouring in, faster than we can follow."

"That actually sounds ominous," said Jerry. The girls merely gazed at Skye, completely lost.

"I think Harold would heartily agree."

"Didn't you say that the original big investor was Saudi Oil?"

"Yep. Their investment stands, but their share holding has decreased as others have bought in. It is one of the many anomalies."

"Have other oil companies taken an interest?"

"Yes, now you mention it."

"Big coal? Mining?"

"Yes. Why?"

"Back in the day, big tobacco sponsored sport, particularly for the young, as a way of cleaning up their increasingly grubby image."

"I see what you are getting at," Skye said slowly. He was staring at Jerry with his wine glass poised halfway to his mouth. "You think it is the big polluters cleaning up *their* image."

"Stranger things have been known."

"True. But there are also that private bank I have never heard of lending huge amounts – but why? Is it run by eco-freaks?"

"You said Cyprus?"

"Yep."

"Then the owners could come from anywhere. Chinese?"

Skye thought about it as he sipped. "I'll check," he finally said.

Silence fell. The yacht bumped and lurched every now and then, and they listened to the rain pouring down outside. Agnes arrived, and much to Kate's fascination, she laid a dampened cloth on the coffee table.

"Things will not skid now, okay," she said, and smiled.

Then, when she had gone, MJ arrived to top up their glasses. "Getting very rough," he said, smiling as sunnily as ever. Skye, studying him consideringly, wondered how much of the last conversation the bar manager had overheard. And Agnes? The shipboard grapevine was just another weirdness in this very strange voyage.

Any day now, he thought sardonically, he would be offered another flash drive, or maybe even a job on board.

As MJ went away, the yacht executed yet another soar and plunge, so that even that surefooted seafarer had to grab for a handrail. Something fell with a big thump in the suite. Maggie gave Kate her glass to hold, and stood up to see what it was.

"My portfolio," she said, coming back from the stateroom.

She sat down again, and opened the folder. Another lurch, and drawings slid out and all over the floor in a riot of color. Parrots, roosters, feathers, great swathes of ferns and banana leaves, all shot through with black and dark, iridescent blue, with streaks of shining gold.

"You've been painting," Kate said with delight. She gave the two glasses to the men to hold, and dropped down on hands and knees, spreading the sketches over the floor.

"Designs for fabric," Maggie said, taking back her wine, and sipping to salute herself. "I was inspired by Nuku Hiva, so very inspired. That wonderful light, the warmth of the colors. Even blue and green were warm. And all those curves, everything curved. You like them?"

"They are fabulous. For scarves? Or what?"

"Anything! Scarves, dusters, jackets, tunics, cushion covers. I'll design the garments next, and hope that Bellissimo loves them."

"How could they help but love them?" Kate said, and took back her own glass.

And then the yacht dropped dead in the water. The engines had silenced.

When Skye got down to the engine control room, Sarah was addressing the port engine with a great deal of colorful language. The two Scottish engineers merely looked dour.

When Captain Castellano arrived he looked harried.

"What is it?" he said.

"The bloody oil leak in the port engine, sir," said Sarah.

"I thought it was fixed."

"It was fixed," said the chief engineer, sounding wounded. "But the heavy sea set the oil tanks sloshing, and so the pumps stopped. It was an automatic shutdown, sir, triggered by an automatic alarm. And when we checked the oil, sir, the port engine had the same old leak."

The yacht swayed as it wallowed in the trough of a wave, and Captain Castellano grabbed a handhold. "What about the starboard engine?"

"We are worried that it might go the same way, sir."

"Well, it has to work. I need at least one engine."

"I daren't run it at full speed, sir."

"Then don't. Just keep it running fast enough to keep steerage way, please. And get the port engine fixed, for God's sake."

"We have to make a harbor, sir. There's no way we can get to New Zealand as we are right now."

The captain looked at Sarah. She shrugged, and said, "Vavau or Rarotonga, sir. Avatiu at Rarotonga has better chandleries, but we should make for whichever is closer."

"Thank you," he said with a sigh. "*Grazie.*" And went off back to the bridge, muttering to himself in Italian.

By the next afternoon it was very rough indeed. The yacht, though keeping a steady course, was behaving like a surfboard, soaring up one side of a wave and then plunging down the other, travelling much faster than could be expected with just one engine working. Every time a wave was breasted, the yacht came down with a crash, sending everything flying. The girls were advised to move to the lower deck, so took over the doctors' suite, throwing everything that had been left behind into suitcases, and stowing them under the bed.

That night's dinner, when it came, was pizza, being easy to eat in the hands. They crowded into Jerry's room, dragging chairs from Skye's room with them, and clustered companionably around the little table, eating pizza while they listened to cupboard doors slamming and dishes rattling in the galley. MJ appeared with their favorite red wine, and balanced with expertise while they held their glasses out.

"No seasick?" he said.

They all shook their heads. "We wouldn't dare," said Maggie. "The guys would laugh at us for ever."

"Mrs. Pederson very seasick," MJ informed them. "Mr. Pederson, he's okay."

"And Jewel?" said Maggie.

MJ pursed his lips. "Miss Pederson left her shower running. Luiz had to turn it off. She wasn't there, but her music machine was playing."

The Bacchantes looked at each other, because this sounded so odd. They had learned — even if Jewel had not — that despite the desalinators, one did not waste fresh water on a seagoing vessel.

"Is she seasick?"

MJ shrugged, and spread his hands.

"And Mr. Madden?" The Bacchantes had not seen or heard of him since before Tahiti.

It was obvious that MJ had to quench a grin. "Seasick," he said. "Very seasick, but still up on the main deck."

So Madden had been unable to abandon those files. despite being ill, thought Skye. What the hell was the man up to? From all accounts, he had been with Pederson for just two or three months, and he was acting as if he had orders from somewhere else. Skye abruptly wondered how much Madden was emailing, and to whom.

"How is the crew faring?" Kate asked. Waves were dashing up against the portholes, and they were all very careful while sipping their wine. "Are any of them seasick?"

MJ laughed heartily at the absurdity of this. "Much work," he said, smiling as sunnily as ever. "Much tidying and cleaning to do. Tomorrow, when the storm stops, the decks and bulkheads outside will have to be washed and scrubbed with fresh water. Much, much work."

He spread eloquent arms, refilled their glasses, and headed up the stairs.

After pastries for dessert, Maggie went into the galley to help the chefs and practice her French. Jerry settled in the little petty officers' lounge, where he made himself coffee and chatted amiably in Tagalog with any steward who had the time to talk. Skye went to the engine control room. Sarah was still working on the two tigers, but there was no one else there. Evidently she was spelling the two engineers while they ate their dinners.

"How is it going?" he said, when he got her attention.

She shrugged, and came out of the engine room. "We are getting there. But let's say that we will all be very, very happy when these two monsters are replaced."

"Seasick?"

"Are you joking, or trying to insult me?"

He laughed. "Are you hungry?"

"Is a lion?"

Skye went to the galley, where the scene had changed. Jerry and Kate were now washing and drying pans and plates, and François merely smiled when he scooped three slices out of one of the pizzas on the counter. He took these with a large glass of red wine to the engine room, and Sarah said, "I think I love you."

"*You* are joking."

"Of course I am. But a man who feeds and wines me deserves a little affection."

By morning the wind had moderated to a stiff breeze, though there was still a heavy swell. The sun shone and white clouds scudded in a bright blue sky, but Captain Castellano's mouth was pulled down as he studied the NOAA satellite screen. The thunder belt had enveloped Tahiti and her islands for two days now, and he could imagine the flooding. It was lucky they were away from that, he thought, but, very ominously indeed, the equatorial top of the comma-like thunderbelt was thickening and starting to spin. There were warnings of a developing tropical cyclone, which had now been given a name — tropical storm Giuseppe.

Outside, by contrast, there was much laughter. The Bacchantes, bare-footed and in saturated shorts and tops, were helping the three deck stewards wash down the bulkheads. Stainless steel and glass had to be rinsed repeatedly with fresh water before the sun scoured the salt into their surfaces. Normally, it was a tedious job, but the Bacchantes had turned it into fun.

Luigi shook his head, straightened his indulgent smile, and called Beni over. They consulted the charts, watching the constantly changing satellite image at the same time. Finally, he called Sarah up to the bridge, and she arrived looking sweaty and very dirty with grease.

"How is the port engine?"

"Still giving trouble, sir, but believe me, we are working on it."

"I'd like to have it going within the hour. Is that possible?"

She pursed up her mouth and said, "You will have to check with John, sir. Are we expecting more bad weather?"

"I fear so." Then he was interrupted by the lookout, who gestured to the northern horizon.

The seaman, looking stunned, said, "It's back, sir, it's back!"

"What?"

"The brig, sir."

Captain Castellano took the binoculars, stared for a moment, and then handed them to Sarah. The two white blobs of the brig's topsails were clear and unmistakeable.

"They still haven't turned on their AIS," said Beni Boulez.

"Even weirder," said Sarah, "is that they should be a long way ahead of us. They left two or three hours before us, and while the south-east trades were gale-force twenty-four hours ago, with good sail handing they were in the brig's favor. The South Pacific current is with them, too. They've had two days to reach their destination. It seems so strange that they haven't swung northwest to get to Suwarrow."

"Suwarrow?"

"That remote atoll in the northern Cooks. It was suggested, if you remember, sir, that they might be transporting illegal drugs there, to hand on to other smugglers."

Luigi nodded. "And if they are not carrying drugs?"

"Then a swing northwest would take them to Samoa."

"Not New Zealand?"

"That would need another voyage, southwest from Apia, sir."

Harold Pederson came onto the bridge, and said, "Is there a problem?"

Luigi pointed at the radar screen. "The brig is back with us."

"What?" The owner frowned. "They are shadowing us still?"

"Not for long. We think they are making for Apia, while we have to make for Rarotonga, to do some more work on the engines. We'll head for Auckland after that."

Harold Pederson scowled at Sarah. "Why wasn't the repair done properly in Papeete?"

"We did our best, sir."

"Well, obviously it was not good enough."

"I apologise, sir." The words were gritted out.

There was a sudden jolt as the yacht breasted a wave that was steeper than the last. Captain Castellano pointed at the windows, where the deckhands and the Bacchantes were still scrubbing away, and said to Beni, "Better call them in."

"Aye, captain."

"And tell the crew that we will have to batten down again."

Luigi distinctly heard the bosun swear under her breath as she hurried out. Damn engines, he thought, too old for this long voyage. Having one give out was bad enough, but to have both give out was unthinkable. What the hell else was going to go wrong? Those who wanted to learn how to pray, he thought, needed to go to sea.

And, on the heels of that thought, Constantia burst onto the bridge, looking more harried than he had ever seen her before.

"Captain," she said, but had to stop to catch her breath.

"What is it?"

"*May malaking problema tayo.*"

"What?"

"We have a big, big problem."

"Oh, *per l'amour di Dio*, come out with it."

"Miss Jewel is not on board."

Chapter twenty-three

O Dio, questo non può essere vero, Luigi thought with near panic. He had never, ever, never in all his seafaring life, left a passenger behind. A single glance at the satellite image of the weather confirmed that the passage back to Tahiti was impossible. So what the hell was he to do?

Struggling to sound calm, he said, "Are you certain?"

"We have looked everywhere." Constantia was wringing her hands. "She has gone."

Harold Pederson was standing rigidly, having as much trouble as the captain to comprehend the enormity of this. He said, "But she must be on board. I heard her shower running after we sailed."

"Luiz told me that he had to turn her shower off. But her music machine was playing," Constantia added.

"Better bring Luiz up here," said the captain, and Constantia radioed to the room steward.

Luiz, when he arrived, looked on the verge of suicide. "I was so sure Miss Pederson was with us when we sailed, sir," he wailed. "Very sure, really, sir."

"Because the shower was running?"

"No, no, sir, she was gone from her room. Her room was in a big mess and the shower was running and the music was playing. I tapped on the bathroom door many, many times, and then Rosa came to the suite, and she opened the door, and Miss Pederson was not there, but the shower was running so I turned it off. But still, sir, the music played. Then last night I was certain that she had been moved for safety to the suite that the doctors had occupied, because I heard movements. But this afternoon, sir, when I went into that suite to make the bed, it was already made, and no one was there."

Maritime regulations were running through the captain's head. "We must have a head count, and make sure who is on board," he said. "In the main lounge. Can you manage that, Constantia?"

Constantia did manage it, miraculously without having to sound the general alarm. The Bacchantes arrived barefooted and wet, looking bewildered. The stewards were huddled in a group, as if for mutual support. Madden came out of the owner's suite, having evidently been in the office, and was followed by Mrs. Pederson, swathed in a bathrobe, and looking very pale.

Captain Castellano, who had left Beni in charge on the bridge, took the head count himself. Within minutes it was plain that Jewel Pederson was the only one missing. He called Luiz to the front, and asked him to repeat the story of the shower, the music, and the noises in the doctors' room

"That noise in the doctors' suite was Maggie and me," said Kate. "Gladys advised us that it was safer to sleep down there. I'm sorry; I thought everyone knew. And we made the bed to help out."

A long pause. Then Skye said, "There is the horrible possibility that she fell overboard during last night's storm. But has anyone actually seen Jewel since we left Papeete?"

The stewards and deckhands looked at each other, and then shook their heads. The bosun and the engineers and the chefs did the same.

"So," said Skye, "we don't know if she came back on board at Papeete at all."

Harold Pederson objected, "But I heard the shower."

"The shower and player could have been turned on to fool us,"

Skye said in a flat voice, and Helen Pederson put her face in her hands and began to cry. Harold winced, and put his arm around her.

"Which means that she is back in Papeete," Skye concluded. "And we need to radio the gendarmerie."

Kate ventured, "Has Jewel ever run away before?"

Silence. Then Helen Pederson reluctantly nodded.

"So we had better make sure that she has her passport. And a credit card."

"Can you search her room?" Captain Castellano asked Kate.

"Of course. I'll get dressed and do it right away."

"And the chief officer can break the news to the police," he said heavily, and went back to the bridge.

Within an hour it was plain that Jewel had taken not just her passport, but a great deal of cash from her mother's purse, as well as a credit card and her mother's phone. Basic clothes were missing too, along with cherished cosmetics.

"This wasn't a spur of the moment decision," deduced Kate to Maggie, who was helping her search. "It looks as if she had been planning to run away for quite a little while, and she got her chance at Tahiti, when we were all preoccupied with the funeral."

"She never got over her fury about the confiscation of her phone," Maggie sighed. "Do you remember the screaming rage? But I am amazed she got away with it. If it hadn't been for that storm, she would have been found out in time to turn back."

"And we can't turn back now?"

"Skye says there is a huge thunderburst at Tahiti, with lots of flooding. And there is another big storm on the way. I'm sure it's too dangerous. We have to leave it to the police."

"So how is Jewel coping?" Kate wondered aloud. She was very concerned. "She is such a *child,* and I don't think she speaks French

— and if the weather is foul for any length of time, she could be in a bad way."

It proved to be a pointless worry. That evening, while the Pedersons and the Bacchantes were eating dinner in the owner's suite, and the awful silences were only interrupted by bits of random talk, Harold Pederson's phone pinged.

The ransom demand had arrived by email.

"She's been *kidnapped*?" cried Helen.

"By the men on that bloody brig," said Harold, staring at the screen. "They want fifty million dollars deposited in a nominated bank account before they will send her back."

"Pay it, Harold, you *must* pay it."

"Of course," he said, but only absently. He was still glowering at his phone.

"Do they say how you get the money to them?"

"I will have to wire it to the number they've given."

"Then do it, Harold, *do* it!"

"That's no problem," he lied. "What worries me is how they are going to get her back to the yacht. I have to see the captain," he finished abruptly, and left the table, heading for the stairs to his office and the bridge. At the bottom step he hesitated, turned, and jerked his head at Jerry.

"I'd appreciate it if you came with me," he said, and Jerry, though surprised, nodded and joined him.

When they got to the bridge, and had closed the door, Pederson said in a low hiss, "They used her bloody phone."

"Jewel's?"

"No, of course not. I have it under lock and key."

"Your wife's?"

"Yes!"

Jerry already knew just what Jewel had stolen before she left the yacht in Papeete. He said very slowly, "That could put a different complexion on it, I'm afraid."

"Yes indeed." Pederson's mouth was set hard.

Captain Castellano looked at the message for a long moment, and then silently handed the phone to Beni Boulez, who whistled when he read it.

"So that was their game," he said. "Not drugs, but a kidnap. They probably planned it well ahead — sail randomly until a luxury motor yacht was encountered, find out who was on board, and take it from there."

"Here, in the south Pacific?"

"The Caribbean would be too close to various authorities for them to get away with it. And the south Pacific has become popular with the mega-yacht set."

"Really?" said the captain.

"Dozens, according to what I was told in Tahiti and Taiohae."

"So we were chosen at random?"

"Of course it was opportunistic, sir. The scenario would work with any millionaire's yacht. First, find the right yacht. Then kidnap someone close to the owner. Then, once they have their hostage, demand that money be wired to an account — just as they say here. Undoubtedly, the instant the money is in the account, it will be shifted somewhere else to avoid detection."

Very feasible — and even more profitable than drug smuggling, thought Jerry. And, in these circumstances, much less dangerous.

"They have internet on board, and probably a satellite link, too," he said. "That takes expertise. It's a well-planned operation."

"They probably broke their desalinator on purpose," agreed Beni, expanding on his theory. "It was an excuse to board us, *une raison croyable,* after claiming the help due from any other seafarer to any seafarer in distress."

Remembering how the two men had talked their way onto the bridge, and then blundered through the upper deck lounge onto the star deck, Jerry thought the chief officer had it exactly right. The looks on the intruders' faces as they rapidly looked around had been assessing, he thought. Then Jewel had danced out onto the open deck below, while they were hanging over the rail to check their rubber boat, and had presented herself as the perfect target.

A willing target, he strongly suspected, and thought Harold Pederson felt the same.

Captain Castellano sighed deeply. "They had incredible luck, as well. If we had discovered she was missing before leaving Tahiti, we could have contacted the authorities. But we were in a hurry, the storm was impending, and we didn't have the time to make a proper head count."

"But we would have assumed that she was in Papeete," Jerry objected. "So days would have been wasted before we started wondering about the brig."

"Their fortune continues," said the captain. "We are far away from any police force, in the middle of empty waters. Too far out for a helicopter, even if one could be summoned."

"They planned it that way," Beni decided with grim relish. "Once they had their hostage on board, they would wait for that kind of distance before making their demands."

"But," said Captain Castellano, and pointed at the screen with the NOAA update, "they did not take into account the weather."

The weather? Jerry frowned, but then noticed the increased movement of the yacht. Another heavy swell was developing. When he looked at the screen he saw a comma of storm with a thick centre that looked on the verge of starting to spin.

Luigi confirmed this, saying, "Another storm is on the way, and I fear it will be a much more severe one. And I think it will take a long time to organize the money, no?"

"No one has fifty million sitting idle in a bank account," Pederson wryly agreed. "I will have to sell a lot of shares, and call in several debts. It will definitely take time — quite a lot of time."

"So," said the captain. "by the time we have agreed to their demands, and the money has been wired to their bank, it will be impossible to launch a boat. Even now, it would be so dangerous that I would not like to authorize it."

As if to emphasize his words, a wave loomed, soared, and broke over the bows, splashing up as far as the bridge windows before it was washed away by the automatic wipers. The sky was wild with scudding black clouds, and the moon had an immense halo. The stars flickered out only now and then.

"How big a storm?" asked Pederson.

There was a rolling crack of thunder in the distance, and the horizon was lit up for a blinding second.

"Very big. Big enough to have been given a name."

The birth of Hurricane Giuseppe was the same as that of thousands of its murderous sisters. A low pressure centre formed in the intermittent calms and deceptive light variable breezes of the doldrums, and then began to spin as cold air rushed in from the rim, forcing gigantic pillars of warm sea-saturated cloud up and outwards. Up the shafts of air went, charging through atmosphere that had already been agitated by the thunderstorm, and on and on the low pressure centre revolved, the air around it becoming more turbulent with every second.

As more and more air rushed in, the typhoon was whirling faster and faster, cold air in, warm air out and up, spilling great cataracts of rain. Gigantic forces were forming within it, reaching the megatonnage of an atomic bomb with every pulsing second. It was fuelled by plummeting pressure, by the rain it spewed in its path, by the whirling gales of the hurricane itself, as it whirled about its miles-wide clear eye. And now the monster was striding across the South Pacific, torturing the tides and lifting the seas, impelled by the spinning of the earth, arrowing slowly but surely for the motor yacht *Odyssey*.

On board, the night was an uneasy one, with the underpowered yacht lifting up and then sliding down the heavy waves. Each time it dropped, there was a mighty lurch. It was as if the boat were a flat stone being skipped over the surface by some invisible titan. Thunder rumbled constantly, yet in the morning the sun was shining, which was even more weird, as the air was heavy, hot, and menacing.

When the girls got to the rail of the star deck, the unbroken waves were oily in the bright early light. The brig was shockingly close by, just five hundred yards off and keeping pace with the yacht. The sight as she plunged and lifted through the waves was compelling; it was hard not to watch the brig all the time.

"This is a much more organized operation than it might appear," said Jerry at breakfast. "They are certainly not opportunistic hippies." Because it was fine, though so hot already, the Bacchantes had opted to eat outside, under the awning.

"But it seems odd that they should have used anything as attention-getting as a sailing ship," said Kate.

Jerry sniffed. "The brig's only a replica, with a steel hull and masts. If she ever sank, she would go down like a rock."

"That's not the point I was trying to make," she protested. "It just seems strange that criminals would use a ship that is so easily identified and remembered."

"I agree," said Skye. "But when you think of it, a sailing ship would attract what could be a lot of the right kind of attention, as people from mega-yachts would be as likely as anyone else to want to have a tour on board. It would make sizing up a victim much easier. It would also make them look unlikely to be up to anything underhand. They were hidden in plain sight, as it were."

"Jewel would certainly be fascinated by anything so exotic," mused Maggie.

"Do you think they are treating Jewel well?" Kate worried aloud. "I mean, she literally walked into a trap. A poor fly, lost in a spider's web. If she took all that stuff, including things she had stolen from her mother, there must have been an arrangement for her to meet them in Papeete."

"I think she knew exactly what was going on," Jerry flatly stated. "It was not just the brig that intrigued her. She was fascinated by those two characters who came on board, and she has been very, very angry with her father all along, not just when he took her phone away. Remember how he yelled at her when she put on the music and danced? For her, it would seem like sweet revenge."

"So you reckon it was arranged while she was on the brig in Taiohae?"

"I would not be at all surprised if that was what happened. It was far too dangerous to capture her so close to the gendarmerie, but it was a chance to feel her out. After Pederson confiscated her phone, they would have had to play it by ear, but they had a very willing victim."

"If he pays the ransom, do you think she will agree to come back?"

Jerry pursed his lips. "That is a very good question."

"You think she expects a share of the ransom?"

"Who knows what goes through her head," Maggie muttered. Her tone was brooding.

"Fifty million is a hell of a lot of money," said Kate. "Do you think they truly expect that much?"

"Oh yes," said Jerry. "Captain Castellano has informed the authorities, of course, but out here the kidnappers are out of reach, and can afford to wait for Pederson to transfer that money, no matter if it takes days."

"It's an academic question, anyway," said Skye, gesturing at the sea with his fork. Though the waves gleamed with light, and the sky was blue with racing clouds, the space between the brig and the yacht bulged and sank with heavy swells. "There's no way Captain Castellano would launch one of our boats in this."

As if in reply, MJ arrived, accompanied by two deckhands and looking apologetic. "We must take down the awning," he said.

"The captain expects worse?"

"*I* expect worse," said MJ, and smiled serenely. "Much, much worse."

Then, when Maggie stood up, she pointed, and cried out, "Look! We have company! Sharks!"

They all went to the rail, to see triangular fins cutting through the water between the yacht and the brig, coasting up the swells and then flipping over the other side.

"Dolphins, not sharks," said Skye. "Look, they are playing."

And even as he spoke, Maggie could see the short bursts of their spouts. Black above, and gray below, the dolphins looked like surfers in wet suits, and they seemed to be having the same fun. When one came close to the yacht, she could see the famous dolphin smile.

"They are laughing at us because the sea is our enemy right now, and for them it is an eternal friend," said Kate.

"No, no, very good luck," said MJ. He was at the rail, too.

"Very okay," agreed Agnes, who had arrived to take their plates.

"Not necessarily so," said Kate, much more soberly. "Some Maori in New Zealand think they carry messages from the dead."

"Florida?" said Maggie. "Trying to tell us something? Do you think Dr. Green has died, too?"

Men were at the rail of the brig, watching and pointing. A flash of color — Jewel. She was laughing, Maggie was certain. A very willing hostage, she thought sadly, and then thought that this almost made it credible that the doctor who had tried so hard to fix Jewel was now sending them a message.

She shivered, and as if in response the dolphins vanished. They all dived as one.

Chapter twenty-four

On the bridge, Captain Castellano and his first officer were watching the dolphins, too. "Back home," said Luigi at last, "they would be considered a lucky omen."

"But here, said Beni gravely, "they are more likely to be heralds of the storm. See, they were laughing at us, because we are going to have a very rough time, while they will be playing in the deep."

The captain was equally gloomy. Both the wind and the sea were coming from the east, so the safest plan seemed to be to run west-southwest, skirting Mauke to get to Rarotonga, but the messages on the screens and on the radio told him that it was going to be very, very rough indeed.

By noon the *Odyssey* was plunging and lifting more heavily in the swells, and the gusts were coming at shorter intervals, while the sound of the wind had risen to a moan. Deckhands were hurrying about securing deck furniture and taking down awnings, and inside the lounges the stewards were lashing the handles of drawers and cupboards, so that they would not be shaken open and release all their contents.

"Can we help?" said Maggie to Agnes.

"Yes indeed, Signorina Maggie. If you would go into the guest suites, put towels in the rubbish bins, and carefully place all the glasses and other breakables inside those towels, it would be very helpful indeed."

At three in the afternoon the wind abruptly became a full gale.

The brig was so near that Captain Bacchante was able to watch the seamen on the brig take in sail. Men were hauling hard on braces as they visibly skidded from one part of the deck to another, while on the yards other seamen fought with the canvas, which had blown into great bags of wind.

While for the crew on the yacht the sound of the storm was a whistle, whine and moan, on the brig there must be a great slamming of canvas and spars, to match the slamming of the waves. Captain Bacchante saw a great breaker engulf the deck and then foam away, leaving several men struggling in the scuppers. He thought of his country's long history of roaming the seas under sail, and felt an unwilling respect.

Dark arrived early. The *Odyssey* soared up unseen waves, and then crashed down the other side. The helmsman struggled to keep her on course, but with a following wind and a sea pushing at her heels, she refused to inch to the south. What was it like on board the night-shrouded brig? *Povere anime*, thought Captain Castellano.

Helen Pederson was in bed in the owner's suite, with the sheets tucked tightly across her, both Gladys and Rosa working to get her swaddled safely so she would not roll out.

"Constantia?" she asked.

"You want her, Mrs. Pederson?" said Gladys. "I will fetch, okay?"

"No need," said Helen, with a reluctant smile. "But she tucked me in like this in another hurricane, oh, so long ago. Tell her I remember her kindness."

"Okay," said Gladys. "She will be happy to hear that." And the two Filipina girls hurried away, intent on other precautions for the oncoming ordeal.

For Kate and Maggie, it was not too bad while they were busy helping the stewards, but there came a time when they were banished to the suite where the doctors had been, for their own safety. There, on the lower deck, they sat on the floor with their backs against the bulkhead, and their feet braced firmly against the bed. It was a time of fraught suspense, while they listened to the crash of the waves, the suck and roar of the gusts, and thunder that had been distant but then moved closer. The yacht soared and then thumped down, and Maggie's water bottle shot into the air, hit the deckhead, and like an aimed arrow dashed straight into the trash bin, smashing the glasses the girls had nestled there, and then leaping out onto the floor.

Their laughter was a little hysterical. Maggie struggled to her feet, crept over to the bin, and gripped the towel inside by the corners, trapping the broken glass. Straightening up and hanging onto handholds, she made her way to the galley, where François and Jean-Pierre were securing locker handles so that the doors would not slam back and forth. Outside the single porthole, the crash of waves was deafening.

Hanging onto the doorframe with one hand, she held out the towel with its load of splinters, and made a gesture of apology. François waved the silent apology away, and pointed to the bin for broken glass. Then, when she had tipped it in, he pointed at the bin for laundry, and after she had rid herself of the towel, he smiled broadly, and indicated a drawer. It was a heated drawer. When she opened it, there were plates of warm pizza.

"I don't think I will ever eat pizza again," she said to Kate, when she crawled back to her place on the floor beside her.

"Do you remember the time Jerry came home to the vineyard with a huge bank draft in his pocket, and went out and bought a commercial pizza oven? You said that back then, too, after a week of the men trying the oven out, with some good results and some very bad. I think all the Bacchantes went off pizza, for a while."

Maggie laughed. It was a good memory, and the pizza in her

hands tasted pretty good, too. When she had eaten, she struggled to her feet again, and took the empty plates to the galley, where she grabbed more pizza and carried it, sidling inch by inch as the yacht rocked, plunged and rolled, to Jerry's suite, where he and Skye were sitting on the floor with their backs against the foot of the bed and their feet braced against a bulkhead, drinking wine.

Naturally, she was hailed with delight. It was impossible to talk, so she went back to join Kate, grabbing a bottle of wine on the way. Like Jerry and Skye, they didn't bother with glasses, but took turns drinking from the bottle. If they slept, they slept sitting on the floor, feet braced, and heads on each other's shoulders.

And so the long night dragged on.

The day dawned with driving rain. The dark gray clouds were rent at intervals with lightning, but if there was thunder, it was impossible to hear it, because the wind shrieked like a demon from the depths of hell. The growing light revealed a tormented sea that was constantly heaved up into huge white-capped breakers. Luigi Castellano stared out at a scene that was out of a mariner's hell — and yet it seemed there was worse to come. There was an even blacker bank of cloud on the horizon, torn at the edges, progressing rapidly towards them.

Weirdly, the top of the bank was rimmed with gold, as a sign that somewhere, away from this tortured ocean, the sun was shining in a happier place. Then, with terrifying speed, the bank of cloud arrived, and the world was abruptly dark again. The wind roared in vicious gusts, howling in fury, skipping the tops of the waves into white mist, dashing with lethal force at the bridge windows. Only the monitors gave any indication of what was around them, and a lot of that was faltering.

The IAS monitor showed no sign of the brig, and in the pauses between squalls it was nowhere in sight. Obviously, once they reduced canvas, the yacht had left them behind. Poor souls, thought Captain Castellano again. It was impossible to imagine climbing the masts to work the sails, or how they were keeping the ship to the wind. Falling off to any degree would mean that the brig was doomed. Or perhaps the brig had foundered already. He shuddered at the thought.

His eyes were red, and his face was stubbled; he was convinced that when he looked into the mirror again, his hair would have turned white. Two storms! — he couldn't believe it, that an even bigger storm had followed the first. It was a terrible test of a shipmaster. All night the worry had nagged at him that the wind had not altered direction at all, which meant that they could be running straight into the eye of the storm. There was nothing to be done, as turning back would guarantee disaster. When the gale finally began to fluctuate, fluttering around the compass, he took a great breath of relief, even though the wind was still wild. Given immense luck, the centre of the cyclone would pass to the north, and the worst would be over.

With the confused gale the sea became confused too, the waves coming up in towering lumps before they broke. As the yacht was so close to the water, they were thankfully not making much leeway, but were nevertheless being tossed about like a cork. Each time the bow thrust upward as the *Odyssey* rose up the side of yet another huge breaker, it was a case of hanging on to walk uphill, and when she came crashing down the other side, it was a stumble downhill that too often went out of control. Like all his crew, Captain Castellano had cuts and bruises from being thrown around. *Grazie a Dio, non ci sono ossa rotte*, but perhaps it was just a matter of time before someone was seriously hurt.

At last it was as light as day, revealing men who were as haggard and red-eyed as Castellano felt. Even the normally immaculate Beni Boulez looked fraught. But the black clouds were flying north, confirming the captain's hopes. He even started to relax a little, but then the door to Mr. Pederson's office opened.

Luigi winced, and called out, "No!" But the yacht's owner came in, followed by his wife. They both looked white and drawn, and she was wearing a bathrobe. Mr. Pederson was wearing the same as he had the day before, but very crumpled, making it obvious that he had slept in his clothes, if he had slept at all. It was possible to smell their nervous sweat.

They came in, hanging onto the door frame, and then gripping the chart table. Captain Castellano moved so they could wedge themselves into a corner, and then, before he could speak, Mrs. Pederson cried tremulously, "The brig – where is the brig?"

Luigi opened his mouth with no idea what he was going to say, as the brig could not possibly have survived the tumultuous sea. But then Mr. Pederson shouted, "Look!"

And there was the brig, as close by as before. The masts were bare, with just tatters of sail clinging to the yards. Though poised on the top of a wave, the vessel was much lower than the captain expected. They had taken on water; there were leaks, he grimly realized. If the hatches had gone, tons of water must be pouring into the hold.

All the deck houses had been torn away, except for some struts that evidently had sheltered the access way to the after quarters. Then he saw a great wave towering to windward, as high as the lower yards. It crashed down on the decks, sending water foaming in great gallons down the sides.

It was impossible to believe that there was anyone alive on board, but then he glimpsed two men hanging onto the helm. There was a weird lull in the storm, and he could hear a bell tolling. The brig's bell, he realized, hanging from above the helm, and swinging free.

Tolling for whom? A superstitious shiver lifted the hairs on the back of his neck.

A furious gust attacked the yacht and Captain Castellano had to grab the chart desk to save himself from tumbling. He could hear something smashing in the office beyond the owner's door, and hoped it was not a vital computer. Forward, deck furniture broke tight lashings, and crashed across to the railing, and fell into the water.

A second gust reached the brig, sending the hull far, far over. One bulwark was high, the other plunged deep, so deep that the ends of the lower yards were deep in the water. Would the ship come back? Luigi was holding his breath, his nerves torn with impending horror. Almost – almost the brig recovered, but then another vicious blast arrived. He could see the brig shudder before falling further. And then over went the little sailing ship, and the hull sank, sank, until only the tips of the yards could be seen.

The last vestiges of the brig plunged down into a vortex of tormented waves. Tears were running down the captain's stubbled cheeks, in his natural seafarer's grief at the loss of any ship, even one with criminals on board. And Mrs. Pederson was wailing with inconsolable heartbreak, while her husband held her close to his chest.

Chapter twenty-five

By some cosmic irony, the hurricane subsided to a merely strong wind just hours later. There were still sharp squalls, but the sea, though high still, was running true. By teatime the deck stewards were returning the outside of the yacht to something like its pristine self, and the room and table stewards were busily fixing up the interior. The Bacchantes were helping both squads, like the members of the crew they had become, dear souls. And, after instructing Beni Boulez to report the dreadful aftermath of the kidnapping to the authorities in Tahiti, Captain Castellano was able to turn to the much more pleasant job of charting a course to Rarotonga.

Then he was at last able to retire to his berth, leaving Beni to another job, that of preparing the necessary formalities for entering that island. This included emailing advance notice of their arrival, though with a warning that they would probably be earlier than the forty-eight hours required, as the yacht was in dire need of service, being likely to break down at any moment.

They made Rarotonga the very next afternoon, twenty-four hours early. The difference in the weather was incredible. Outside the reef the rippling sea was a dark, deep blue, and a heavenly turquoise within the lagoon. The sky was also blue — completely blue, except for a halo of little white clouds about the double peak of the single mountain. Green plantations ran down the lower sides of the mountain to white beaches and coconut palms, and the air smelled of warm dirt and frangipani flowers. As the yacht motored through the gap in the reef to the quay at Avatiu, the contrast to the morning before could not have been more extreme. Even the port engine was running, making their excuse for a premature arrival seem rather lame.

Skye was on the bridge. For once, Mr. Pederson had not summoned him. Instead, the owner was in his stateroom, trying to comfort his wife. Despite the absence of his employer, Madden had taken his usual place in the office, and Skye could hear him shuffling paper and rattling keyboards. He would have liked to be there, too, just to watch what he got up to when Pederson wasn't there. The captain, however, had asked him to join him on the bridge, as Beni Boulez needed to take a break, and the bosun, who often took over as second mate, was preoccupied with the port engine, just as she had been throughout the turmoil of the storm. The fact that Skye was a New Zealander and Rarotonga was an outlier of New Zealand was also an advantage, or so the captain announced.

They arrived. Deckhands threw ropes, and then jumped after them, but there were local Maori stevedores there too, ready to secure the lines around bollards. The locals then stood back, staring up at the yacht with awe. Obviously, luxury mega-motor yachts were not a common sight around here. Beyond the wharf, with its welcoming sign, there was an office, and a chandlery, and the double lane of the road into town. It was civilization as known in the south Pacific.

Captain Castellano looked particularly marvelous in his white uniform, crisply starched and ironed, his black epaulettes flaunting the four gold bars and gold fouled anchor of his rank. His peaked hat was on the chart desk, and to Skye's hidden amusement, his shoes were glossy black patent leather. The guest passports and the crew list, plus the crew passports, were neatly piled next to the hat, along with the completed paperwork.

Skye had fully expected that they would go on shore right away, even if just to feel the stable earth beneath their feet. But Captain Castellano seemed immovable.

He queried, "What happens now?"

The captain turned tired, reddened eyes, and blinked. "We fly the Q flag and wait. That is what the papers say."

"Someone will come to inspect us?"

"Yes."

They waited.

Agnes brought coffee. It was very quiet. The helmsman had gone below to get overdue sleep, along with the lookout. Only the screens were busy, ticking off the status of the ship, and the weather, and the ocean, working just as well as they had before the superstructure was hammered by the storm, something that Skye considered a miracle. He and the captain made idle conversation, but it was obvious that Castellano was very tired, while Skye himself was preoccupied, wondering what was happening down in Pederson's office.

At five in the afternoon two customs officers arrived, along with a policeman, and the biosecurity officer. They were all very impressed to be on board a luxury mega-motor yacht, even if it had reported engine problems, and were very chatty about it. For Skye, it was almost like being at home. Like many officers in New Zealand, they were stalwart Polynesians, and they wore familiar uniforms. They even had the same accent. The only difference was that the customs officers had frangipani leis around their necks, which they took off and put round the necks of the captain and Skye. They smelled very fragrant, but to Skye's discomfort, they were wet. He also wanted to sneeze.

Agnes and Rosa brought in coffee and plates of sandwiches and cake, and the visitors ate with relish. They discussed the latest Super Rugby scores with Skye, having a natural lively interest because so many Cook Islanders had played with the All Blacks. After that, they wondered at length whether Pasifika teams like Manu Samoa might make the competition. Then finally they got down to business. The forms were the same as many Skye had filled in, in the past. The biosecurity officer went down to the galley to check the refrigerators and cool room, and came back with flakes of pastry on his chin.

Everything was in order. Clearance papers were stamped and handed over. The *Odyssey* was free to spend up to thirty-one days in the Cook Islands, though there were very steep fees to be paid. Suwarrow, however, was out of bounds. There had to be a special customs inspection if they had any plans of going there. Skye communicated their total lack of desire to visit that atoll. Then he asked for the policeman's card.

"I believe you have the same rights and duties as in New Zealand?"

"Absolutely, sir."

"Excellent. I will come and talk to you in the morning."

At last they went, and all souls on board the *Odyssey* were now free to land on Rarotonga. But the tropical sunset was due, along with a much-anticipated dinner. Skye collected his phone from the office, and then went down to have a shower.

Maggie had spent the last twenty-four hours in tears, struggling with guilt. "I was so impatient with her," she wailed to Kate. "I only thought about my work, and how she was treating my sketches, and she was in such need of a friend, yet I didn't understand."

"Nonsense," said Kate. "You could not have been nicer."

"But inside I was angry with her. Do you think she sensed it?"

"Of course not."

"Oh Kate, could I have ever survived without you?"

Kate laughed, and shook her head. "We're joined at the hip, you and I, and one can't do without the other."

"But I do feel so bad about Jewel, and how I let her down. Poor Helen — how must she be feeling!"

"Harold is looking after her. Come now," Kate said bracingly, "the guys need our company."

"Not at the big table — I don't think I could stand that."

"No, no. It is going to be like old times, on the star deck."

And Maggie, sniffing back tears, smiled mistily and said, "Really?"

"Yup, under the moon and the stars."

"Oh Kate," she said, and then was blessedly silent.

It was indeed like old times. There were little lights on their table, and lanterns hung in the miraculously restored awning. Altogether, it was magical, though Kate noticed that Jerry looked as if he had shed tears, too — as if the deaths of the brig and the girl had affected him personally.

The first course was sashimi, just the way the girls loved it, with chopsticks, dabs of wasabi, and little pots of soy sauce. Fresh fish? Already? "The biosecurity officer brought a tuna as a gift, so nice," said Agnes. So Polynesian, thought Skye, with a smile.

MJ materialized with a bottle of wine, as sure-footed and sunny as ever. "That was a very big storm," he said as he deftly poured. "Very sad, Miss Jewel has gone to heaven."

He didn't look particularly sad. Jerry wondered how the crew really felt about it. Jewel had been a big problem for them all, and as well as the natural resilience of Filipinos, their religion was a reliable panacea. Throughout the years with Rosita, his Filipina ex-wife, he had been constantly amazed at the ability of the people to smile and be happy no matter how awful the latest disaster, and he supposed this was the same.

"It must have been a nightmare on board that brig," Kate meditated when MJ had gone. "It was bad enough on this yacht, but on a sailing ship —"

"Very noisy," Jerry agreed. "And very wet." He looked around at the silhouette of the mountains, the stars and the moon, and shook his head. "What a contrast to yesterday and the day before, and the day before that — what a difference a day makes," he murmured. "It's just not the same sea."

"Those who have not been to sea have not seen God," murmured Kate.

"You have to admire the helmsmen," said Skye. "If they had fallen off at all, the end would have come a lot sooner."

"Indeed," said Jerry sadly. "But it only prolonged the agony."

Agnes arrived with their salads. Like MJ, she was as jaunty as ever. "Very tragic what happened to Miss Jewel, but she is in heaven now, problems all finished, so okay for her, don't you think?"

"It's certainly a wonderful thought," said Maggie, though there were tears running down her cheeks again.

Agnes went off, leaving the usual aura of her smile behind, and returned with their plates of pasta. "And tomorrow afternoon we all go to church for a memorial service for Miss Jewel," she said, as MJ poured more wine.

"We do?" said Kate, astonished.

"Mrs. Pederson has organized it. There were telephones to the church minister. The officials who came on board arranged it, at Mrs. Pederson's request."

They all stared at her, while Agnes smiled serenely back.

"A memorial?" said Maggie.

"Yes of course, and we will all go. Constantia said so. She is adamant that we should all go, no excuses taken, but that is okay. It will be very strange, on a distant island and with no coffin, but we will give Miss Jewel a proper memorial. Mrs. Pederson will feel much better, and so will everyone else."

"Good lord," said Skye.

"Which church, I wonder?" said Kate.

"The missionary church," said Agnes, when she arrived back with fruit and pastry. "The old one. I don't know what kind, but it is historic. And the ladies must wear hats, not like Manila, no bare heads. Coffee in the lounge okay?"

They all nodded, but when the girls finished eating and had stood up to go, Skye said, "We'll join you later." Then he said to Jerry, "Stop a moment. I have something to show you, and need your advice."

It was his phone. He had propped it on a desk before he had joined Captain Castellano on the bridge that afternoon, and had left it running. Unobtrusively, it had been aimed at the computer that Madden habitually used.

They watched. It took a lot longer than a moment — half an hour, but not a word was said. When it came to a stop, Jerry stretched, yawned, and said, "My mind is not the sharpest tonight, Skye, but that is plain enough. Madden was copying something — or everything — onto a flash drive. But what?"

"That is indeed the question. But he did it during one of the rare times that Pederson is not in the office. He's put the flash drive in his pocket. Do we need to get hold of it?"

"It's odd that he uses flash drives at all," Jerry ruminated. "It would be easier for him to save it to some secret account in the cloud — but then it would be easier for us to find out exactly what he has stolen. All we would need is his password."

"*Stolen?* That's a big word."

"It looks a lot like theft of intellectual property, to me."

"More like trade secrets. Industrial spying. There is a whole lot of British — and New Zealand — law that covers that."

"Does that law apply here?"

"Yes indeed. I checked. Though the Cooks are autonomous, they function as a dependency of New Zealand. He could be charged while we are here."

"Why not wait until we are in New Zealand? Then we can bring charges, and request the confiscation of his laptop."

"Your mention of saving to the cloud worries me. It could be better done sooner rather than later. When we get to Auckland he might simply vanish with all the data. It would be easier to disappear with the evidence there than it would be here."

Jerry paused a long time. Then he said, "I agree that it seems very clear that Madden is working for someone or something else, but we need more than this recording. And if he is saving to the cloud, it's too late anyway. Unless," he added thoughtfully, "we do manage to get the password."

"It's a pity that you didn't keep that flash drive."

"Oh, but I did. Now, if I could only remember where I put it..."

Skye snorted with laughter. "Jerry, you can be such a bastard."

Jerry grinned, looking more cheerful than he had for days. "We have to consult with Pederson before we do anything, anyway. He's the guy who is being bilked."

Chapter twenty-six

The weather in the morning was idyllic. The sky was blue, the tall mountain was clothed with plantations almost to its wild summit, and inside the reef the lagoon was turquoise, rippling but calm enough to reveal the stones and coral and crabs and flowing weed and swimming creatures within it. It was as if the storm had merely been a nightmare.

Once at the head of the quay, it was just a short walk along the road to a shop where a car could be hired. The man behind the counter looked at Skye's New Zealand driving license and asked about the latest rugby scores, which luckily Skye knew because the customs officers had told him. Nevertheless he was charged twenty-five dollars for a Cook Islands version, which he paid happily, thinking of it as a souvenir. Then he was told never to park under a coconut palm.

Having assented to that, he was given a key. The car turned out to be open — what they called a 'fresh air' car, which he considered drafty, but when he picked up the girls at the wharf they thought it was wonderful.

They wanted to shop — for hats, they said. Constantia, who seemed to be a bottomless fount of local knowledge already, had said that the hats had to be fine pandanus hats, and have fresh flowers decorating the brims. There were shops in the little main town, Avarua, where Agnes and Constantia and Rosa and Gladys were already browsing, having traveled by the round-island bus.

Skye dropped the girls, who assured him that they would get back to the yacht by bus, just like the stewards, and then he found the impressive frontage of the police station, just beyond a great flame-of-the-forest tree, drove there, parked and went in. An hour later, when he drove out feeling pleased with himself, Kate and Maggie were parading through Avarua with the stewards, led by Constantia. The women were all wearing amazing white pandanus wide-brimmed hats, with amazing fresh floral garlands. When he tooted, the girls merely waved, very happy to catch the bus. Within an incredibly small amount of time they had adopted the local way.

Once on board, with a sense that everything was working out at last, he found Jerry, who had quite a lot to report. After he had told the whole story to Pederson, the tycoon had readily agreed to make arrangements. This morning, Madden had been sent into town to hand in more papers to the Ministry of Agriculture, just as the biosecurity officer had requested the previous day. And this afternoon, Madden was going to the memorial service. He had not been keen to attend, and had pointed out had not been at the funeral for Dr. Sullivan in Papeete, which did not seem to have been a problem. But, as Jerry reported further, Harold Pederson had barked that Madden must be there, as a proper gesture of respect to both the owner and his wife. After all, the memorial was for Harold's daughter.

And Madden had reluctantly agreed.

The girls arrived back for lunch, loaded down with purchases that they had made with the New Zealand dollars they still had in their bags. Agnes served them, and MJ plied the wine. The two stewards were excited, talking about getting back into that enticing little town that afternoon for a little more shopping before walking to the church, which was very handy there.

Kate and Maggie planned to go with them on the bus, but Skye insisted on giving them another ride in the fresh air car. Jerry sat in the back seat with Kate. The girls had their amazing hats on their knees, and they put them on when they arrived at the church. When they walked up the path through the graveyard, Skye was surprised how many locals were there. The story had got around, and the luxury mega-yacht had such charisma that many, many wanted to witness the service for a girl none of them had known. But then, he thought, perhaps that was not quite the reason. Rarotonga was surrounded by the ocean, and had been the last stopping place before the first Polynesian voyagers had sailed to New Zealand, a discovery voyage that was such a massively dangerous venture that they felt great sympathy for anyone who was lost at sea.

The church had a very English square bastion, and a very English graveyard, but the singing was purely Polynesian, sung from the heart in Maori, rich with baritones, soaring to the skies. All the women, just as promised, were wearing fine straw hats adorned with great garlands of flowers. Both girls were crying, tears running down their cheeks, and Helen Pederson was weeping with emotion too, her husband's arm around her shoulders. Only that morning, Helen had learned that Trevor Green had joined his soul mate in the afterlife, so the memorial was for him, as well.

Would Jewel have appreciated and understood the service? Skye very much doubted it, and didn't think that a scientist like Dr. Green would have understood the emotion of the service, either. But as he watched Helen's profile lifted to the tall windows, he thought she felt better for the experience. The girls looked more serene, too. And the preacher, definitely, had found the right English words.

Afterwards, in true Polynesian style, there was a huge repast, with fried taro, Polynesian bread, pork cooked in an underground oven, and local fruit. Skye slipped away to the yacht. After prowling around the lower deck he found Sarah and the two engineers down in the engine room. They were prodding oily cavities and heaving new parts into the tigers.

"My God, you must be tired," he said, but when Sarah looked up at him, she was just the same as ever, though perhaps even more stained with grease.

"The chandleries here are useful?"

"Very," said John, but otherwise they paid him no attention.

Skye went up to the sun deck bar. MJ wasn't there, so after exercising in the gym he found the beer refrigerator. Holding a can, he wandered down to the owner's office. All the computers were running idly, and when he ventured down the stairs to the owner's suite, there was no one there, either. So he went back to the bridge, waved amiably at Beni, who was on watch, and opened the crew door to the upper deck lounge, where he sat and enjoyed his drink.

It all felt so empty, as if he and Beni Boulez and Sarah and the two engineers were the only souls on board. But then, with a lot of laughter and chatter, he heard the deckhands and stewards come back, along with Jerry and the girls. When he went out to the star deck he saw that Kate and Maggie and the Filipina women were still wearing their flowery hats. He called out, and in due course the other Bacchantes joined him in the upper deck lounge.

"You've been drinking," accused Jerry.

"Only a very little, and I have not been fed, either."

Agnes, as attentive as ever, came in with a platter of olives and cheese and salami, followed by MJ with a bottle of wine. "The feast after the memorial was very okay," she opined, "but perhaps you are still hungry?"

"Sashimi?" said Maggie hopefully.

"Of course. There is still some of that tuna."

"Wonderful," said Kate, and Agnes vanished, to come back in a miraculously short time with a platter of finely sliced tuna in one hand, and a plate of fresh French bread in the other.

"I want to take you home," said Kate when wasabi and soy sauce were produced, but Agnes merely smiled. They nibbled hungrily, and were only just starting on their second glass of wine when the door to the bridge slammed open.

Madden stood there. He was whiter than ever, and furious. There were scarlet patches high on his white cheeks. He snapped, "Someone has stolen my laptop."

"Really?" said Skye.

"Are you sure?" said Jerry.

"I've looked everywhere! Some thief must have come on board while we were all at the church."

"In that case," said Skye, "it is a local matter, and we need to report it to the police."

The men got into the fresh air car, with Madden in the seat beside Skye, and Jerry sitting in the seat behind. The drive to the police station in Avarua took only a few moments. The sapphire sea rippled gently to their left, and to the right the mountain reared to the sky, clothed with green growth. There were banana plantations all along the landward side of the road, and coconut palms along the beach. The air was cool and warm by turns, and smelled all the time of good things, fruit and growing palms, and warm dirt and flowers.

Skye zoomed deftly around the roundabout with the flamboyant tree in the middle. They arrived at the forecourt of the very modern police station, and parked. Then Skye led the way past the reception desk with a nod to the clerk; he knew exactly where he was going. When he opened the door of the right office, having tapped and received the right grunt in reply, there behind the desk was the police inspector he had interviewed that morning.

Beside the inspector was a policewoman ready to take notes. Harold Pederson was sitting at the end of the desk in one of the visitor chairs. And Madden's laptop was on top of the desk, the lid open. It was running.

Madden looked, paused, and then visibly deliberated how to react. Skye watched various emotions chase each other across his white clerk's face. Then, having decided to be aggressive, the personal assistant snapped, "What is all this about?"

The policeman said very politely, "Please sit down, Mr. Madden."

There were more chairs in front of the desk. Reluctantly, looking hunted, Madden sat, and Jerry sat on one side, and Skye the other.

"You are Steven Madden?"

"I am. I believe my passport has already been scanned."

"That is so, sir. Have you come in to report a crime?"

Madden hesitated. Obviously, he had come in to report the theft of his laptop, but there it was right before him. Finally, he said, "My laptop — that one there — has been confiscated by persons unknown, for reasons unknown."

Jerry said, "Guilty, Mr. Madden. I took it out of your suite while you were at the Ministry of Agriculture, and delivered it here, to the police station, as evidence of a crime. Then I went back to the yacht, and after that I went to church. Don't you think it was a touching service?"

Madden ignored this last, snapping, "I don't know what the hell you are going on about, and I want my property back."

Harold Pederson moved so that his head was facing Madden directly, his expression menacing. "I have a video of you saving data from my computers onto a flash drive."

"That was a security measure, just in case of a computer failure in the night."

"And I also have a flash drive of yours, containing private files pertaining to my business, Pederson Strategic."

Madden stared at him, his mouth hanging open. Then he said, "But how — and that is nonsense — why would I —?"

And the inspector said gravely, "Steven Madden, I am about to arrest you according to Section 230 of the New Zealand Crimes Act, for the crime of taking, obtaining, or copying trade secrets."

Then, looking down at his notes, he solemnly recited, "And, furthermore, I must warn you that anyone who is found guilty of intent to obtain any pecuniary advantage or to cause loss to any other person, dishonestly and without claim of right; who takes, obtains, or copies any document or any model or other depiction of any thing or process containing or embodying any trade secret, knowing that it contains or embodies a trade secret; or dishonestly and without claim of right; who takes or obtains any copy of any document or any model or other depiction of any thing or process containing or embodying any trade secret, knowing that it contains or embodies a trade secret, is liable to imprisonment for a term not exceeding five years. Do you have anything to say in your defense?"

"Jesus Christ!" Madden leaped out of his seat. "I'm not committing the crime around here!" And, fishing about in his coat, he produced a badge.

"Department of Justice," he pronounced, with an audible sniff.

Skye and Jerry peered at it. "Dear lord," said Jerry in disgust. "The man's a public servant."

The inspector said, "Which Department of Justice?"

"For God's sake!" Madden cried. "Of the United States, of course! An SAR was filed against Pederson Strategic four months ago! And I was assigned an undercover role. Pederson's personal assistant was persuaded to resign, I took his place, and since then I have been gathering incriminating data."

The inspector's brows lifted. "An SAR?"

"Suspicious Activity Report! He's a money launderer! He cleans up money committed in crimes, by passing it on to innocent-sounding eco-friendly organizations! Pederson Strategic is a money laundering operation!"

Harold Pederson had gone puce in the face. He roared, "I am most certainly not a money launderer! I want to sue that man for slander!"

But, after a lot of phone calls to the United States, the policeman was obliged to release the fuming Madden. However, he was not allowed to take his laptop, which was firmly wrapped up as evidence.

Chapter twenty-seven

The next night's dinner was the last the Bacchantes and the Pedersons had together. There were just six at the table, and there was a sense of completion. Jewel had been spiritually laid to rest during the memorial at the old Rarotongan church, which, as Agnes had told the Bacchantes, was definitely okay.

All the Filipinos agreed with that, Constantia in particular. And Madden had gone. Harold Pederson had flatly refused to pay for his ticket home, and it had taken the undercover agent a lot of yelling on the phone to get the fare out of his very angry bosses. They had received the file of his crimes and the warrant for his arrest, and considered it a department embarrassment.

Most unusually, Harold and Helen Pederson sat side by side at the dinner table. She looked recovered, as if she had resigned herself to life after losing her daughter. They murmured together, making plans, smiling often. They were booked on a flight back to California in the early morning, and had their cases packed already. There were many other flights ahead of them, including a crucial one to Geneva, but now that Pederson knew exactly what the problem was, he had taken on new energy.

Skye said, "You know you can call on me as a witness."

Harold Pederson nodded. "I know I can, and it's likely that I will call in the favor. I need to find out who or what is behind that bank in Cyprus and this attempt to siphon dirty money into Pederson Strategic. It will not be easy, but I will do it — and I will indeed need your auditing help at some stage."

Skye hesitated. The advice he wanted to give was to turn Pederson Strategic into a charitable foundation, which should be beyond investigation, but he decided against it. Not only was it probably a lot more complicated than it looked on the surface, but there could be many so-called charitable foundations that were actually fronts for criminal organizations. It could be an excellent means of laundering profits from drugs, extortion, and a whole list of other crimes. What did he know? The world of wine-making was so innocent by contrast.

So he raised his glass and said, "The best of luck. It really should be straightforward to prove that you aren't guilty of this, and I hope it will be that easy."

"Whatever, Bacchante wines has my business."

Skye smiled, but Kate thought she saw the doubt in his eyes.

She said to Harold, "I'd be grateful if you forgot the ten million you were going to pay me. I don't need or want it. Very romantically, I thought I'd strike out and found my own publishing business, but now that I've seen what big business is like, it's the last thing I want. So I will accept the publisher's offer. And," and she smiled brilliantly, "I know they are going to be absolutely thrilled with the first draft I wrote on this voyage."

Helen laughed — she laughed with spontaneity, and the grief fell away from her face. In that fleeting second Skye saw a distinct resemblance to Kate herself. Dear God, he thought, she really did take the wrong baby; Jerry was absolutely right. And Pederson was not so crazy, after all. It was on the cards that he had taken DNA tests at some time in the past, and had known the truth all along.

"I can't wait to read the book," Helen said gaily. "And promote it, too. That party in New York is only postponed, you know. We're going to be such great friends, my dear."

"And forget my ten million, too, sir, because I don't want or need it, either," said Maggie to Harold Pederson. "I heard from Bellissimo and they are thrilled with my fabric designs."

"Wonderful! I am so happy for you. I can't wait to see the showing." Helen Pederson clapped, and they all raised a glass.

"Enjoy the rest of your cruise," said Pederson, and they shook hands, hugged, and kissed all around.

Next morning, as the *Odyssey* sailed from port, the Bacchantes watched the States-bound plane fly off overhead. The sea was calm, the winds kind, and the two engines purred as if they were new.

Captain Castellano and Beni Boulez took turns to have dinner with the Bacchantes on the star deck, and so news of the crew's various plans was exchanged. They were all looking forward to the vacation that was due to them after arriving in New Zealand, and, as the Bacchantes learned, they all had big ideas.

Beni would head back to Tahiti, as he wanted to see more of the islands that were administered by his country. The French chefs, by contrast, would go back to their homeland, to check on the three-star restaurant they had founded. Sarah Murray would stay in Auckland to oversee the overhaul of the *Odyssey* as the owner's representative, while the two Scots engineers planned to climb a few mountains in the Highlands. The rest of the crew had tickets to their various homes in the Philippines, where the stewards and deckhands all looked forward to the first big meal with their families. And Constantia would visit her orphans.

And the captain? He was going to Malta to race motorcycles. It was his hobby and his passion. "What else should one do for fun, after dawdling along for weeks at twenty miles an hour?" he demanded.

"And that's only when the engines work," murmured Skye.

One week later, the Bacchantes were driving towards Homerville. Skye was at the wheel, and Kate, Maggie, and Jerry were in the passenger seats. Kate and Jerry both held bunches of flowers.

About them were farms. There were a few houses and sheds and barns made of wooden planks with roofs made of painted tin, but the scenery was mostly flat fields, holding silly sheep, nervous deer, and cud-chewing cows. Well-maintained wire fences surrounded those paddocks, along with windbreaks of macrocarpa pines. The cropped grass was dotted with salt tubs, water tubs, and big rolls of hay in green plastic wrappers. The sea whispered, mostly unseen, hidden behind dunes.

The little town was unrecognizable. The hospital had never been replaced, and the wharf where the *Odyssey* had tied up twenty-one years ago was a wreck. They had to go into the general store to ask the way to the church.

The church was locked, so they had to find their own way about the graveyard. But there were not many graves. There was one dedicated to a nurse named Betty, who had been killed in the hurricane, and next to that was a plain stone, with just the name *DEBBIE PARKIN* etched onto it, along with dates of birth and death.

Jerry hunkered down in front of it, put down his flowers, and raked weeds away with his hands. "That was the name in her passport," he said. "She must have had it with her."

"It was Kelly's real name?" said Kate.

"I guess so. But she always referred to herself as Kelly. One of her stepfathers, Seamus Kelly, was apparently the one who had been kindest to her. But the poor girl was used to abuse. Hell, she had a hard life, and being lovely to look at must have made it worse."

Maggie said, "And all this time she has been buried here?"

"*Si, piccolo*. When I asked about the young woman who'd been moved to a house after the birth of her baby, they said they were sorry, but she had gone."

"Gone?"

"Yes. Gone." He laughed wryly. "They talked about something called eclampsia, but I didn't know what they meant, so I just assumed she'd run away. According to her stories, she had run away often before, just to get away from impossible situations, and she would certainly have reckoned that taking care of an infant would be impossible, considering her lifestyle. So that's why I looked out for her in London, Auckland, Sydney, but never thought of Homerville. It was only just lately, when we were at the hospital in Papeete, that I realized that when they said *'we're sorry, but she's gone'* they meant she had passed away."

There were tears in his eyes, and he turned to blink them off.

"She moved so beautifully," he finally went on, with quiet passion. "She was so lovely to watch when she danced. And I suppose that though it is so sad that she died so young, it's a comfort to know that she never had to get old, gray and awkward — something that is bad enough for the rest of us, but very, very hard on beautiful young dancers."

There was a long silence. Maggie was gripping Kate's hand. Then Kate whispered, "Thank you, Jerry. It's so good to know that you loved her."

She laid her flowers at the foot of the cleared headstone, and then they all got back in the car and drove back to the vineyard and the warm welcome of the *famiglia* Bacchante.

If you enjoyed *Daughters of the Storm,* look for the next in the Bacchante series, *Storm Swept.*

Harold Pcderson's discovery ships are in trouble. Specializing in exploring remote estuaries and photographing endangered wildlife in South East Asia and the western Pacific, his fleet ventures into waters that are rife with pirates.

When Jerry Giacomo is hired by Pederson to make his ships more secure from pirates, he finds that the situation is even more precarious than envisaged. The terrorist organization Abu Sayyaf is master-minding the kidnapping. Then *Storm Swept,* with all the Bacchantes on board, is requisitioned by the British navy to take part in an exercise up a remote river in Borneo, where survival is not a given.

At the same time, Helen Pederson is trapped in a remote village in Mexico, being blackmailed by her first husband. When she confides her dilemma to Skye and Jerry, they are forced to face yet another great challenge. The paternity of Kate Giacomo has been brought into question yet again. Just who was the man who fathered her?

The answer could be dangerous.

Acknowledgements

First, I want to acknowledge the technical help of Lindsay Druett and Rick Spilman. They countered many questions about diesel-electric engines, telecommunication at sea, and automatic vessel identification systems. And, as always, support from other Old Salt Press authors has been bracing, reliable, and extremely well informed. The mistakes are all mine, and the credit is all theirs.

Rick Spilman is the founder and manager of Old Salt Press, an independent publishing company that provides the umbrella for a number of my books. As well as keeping up a hugely popular blog, "Old Salt Blog", Rick has published three very successful nautical books — *Hell Around the Horn*, *The Shantyman*, and *Evening Gray, Morning Red*, plus a novella that I have read at least ten times, *Bloody Rain*. *The Shantyman* won a Kirkus Reviews Indie Book of the Year award, and deservedly so. All four are absolutely firstclass reading.

Alaric Bond, an English Old Salt Press author, is the producer of the hugely popular Fighting Sail series, the latest page-turner being *Seeds of War*. He tells me that he is working on the fifteenth book in the series, which makes me very happy. He has also produced three stand-alone books, *The Guinea Boat*, *Turn a Blind Eye*, and *Hellfire Corner*. I am particularly fond of the third book, as we were in Dover with the author and his lovely wife when he was embarking on the research.

Another very successful English Old Salt Press author (and blogger) is Antoine Vanner. His Dawlish books — all with 'Britannia' in the title — are compelling yarns about the Royal Navy in the early steamboat years, which feature a complex hero as well as high adventure. When I read *Britannia's Wolf*, I was so impressed with his expertise that I wrote a rave review, calling him 'The Tom Clancy of Maritime Fiction.'

I first came across Linda Collison when I read *Star-Crossed*, and was so intrigued that I got in touch with her. Linda has also published a number of other works independently, including biting satires under the 'Knife and Gun Club' banner, and *Redfeather*, which was a finalist in Foreword's Book of the Year Award. *Water Ghosts*, a haunting tale that was a number one Amazon bestseller in the Young Adult category, is with Old Salt Press, and I look forward to more.

A Canadian author who has joined us relatively recently is Seymour Hamilton, the creator of The Astreya Trilogy. I thoroughly enjoyed *Angel's Share*, which was beautifully illustrated by Shirley MacKenzie. His work, though maritime, is reminiscent of Tolkein's carefully wrought fantasy worlds. I look forward to his further contributions to the Old Salt Press list.

The list also features V. E. Ulett, the nom-de-plume of a very successful Californian writer who normally specializes in steampunk adventures. Her three maritime novels, all proudly presented under the Old Salt Press colophon, are *Captain Blackwell's Prize*, *Blackwell's Paradise*, and *Blackwell's Homecoming*.

Joan Druett

Joan Druett became a maritime historian by accident. In 1984, while exploring the tropical island of Rarotonga, she slipped into the hole left by the roots of a large uprooted tree, and at the bottom discovered the grave of an American whaling wife, who had died in January 1850 at the age of twenty-four. It was a life-changing experience, leading to much travel and much research. Because of this, Joan became a noted expert in the history of women at sea.

Daughters of the Storm is her tenth novel, and the first with a modern setting. *Abigail* (republished as *A Love of Adventure*), *A Promise of Gold, Finale* and *The Money Ship* were all very warmly reviewed. And then there was the very popular Wiki Coffin mystery series, featuring a Polynesian sleuth on board the United States Exploring Expedition. Wiki has also been featured in *The Alfred Hitchcock Mystery Magazine*.

Joan has also published many award-winning nonfiction books, including the bestselling *Island of the Lost*, which is now a classic in the castaway genre, and a popular true crime story, *In the Wake of Madness*.